PENGUIN CRIME FICTION

THE LAST TWO WEEKS OF GEORGES RIVAC

Geoffrey Household's life began innocently enough. He was born in 1900 in Bristol, England, into "a conventionally and mildly cultured environment," educated at Oxford University, and slated for a respectable career in international banking. But one day he jammed his umbrella into the grillwork of the bank's gate, placed his bowler on the handle, and boarded a night train for Madrid. In the years that followed this break for freedom, Mr. Household sold bananas in Spain and ink in Latin America and spent five years during World War II as a British Intelligence officer in Rumania, Greece, Syria, Iraq, Palestine, and Germany. He is the author of many celebrated novels of adventure and suspense, including *Rogue Male, Watcher in the Shadows, Red Anger, Hostage: London,* and *Dance of the Dwarfs,* all published by Penguin Books.

D1565340

Books by Geoffrey Household

NOVELS

The Third Hour	Watcher in the Shadows
Rogue Male	Thing to Love
Arabesque	Olura
The High Place	The Courtesy of Death
A Rough Shoot	Dance of the Dwarfs
A Time to Kill	Doom's Caravan
Fellow Passenger	The Three Sentinels

The Lives and Times of Bernardo Brown
Red Anger
Hostage: London
The Last Two Weeks of Georges Rivac

AUTOBIOGRAPHY

Against the Wind

SHORT STORIES

The Salvation of Pisco Gabar
Tale of Adventurers
The Brides of Solomon and Other Stories
Sabres on the Sand

FOR CHILDREN

The Exploits of Xenophon
The Spanish Cave
Prisoner of the Indies
Escape into Daylight

THE LAST TWO WEEKS
OF
GEORGES RIVAC

By Geoffrey Household

PENGUIN BOOKS

Penguin Books Ltd, Harmondsworth,
Middlesex, England
Penguin Books, 625 Madison Avenue,
New York, New York 10022, U.S.A.
Penguin Books Australia Ltd, Ringwood,
Victoria, Australia
Penguin Books Canada Limited, 2801 John Street,
Markham, Ontario, Canada L3R 1B4
Penguin Books (N.Z.) Ltd, 182–190 Wairau Road,
Auckland 10, New Zealand

First published in the United States of America by
Little, Brown and Company in association with
the Atlantic Monthly Press 1978
First published in Canada by
Little, Brown and Company (Canada) Limited 1978
Published in Penguin Books by arrangement with
Little, Brown and Company in association with
the Atlantic Monthly Press 1979

LIBRARY OF CONGRESS CATALOGING IN PUBLICATION DATA
Household, Geoffrey, 1900–
The last two weeks of Georges Rivac.
I. Title.
[PZ3.H8159Las 1979b]   [PR6015.07885]
823:9'12   79-18121
ISBN 0 14 00.5273 9

Printed in the United States of America by
Offset Paperback Mfrs., Inc., Dallas, Pennsylvania
Set in Primer

THE LAST TWO WEEKS
OF
GEORGES RIVAC

I

Until five in the afternoon when Karel Kren arrived May 21st was a Saturday like any other. Georges Rivac, since his clients mostly observed what they called *le week-end anglais,* was free to attend to his office work without the distraction of his secretary and was about to get down to the unwelcome business of checking her statement of profit and loss. He was an active young import agent, jumping with energy and switching back and forth between excitement and depression according to the prospects of new business and the state of his overdraft. He preferred to be out selling. Accounts bored him; they measured success but had nothing to do with it.

He had had no warning that Kren was coming to Lille and was surprised to see him. A trade delegate from Czechoslovakia of obvious importance could not be expected to call on a minor provincial agent. Rivac had met him two months earlier and sensed a mutual sympathy. He had been impressed by this tall well-dressed man with white hair and mustache who would pass as an experienced diplomat or distinguished soldier rather than a factory director in a communist economy. Though a little too serious, Kren had been helpful on questions of foreign exchange and seemed as sound a businessman as any capitalist.

Rivac received the unexpected visitor with a formal courtesy which owed more to early training in Spanish manners

3

than to the long line of enterprising French bourgeoisie on his father's side. He had the impression that Kren was in a hurry, as well he might be if on his way to more important agents in Paris or Brussels. But even a hurried visit was to be commended; when a manufacturer needed reports and suggestions from buyers in a new market, direct contact with the grass roots of commerce was of more value than talking money in a glass-walled office on a statelier business street.

Karel Kren was full of a new model of the small four-stroke gas engine which Intertatry of Prague was about to market. He produced from his briefcase two advance copies of the brochure, presenting them to Rivac with a pride which seemed to be divided between the layout and the actual product. The brochure was certainly a masterpiece all the way from illustrations to easy diagrams and a comprehensive list of spare parts. After discussing the improvements, Kren told him that Intertatry had several promising inquiries from government buyers. Rivac thought that very likely. The little engines for which he had found a ready market were rugged and cheap. A new model might well serve naval and military purposes as well as industrial. He asked if any of the official inquiries had come from Paris.

"Yes, and London. But over there they have their own methods. By the way, I believe you yourself speak English?"

Rivac replied that when he was a three-year-old orphan at the end of the war his English grandmother had come to the rescue and brought him up. England had been home to him as well as France.

"Did you like it?"

"Of course! Of course! Who wouldn't? But exasperating! Why the devil do they have to be so different from us?"

"Us?"

"I mean Europe."

"Yes. I noticed when I was here before that we shared certain ideals. What do you include in your Europe, Monsieur Rivac?"

"The lot! Of course! Why not? We must make for you — you, our brothers behind what fools call the Iron Curtain — something you can look forward to, something worth serving."

Rivac was an enthusiast for federal union. In his café circle he was tolerantly accused of lack of patriotism. They said it was because he did not know where he belonged with all that chattering over his office telephone in three languages. But he did know where he belonged. His allegiance to Europe was far from mere café talk, and his internationalism did not stop short at the long frontier from Lübeck to the Black Sea. He was a collector of agencies, one manufacturer recommending him to another, and acted as the local representative of several East European factories, among them Intertatry.

Remembering a little late that M. Kren was a prominent figure in the trade of a communist country, Rivac cut short his excitable dissertation on "us."

"But I mustn't talk to you like that. I apologize. Naturally you are a member of the Party and have your own Europe."

"Naturally," Kren replied. "But I understand your attitude. An internationalist does not have to be a communist. Remember always, Monsieur Rivac, if ever you have to suffer for your opinions, that our Europe still shares your blood and traditions."

He dropped the subject and went on to explain that the

import agency in London had no time to waste on general-
ities and sales promotion and wanted precise information
from someone who could answer practical questions on the
spot. The Ministry of Defense was interested.

"I had hoped to call on them myself but I haven't time.
Would you like to do it? As our agent for the North of
France you know quite enough of what we have to offer.
Just fly over to London with these brochures. Charge us
with all your expenses, of course."

Rivac, who was unmarried and could spare twenty-four
hours from his rounds of the customers at any time, said he
would be delighted. When should he leave and whom
should he see?

"The sooner, the better. Now, you can't just drop in and
expect to be received by one of the Ministry's experts. But
I can help you there. A man I was at school with. I was
going to start with him myself. He's a government import
agent and he'll take you around to the right man. Show him
the new brochures and tell him you come from Lukash.
That was my nickname at school. Lukash. Write it down,
Monsieur Rivac!"

"And his name?"

"Herbert Spring. Go straight to his office on the first floor
at Forty-eight Lower Belgrave Street. Ring the bell marked
Bridge Holdings outside the front door."

"Should I suggest any — *mettons* — *c'est-à-dire* — token
of gratitude for his assistance?"

"Good God, no! You are not dealing with an official of the
Lille town council!"

Rivac apologized, saying that he feared he had become
accustomed to rather smaller deals. He then asked Kren if
he would care to dine with him. Very kind, but he had to

catch the flight from Brussels to Prague. Some other time with great pleasure.

"Can I drive you to Brussels? We'll be there by seven — or seven-thirty if there's a jam at the frontier."

"No, no! All arranged."

"And your hotel?"

"No hotel. I had time to waste between planes."

"You must be very tired."

"Oh, I am used to that. I can stand anything, Monsieur Rivac, but pain."

He looked for a moment drawn and much older. Rivac said he hoped there was nothing wrong.

"I meant — just an ulcer, you know."

"A curse indeed! You must find time to take care of yourself, Monsieur Kren. Now, shall I write you a report when I return from London?"

"No, don't bother. I'll telephone you. And take care of these two brochures! It's essential that Spring should study them at length before he accompanies you to the Ministry. If he wants to hang on to them for a day or two, let him do so. You can trust his advice."

Kren left at once. He was evidently a busy man of few words, perhaps more used to giving orders than discussing them. Though there was a lot more that Rivac would have liked to know, he possessed the essentials and they were inviting. He had visions of transferring his office from Lille to London — not that Intertatry business itself could justify a move, but a visit might reveal what chances he had and how many agencies he could take with him.

From Lille the Calais-Dover boat was as quick a route, door to door, as flying to London from Brussels or Paris. The following afternoon he crossed the Channel, spent the night

7

at a hotel and on Monday morning called at 48 Lower Belgrave Street. When he rang the bell of Bridge Holdings, Registered Office, a voice spoke from the panel, asking his business. He gave his name and said that he had called at the request of Mr. Karel Kren of Intertatry, Prague, to see Mr. Spring.

Admitted to the building, he went upstairs to an opulent front door — with a smart brass plate which suggested that Bridge Holdings was in the upper class of Law or Finance — and was shown in by a clerk or manservant, probably the latter to judge by his formal black coat. In front of him was a longish passage with three or four white doors on each side; from the farthest of them a casually dressed man, correct for country as well as town, announced himself as Herbert Spring and cheerfully asked Rivac to come in. The large room he entered, more comfortable than severe, could have been the office of some eminent and genial bank manager.

"And now what can I do for you, Mr. Rivac?"

"I come on behalf of Mr. Karel Kren of Intertatry. Prague."

"Prague, eh? I don't think the Bridge Holdings representative has any dealings with Intertatry."

Rivac explained exactly what was wanted, gave a short description of the new model engine, stopped himself abruptly when he found he was slipping into the enthusiasm of the salesman and presented the two brochures.

"I see. Now who exactly are you?"

"I'm their agent for the North of France. Mr. Kren called at my office in Lille the day before yesterday and asked me to run over and see you. He meant to come himself, but hadn't time."

"He had traveled from Czechoslovakia?"

"Not directly. He had been doing a round of markets, I think, and was changing planes at Brussels. He had a whole day to spare, so he came down to Lille to show me these new brochures. I had been doing some very promising business for the firm, you see."

"And he said I knew him?"

"Yes. He told me you had been at school together and would remember his nickname: Lukash."

As soon as Rivac had said that, he saw the absurdity of it. Mr. Spring was at least twenty-five years younger than Kren.

"There must be some mistake," he exclaimed nervously. "Mine! Of course it's mine! This *is* Forty-eight Lower Belgrave Street?"

"Yes. And I *am* Herbert Spring. I'll try to clear it up, Mr. Rivac, if you'll have patience for a little. Here's this morning's *Times*. And a drink, perhaps?"

He opened a cupboard, full of bottles, and looked a question. Rivac, lost and unhappy, replied that he would like a whiskey and soda. He did not really want it but it was something to do while he collected himself and tried to think how the devil he could have misunderstood Mr. Kren.

In quarter of an hour Spring returned, saying that he had been on the telephone to the Ministry of Defense.

"They know of Intertatry and agree with you that their miniature engines have some exceptional qualities, but there's nothing British industry can't do and no particular reason why they should be imported. It is quite certain, I am afraid, that nobody official has ever sent any inquiry to the firm."

Rivac got up to go but was waved back into his chair. He

9

could see that Spring was curious about him — and, good God, very properly! — but his sharp voice was still kind rather than accusing. Not for the first time he wondered what it could be that made people respond to him when they should have thrown him out.

"Now, suppose you tell me the truth about this visit and I'll see if I can help."

"But I have told you. That's all I know."

"Are you English, Mr. Rivac?"

"No. French. Both my parents died in the last year of the war, when I was three, and I was brought up by my English grandmother till I was fourteen."

"How did they die?"

"My father was a hero of the Résistance. His name is on a plaque in the Rue Feidherbe at Lille. My mother died in Ravensbrück. She was Spanish by birth."

"Then where does the English grandmother come in?"

"I admit that my descent appears complicated, Mr. Spring. But that should be true of every European. My Spanish grandfather — we are clear so far? — married an English girl. They met upon a river in Asturias where they were both fishing for salmon and their casts became entangled — never to be separated, she told me, until he was killed in the defense of the Republic. She then returned to England."

"I see you have the blood of three stern nations, Mr. Rivac."

"Thank you. I am very proud of it. One has to be proud of something."

"Business not doing well?"

"I am content."

"Do you represent Spanish firms too?"

"One or two. I like to use the language."

"You speak that as well?"

"With a touch of the accent of León. My grandmother insisted that in honor of her husband we should speak Spanish together on Mondays, Wednesdays and Fridays. You see, there was no one else she could speak his language to, and she did not want to forget."

Mr. Spring was silent, examining him with a cordial curiosity as if he were a new importation to the zoo.

"This man Lukash, now. Suppose it wasn't just a nickname?"

"Oh, I am sure it was. He said so definitely. What else could it be?"

"What does your Karel Kren look like?"

Rivac described him at length.

"Well, I was hoping that I knew him, but I don't. Give me your address in Lille, Mr. Rivac, and I'll get in touch with you if any explanation turns up. And Bridge Holdings might be able to put something your way so that your journey won't be wasted. Good-bye and good luck to you! Don't forget these brochures!"

Rivac returned to Lille in the afternoon, abandoning his dreams of a London office without any regret. Business in France was at least familiar and profitable. His instructions from Kren, now that he looked back on them, did seem inadequate. That was partly due to Kren's very hurried visit, but more questions should have been asked before dashing off to London. Enthusiasm again — that damned impetuous, instinctive enthusiasm of his!

Before going home, he dropped into his office and found a message asking him to call the police on arrival. He did so and was told that the *Police de Sûreté* would send an agent around at once to see him. Rivac's startled imagination took off. Like any other self-employed businessman he kept two sets of books: one for himself and one for the *percepteur* of taxes; but such small and traditional irregularities were not usually handled by the police. More probably it was a question of imports from Eastern Europe. Once or twice he had had friendly discussions with the *Sûreté* which took the form of warnings not to lay himself open to blackmail and in fact were tactful soundings of his political allegiance.

"It's about the suicide of Monsieur Karel Kren," the agent explained.

Rivac, having settled the visitor opposite his desk and himself about to sit back, shot upright and collapsed back into his chair like a spent rocket.

"Suicide? Good God! When? Where? How? Impossible!"

"You did not see the papers this morning?"

"No. I was in London and came back half an hour ago."

"We identified him from his passport and advised the Czech Embassy in Paris through the usual channels who in turn telephoned Prague. His office had no idea what he was doing in Lille, but said that you represented the firm and that he had possibly called on you. Your secretary then confirmed that he had and that you were in London on some business of his."

"He did call on me — the day before yesterday."

"At what time did he leave your office?"

"A little after six, I should say."

"It was six-twenty when he threw himself under a bus in the Avenue de la République."

"Not an accident? You are sure?"

"The driver, his passengers and passers-by all agree that

it was deliberate. We should be grateful for anything you can tell us. First, where was he staying? We have been unable to find out."

"I asked him that. Naturally I was ready to drive him anywhere. I invited him to dine with me. This is quite appalling!"

"Yes, Monsieur Rivac. Where was he staying?"

"I am sorry. Of course! He told me he could not stop. No hotel, he said. I had the impression that he was changing planes in Brussels and had time to waste. So he decided to come over and see me."

"Any special business?"

Rivac explained. He merely said that the Ministry of Defense in London was not so interested as M. Kren had hoped. He did not go into all the details. Being inclined to reproach himself rather than circumstances, he was a little ashamed of having given up too easily.

"Can you suggest any reason why he should commit suicide?"

"He did say something about not trusting himself to endure pain and added that he had an ulcer. An autopsy — is there to be one?"

"No need. The cause of death was plain. However, I will suggest it. Had he to your knowledge any enemies?"

"I know nothing of his life, private or public. Why do you ask?"

"A trifle. One of those witnesses we suffer from who cannot say what he saw, only what he thought he saw. He is sure that a man jumped out of a car which was waiting at the lights to turn into the Avenue and that he was at once closely followed by another man. When the lights changed the witness crossed the road and did not actually see the accident. He cannot state that the man who jumped from the car was or was not the suicide, and if others noticed the incident they have not come forward. Have you any comment on that, Monsieur Rivac?"

"None. Detained against his will, you suggest? Competitors, perhaps? But it is unthinkable! Intertatry was exploiting new ideas but so far as I know patents were not involved. Frankly, Monsieur, I am sure it was an accident. Kren was overworked and in a hurry. With his mind on trade — you cannot imagine how export/import is frustrated by red tape — he stepped into the path of a passing bus. How nearly have I done it myself! And if you, Monsieur, were then to examine these papers on my desk, you would conclude that it was suicide due to innumerable worries."

The man from the *Sûreté* thanked M. Rivac for his assistance. As soon as he had left, Rivac dashed out for the paper he had missed. It carried a short paragraph on Karel Kren's death in Lille and mentioned Georges Rivac as a young and enterprising agent with international connections whom Kren had chosen to visit England on his behalf. He could not help being pleased. Such publicity was useful.

On Tuesday morning his telephone brought in compliments from casual acquaintances because they had seen his name in the papers. As well as these pointless inanities there was one call of interest from Prague telling him that one of the Intertatry managers, a Mr. Appinger, would visit him in the course of the afternoon.

Appinger turned out to be a very different type from Karel Kren, thickset and of no distinction. His French accent was harsh and his manners oily. After speaking of

Kren's business and personal attractions — almost a funeral eulogy — he passed on to the question of British sales. Could M. Rivac tell them what the late Karel Kren had in mind? He had made some casual reference to it before leaving for Brussels but no correspondence could be traced. Perhaps he had taken it with him?

Rivac told him all he knew. The firm of Bridge Holdings was only an intermediary, so he again omitted his futile visit to Herbert Spring, which could only show him up as inefficient or unenterprising or both. Yes, Kren had apparently had an inquiry from the British Ministry of Defense about Intertatry's new engine; he had meant to follow it up in person but had found himself short of time. Rivac, asked to go over to London instead, had failed to get any good out of the Ministry, which could trace no inquiry and thought it unlikely there had been any.

The manager from Prague put a few casual questions: which was the office he had visited and what were the names of the persons he had seen? Rivac replied that it was in Whitehall — he hoped it was — and weakly invented good English names for imaginary civil servants to whom he had talked.

His visitor abruptly stopped questioning him and became very complimentary over the impression that Rivac would make on any businessman. Both the family and the firm were very grateful for what he had done. Would he care to spend a few nights in Prague, visit the factory and familiarize himself with recent developments? All expenses would of course be paid and it would be a pleasure to show him the restaurants and diversions of the city. He was returning himself in a couple of days, taking Kren's body with him if the formalities could be completed in time, and would be delighted to get a visa and a seat on the plane for Rivac.

This was not a chance to be missed. Though Rivac could not see any reason for Kren's family or firm to be grateful, he readily accepted the invitation. The unfortunate accident seemed to have aroused a lot of interest in him, and more agencies might come his way.

But the day's excitement was not yet over. He dined more lavishly than usual — for it seemed permissible to anticipate future profits — spent an hour with friends at his customary café and walked home in a pleasant glow of optimism and Armagnac. His telephone rang. The musical voice was a woman's, rippling and confident. She said she had failed to get him earlier and had then tried to calculate the half hour between his return and bedtime. She hoped she had.

Rivac was impressed by her air of youth and efficiency, at once deciding that this was not leading to any invitation to share an expensive bed. He had wide experience of receptionists, secretaries and private assistants who had let him in with a smile or turned him away with charm, and guessed that she was one of them. Her French was engaging but hesitant so he tried her in English. She turned out to be fluent.

"I am speaking from Valenciennes," she said, "on behalf of Mr. Kren's English friends."

Rivac allowed himself a cautious "oh, yes?"

"They know him as Lukash — if that means anything to you."

"But, damn it, they didn't!"

"Who didn't?"

"Mr. Spring of Bridge Holdings," Rivac answered obligingly.

There was a noticeable silence before Youth and Efficiency replied:

"Oh, but you ought to have talked to our Mr. Thompson. When he heard of your visit he so much wished he had seen you."

"Is he in Valenciennes with you?"

"No. I came over to deliver a draft contract and some completed forms to the EEC at Brussels, and Mr. Thompson asked me to find your number and telephone you. He was very anxious that you should call again at Bridge Holdings at once."

"Well, I can't go this week. I'm flying to Prague."

"Mr. Rivac, put it off on some excuse! I can't explain now, but you might lose an excellent opportunity. My firm really does want to talk to you, especially after Mr. Kren's sad end."

Rivac said he couldn't be expected to live on cross–Channel boats. He was annoyed. It was a waste of time. If Kren's old school friend wanted to talk to him he could have done it the first time, and Spring might at least have brought them together. Anyway Bridge Holdings was not buying from Intertatry but was simply a useful introduction to the Ministry of Defense. On the other hand it was silly to sulk. Spring had been very kind and in fact had said that his journey might not be wasted.

"If you think it's quicker to cross by sea, I could take the eleven o'clock boat tomorrow and brief you," she offered. "It's more important for you than flying to Prague just to see a lot of old-hat machinery."

He was pleased by that "old-hat" in slightly foreign vowels and enchanted by her manner, though his mind was on business rather than any dreamed-up affair. Rivac was very correct in his womanizing. He was excitably courteous to wives and daughters and only dropped this fidgeting — though retaining the courtesy — in the Lille brothel which he visited once a month.

There was really no reason, he decided, why he should not go. If this Mr. Thompson did not object to talking business after hours he could be back in Lille the next day and off to Prague in the evening or next morning or whenever it suited Mr. Appinger. He put this point to Mr. Thompson's able secretary. She replied that there would be no difficulty whatever. A meeting at the office and a working dinner afterward would suit Mr. Thompson very well.

"And on the boat I shall be dressed in green and red," she added.

When Rivac got up on the morning of May 25th he was thankful that he was a good sailor. Gray squalls were sweeping over gray Lille, rattling shutters and overturning the deserted café tables. On arrival at Calais he could see that he was in for one of those legendary crossings which had impressed upon the French, more profoundly than war, politics or the perfidiousness of Albion, the belief that England was and must be forever separate from Europe. The boat, with no more welcome in her than a drowned white rat, was fairly empty, the few passengers were crowded into the saloon and preparing themselves to pass lying down, if at all possible, the approaching hour of hell. He walked through them and then over the streaming deck but could see no one resembling his imagined picture of Mr. Thompson's secretary. He assumed that she had taken one look at the weather report and sensibly decided to fly.

The handful of passengers who preferred the deck to the saloon were congregated on the port side out of the wind so that he found his bench on the starboard side unoccupied. It was his favorite spot, protected from spray by a lifeboat and an angle of the superstructure and far enough aft to be out of reach of the cataracts sluicing down from the bows. There he settled down to watch the spectacular beastliness of the Channel. It attacked immediately. Outside the breakwater the ship corkscrewed over a sea and thudded into the trough, sending spray over the bridge as dense as the debris of an explosion. A few more passengers appeared, driven from the saloon by the debris of more human explosions.

This was probably the girl, staggering down the deck toward him. It was astonishing that she could still hold herself gallantly as if the crossing of feet, the quick sideways shuffle, the recovery were all part of a complicated minuet. She had a green cap over short, dark curls sparkling with spray and a green tweed cloak covering her as far as the high tops of red boots and concealing arms and hands. He ventured a shy smile.

"Good morning, Mr. Rivac," she said at once. "I am Zia Fodor, Mr. Thompson's secretary."

He had provided her in imagination with an English or Belgian face, pale, pleasant, with fairish hair probably long. That was far from the animated reality contained between the collar of her cloak and the cap pulled down over the forehead. Eyes were gray and steady, mouth smiling and complexion, heightened by the wind, a rich variety of the northern peach rather than the apricot of the Mediterranean.

"Hungarian, aren't you?" he asked.

"How did you know?"

"The name partly. How did you know I was the right man?"

"I think — experience in both cases, Mr. Rivac," she laughed.

"We also seem Channel-proof. Where did you get your sea legs?"

"Someone once slapped my face very hard. He didn't break the eardrum but he disturbed the little what's-it that looks after balance. It doesn't matter which way up I'm put. I ought to be a spacewoman."

"What do you hear from Hungary? How are things there?"

"They are doing their best to make the system work."

"I wish we had something better than we have to offer you in the West."

"To offer us?"

"A real Europe, I meant."

"And if you had, what good would it do?"

"Not much, I suppose. But you could look forward to it."

"Did you ever say anything of the sort to Mr. Kren?"

"Oh, yes! On his first visit when I took on the Intertatry agency I remember he asked me if I had any objection to selling for communists. I said I hadn't and told him why. The closer our interests are, the nearer we are to peace. Europe, that's what matters — a united Europe as far as the Russian frontier. Even in old days it went no farther."

"Now I know why Mr. Kren chose you to represent him in London."

"Do you? The more I think about it, the more I don't know."

"Impulse. A chance. You see, he knew he had no time."

"He killed himself, you think?"

"I am sure."

Rivac wondered how she knew so much about Karel Kren. Her boss must have had a continuing interest in his old school friend Lukash, but never mentioned him to Herbert Spring.

"Is it Kren Mr. Thompson wants to see me about?"

The ship rolled so violently that they had to catch hold of the seat to avoid sliding off it. She only laughed as if they were on some dizzying machine in a fairground. With conversation momentarily broken off she did not reply to his question but asked another.

"Didn't he give you any particular message for Bridge Holdings?"

"Only to tell Mr. Spring to introduce me to the right man at the Ministry of Defense."

"So he didn't ask you to deliver anything?"

"Just two copies of the brochure describing the new Intertatry engine."

"And did you show them to him?"

"Yes. He wasn't interested."

"Of course. He mightn't be at first sight. But I can explain."

"Nothing to explain. If I'd had a chance I could have answered questions myself."

"Have you got the brochures with you?"

"No. No point in it. They were for the Ministry."

"Where are they, Mr. Rivac?"

"In my office somewhere."

"Oh, God!"

"You aren't feeling sick, I hope?" he asked. "That was a fierce one."

Miss Fodor replied shortly that she enjoyed the sea. Her exclamation, Rivac decided, must have been a comment on his thoughtlessness.

"But I cannot be expected — my filing system —"

She calmed him down with a dazzling smile.

"Of course. So long as they are available."

A few miserable passengers were trailing around the deck, huddled in raincoats, one by one experimenting with wind, salt and fresh air as a last defense against the onset of the inevitable. A lonely figure, faceless behind dark glasses and filling a short cloth jacket, belted and furred, which marked him as a Central European, passed them a second time, then halted and made a dash for the rail.

"It's got him down at last," Rivac remarked.

"How do you know? Are you sure?" she asked eagerly.

"He's just put his false teeth in his pocket."

"You're disgusting!" she said. "Please get me a brandy, Mr. Rivac, quick!"

Rivac slipped down to the bar. The only customers were two red-faced north countrymen talking loudly, swilling double whiskies and showing off to the prostrate forms around who were too sunk in misery to notice them. The steward had just served him when he heard the double clang of the engine room telegraph and shouts from up top. The ship shuddered and wallowed. By the time he had negotiated the steps of the companionway without losing more than half the brandy, choosing the port side in case the wind blew out the rest, the ship had nearly stopped. The two white lines of the wake ended in a whirlpool and at one point where waves charged their masses against one another the hurled spray was pink. A lifeboat, already manned, hovered above the seas until it took its chance and cast off. Horrified, he saw it pick up one part of what the propellers had left and cruise for another.

He quickly regained the starboard deck. Miss Fodor was not on the bench where he had left her. The man in the dark glasses had also disappeared. He strained eyes to distinguish what was in the lifeboat. As it turned, the roll gave him a clear view of the well before a blanket was thrown over the body. It was red all right, but the background was gray, not green.

Concentrating on the lifeboat, he paid no attention to the cluster of almost motionless passengers beyond and around the empty davits. When he had time to look the crowd was opening up. Two, nauseated by the motion or the accident, had fainted. The French were exclamatory, blaming the ship; the British were silent and sullen, blaming the sea. Miss Fodor at last came into sight talking to an officer while a woman with a loud, pretentious voice was insisting:

"But this lady can tell you. I saw her bump into him."

Miss Fodor was calm, not even showing contempt. She explained quietly that she had been walking along the deck and had cannoned into the missing man, thrown against him by a violent roll. She didn't think he had even noticed it, and he had certainly not fallen overboard.

"But you, madam, did see him go overboard?" the officer asked his witness.

"Not actually. I was resting, you see, and the movement was so awful that I closed my eyes again."

"So you are not suggesting that the bump was deliberate?"

"Good heavens, no! An unfortunate accident! But I thought it was strange."

"I may be able to help," Miss Fodor said. "I caught a glimpse of him as I turned away to the other side of the ship. He was leaning right over. I think he may have been trying to catch his teeth."

Clever girl! An inspiration drawn from the earlier remark that the man had pocketed them! Rivac made up his mind at once to be a witness. Miss Fodor obviously was telling the truth about the passing bump, but the evidence of this wretched woman could lead to her being subjected to any amount of further questions when they landed, all of them pointless since the man in the dark glasses was heavy and the rail chest-high. No accidental collision could have knocked him over.

"But I can settle it at once," he said impulsively. "This lady was feeling ill and I went down to get her a brandy. When I was just coming on deck again she was not where I had left her and the fellow at the rail was still there. Couldn't you spot from the bridge what happened?"

The officer replied shortly that they had enough to do without nursemaiding all angles of the deck, asked for his name and was of the opinion that the Harbor Police would require a statement from M. Rivac when they came aboard on arrival.

Miss Fodor thanked him very graciously as they returned to their seat. Rivac, in a state of indignant excitement, kept exclaiming against the irresponsibility of women who opened their mouths and shut their eyes. He had no hesitation at all, he yelled into the wind, in telling the necessary lie. She thanked him again, patted his arm and suggested that he should talk less loudly.

When the livid cliffs of Dover were just visible through the flung garbage of spray and rain Rivac was called to the captain's cabin.

"You stated to my officer that you were just coming on deck again when you saw this unfortunate passenger still at the rail and Miss Fodor was not there at all," the captain began.

"That's right."

"Monsieur Rivac, there must have been an interval of perhaps a minute between the time this gentleman fell overboard and the time the alarm was given. You say that you saw him still in his position at the rail; so you must have left the bar well before the ship stopped."

"I suppose I did."

"The bar steward confirms that he served you a brandy but is sure, I'm afraid, that you had only just left the bar when the ship went astern. That is a big difference."

"Oh, he's mistaken! Nobody can trust their senses in this weather."

A very awkward development and the sort of thing which sometimes happened when he was too eager. His account of his movements was far from criminal; but if exposed as a gallant lie the evidence of that detestable, resting, puking female might be taken more seriously. The steward's statement must be challenged. With a sudden inspiration he thought of the two semi-drunks and asked if they could be interrogated.

They had returned to the bar and were easily produced.

"Yes, we remember him," said Number One. "Yes, he'd gone topside before the ship stopped."

That at least contradicted the barman, but Number Two broke in: "Seconds before, Fred. Only seconds."

"You'd just paid a round and we were ready for another."

"Ting-a-ling! Man overboard!"

"Brandy he ordered. Not good for the stomach."

"Knocked your glass over when the ship stopped, Fred."

"Who did?"

"Bloody ship did. He wasn't there then. Must have gone out with his brandy before that."

"Seconds before, Fred."

"Sixty seconds one minute. Minutes before."

Rivac jumped on that one.

"Perhaps minutes," he said to the captain. "As I told your officer, I was just coming on deck and saw the man."

"Matter of second minutes," repeated the two judiciously. "That's right!"

The captain thanked them and turned to Rivac.

"Well, sir, for what it's worth they seem to disagree with the steward. Apparently you could have noticed the man at the rail, yet never saw him go overboard."

"You see, I was trying not to spill the brandy and looking for Miss Fodor."

"Is she an old friend of yours?"

"No. We met on the boat. Very natural! The only two choosing the starboard side in spite of the wind."

"And when did you rejoin her?"

"After the boat had been launched."

"So you were all alone with this man for a moment?"

"I daresay I was."

"Yet you didn't see the accident and didn't hear him yell."

"What, with all that racket going on? Wunk! Thump! Swush! And the propeller out of the water half the time!"

"Twice only, Monsieur Rivac. And that was not one of them."

II

THE VIVACITY OF Zia Fodor had become a habit, so that she could not help giving an impression of enjoying the present even when her mind was occupied by past and future. The present, in any case, was easy enough to enjoy. Like most of her contemporaries she accepted a state which ran smoothly and was full of amusement for youth. Neither she nor her friends talked much even in private about the Russian divisions stationed permanently within the national frontiers; they had to be accepted like the fact of death which seldom interferes with the pleasure of living.

Only once had she come to the notice of the police — for joining a mild demonstration against the dismissal of two popular professors who in their lectures had quietly ignored Marxist dialectic in favor of historical truth. The authorities, unduly alarmed by the precedent of rioting students in France, had reacted violently. She had been arrested — her current boyfriend would have been a better catch — and questioned with purely verbal but insulting brutality. She was so sure of the enduring civilization of her country that she told her interrogator he was unfit to be a Hungarian. The slap in the face which she got for that accounted for her excellent sea legs.

Zia kept her mouth shut about this incident though it was in her power to have set flowing a considerable undercurrent of resentment, for her name was well-known in the athletic circles of the capital. She was a horsewoman approaching international standards and had fenced for Hungary as well. She wanted no protests, public or private, on her behalf; they could only lead to suspicion and careful surveillance when she traveled abroad. It was better that there should be no entry at all — not even an approving entry — on the file which somewhere existed under Fodor, Terezia.

Thoughts, however, could not be filed. Hers as seldom before were dedicated to her father, who died when she was only four. Colonel Fodor had been shot by the Russians in 1956 for the crime of being a socialist in a socialist state. He supported the dictatorship of the proletariat wholeheartedly, as well he might, for it had educated him, spotted his ability and intelligence during military training and opened for this son of peasants the relentless route from corporal to the General Staff. What he did not support was automatic obedience to the hereditary enemy. The open hand of Marxism was just, but the fist too tightly clenched was unendurable.

When Zia left her university, with fluent English and serviceable French and German, she took a job as personal assistant to a director of the Hungarian Travel Bureau. The tours she helped to organize were far from contributing to any love of her fellow Europeans in the mass, but she could not help observing that after all the self-sacrifice and bloodshed of the last thirty years the workers of Eastern Europe under communist leadership were only just reaching the same level of prosperity as the workers of Western Europe under social democracy. She also observed that none of her tourists gave a damn for the governments which had achieved this affluence and were perfectly free to say so as loudly as they chose.

She had not enough solid facts for an informed opinion, but of one thing she was sure: whatever the fears and intrigues of the two superpowers, war that involved the two happily compatible halves of Europe was blinding idiocy.

Zia was seldom indiscreet but one evening she said as much to her uncle — her mother's brother — who had called for her at the Salle d'Armes and proudly taken her out to dinner. He was newly appointed to the command of a division and ought to have the answer.

"It must involve us. It must, Zia," he replied.

"Do you want to go and fight the Germans?"

"That's a professional hazard for all soldiers."

"Well, say with France and England and the rest."

"What else can we do? And if war is non-nuclear we win quickly."

"Do the countries of the Warsaw Pact plan for non-nuclear war?"

"Zia, you really must not ask such questions. The answer is that of course they do. In nuclear war there is no winner. We all know that."

He paid the bill and got up — for other tables were too close — and strolled with her along the Corso, a handsome couple and well aware of it without conceit. In Zia's awareness there was also a fleeting vision of impermanence: of so many passers-by, of the beauty of the sunlit city and the impassive Danube which would outlast them all.

"If I were a soldier, I'd mutiny," she said suddenly.

"Then you'd end up very quickly facing a firing squad or the Arctic. So let's change the subject. Can you go abroad whenever you like?"

"Officially, uncle?"

"Of course. I know very well that you can't go rushing off to Monte Carlo."

"I can when there is show jumping or a fencing tournament."

"That's seldom. What I meant was: can you go abroad at short notice any time? To London or Hamburg or Paris, for example?"

"Somebody in the Bureau can always find an excuse for rushing off and — well, we try to take turns. I'd stand a chance."

"Lucky girl!"

He left it at that. She wondered what was behind his sudden interest and came to the conclusion that in the old tradition of gallant Hungarian officers he wanted either to reward a new girlfriend with a trip abroad or, with Zia's help, to persuade one back from abroad.

It was not until a month later when she was actually and officially in London that she began to see a possible reason for his question. She was at a party at the Polish Embassy; it was primarily for the entertainment of British customers by exporters in Eastern Europe, but not too obviously commercial, for there was also a flattering glitter of politicians, press and diplomatic society. Poles and Hungarians — they knew what a party ought to be.

Zia made herself useful though no special duty had been suggested. The guests seemed fascinated by her — she fully intended that they should be — and it was hard to shake the opinion of the more pressing that she had been invited for their continued entertainment at a later hour. She regretted, she told them, that she had nothing to offer but tours of Hungary, her frankness and laughter sending them home with enduring memories of this young executive who could swing her skirt so provocatively, smile so deliciously and pinch an ear with the sort of casual affection one would expect from a flirtatious young aunt.

After an hour of dutiful sociability she found herself occupied by a Polish colonel. Though nearly double her age he was the kind of man she liked to be seen with, whose opinions would be worth hearing and whose surface repartee would be as light as her own. It was a disappointment when he handed her over to a dull Czech businessman named Karel Kren, pointedly saying that Kren had been a friend of her father. Instinct told her that there was more to it than that. Probably the man, who spoke faultless Hungarian, had new ideas for combined tours of Prague and Budapest and wanted to talk routes and prices.

When the party broke up she found herself dining with him, though not entirely clear how it had happened. The Polish colonel and a Romanian friend of his had captured her, again drifted off and left her with Kren. He seemed too serious. As if he had read her thoughts, he admitted that Czechs could not compete with Poles and Hungarians; they had not the heart to face fate so graciously.

"What fate?" she asked, giving nothing away.

He might be, for all she knew, employed to test the allegiance of businessmen and women who traveled freely abroad. He looked suspiciously international — a faintly smiling, prosperous manufacturer from anywhere at all. The prematurely white hair and the air of distinction were out of the common run. It was possible that he was a showpiece to impress the foreigner.

"I meant the fates of life and death."

How like a Slav, she thought, to bring up life and death

with Sole Mornay and a heavenly Moselle! She did not put it so baldly as that but she did stress wine and gaiety.

"Grapes trodden by the exploited peasantry of France in conditions of appalling squalor," he said.

"Who told you that?"

"It was told to his readers by a government hack when some young fool suggested the importation of French wine which we can't afford anyway."

"Aren't Hungarian wines good enough?"

"I prefer them to the Russian. Miss Fodor, you remind me so much of your father."

"Tell me about him. Where did you meet him?" she asked, getting on to safer ground.

"We were testing a new pressed steel support for a heavy machine gun — he acting for the Hungarian Army and I for the factory. Thereafter we met more often."

"You know how he died?"

"Yes. My mother died of the same disease, caused by a different virus. But I thought you didn't want to talk of life and death and fate. Yet you talk of them with your uncle, I believe?"

"Philosophy?" she replied, parrying the thrust. "No, we usually talk about horses. Do you know him too?"

"I have never met him. But one might say we belong to the same club."

"I suppose women aren't allowed to join."

"They wouldn't be quite at home there, Miss Fodor. It's a very male club. We even play with railways and soldiers."

"Model soldiers?"

"They are not very reliable."

"I am sure you will soon catch up with Western manufacture."

"Miss Fodor, I am not surprised you fence for Hungary. I have admired the way you never commit yourself till I have. Now I shall. Has it ever occurred to you that the armies of the Warsaw Pact are the greatest guarantee of peace?"

"My uncle once told me that in non-nuclear war we win quickly."

"Possibly. But suppose the enemy — the nominal enemy — can hold. Their strength is in antitank weapons and it might take longer for the Russians to overrun Europe than they think. In that case they cannot be sure of their allies. They could be faced with insurrections in Poland, Hungary, Romania and my country. At the best that means trouble for them on the lines of communication; at the worst some of our troops engaged in the front line might go over to the enemy. Yes, we might risk in battle what we dare not do in peace. And they suspect it."

"Was it my uncle who said you could talk to me like this?"

"Not directly. His suggestion came a long way around."

"What do you want from me?"

"Nothing, except to remember that you were bored stiff by a dull Czech who could only talk about business. But if ever your uncle wants some little service from you, give it!"

"He must know I would. He could have asked me himself."

"Miss Fodor, in a club the members suggest and the committee decides. For example, you wouldn't put somebody's favorite niece in charge of a tour without personal inspection."

"Sometimes I am ordered to put people in charge of a tour whom I do not know."

"That of course is another point to be considered. Always remember their faces! Always! And now I will try not to be a dull Czech anymore and remember I had a Romanian mother."

The rest of the evening was easy and pleasurable, for Kren had wit which fully compensated for his lack of humor. Determined and even ruthless, she guessed. Undoubtedly a man's man rather than a woman's. He made no further reference to his club except when they parted. Eyes directly meeting hers and again somber, he said that hatred was a poor thing and often unfair; one did not serve from hatred but from love of Europe. He hoped that they might meet again.

They never did — at least not to speak to each other — and the only effect the conversation had on Zia was that she became more alert to innocent chat which might not be innocent. However, there was no sequel to what had seemed an invitation, so that after a couple of months she began to wonder whether the presumed probing and acceptance of her had after all been no more than indiscreet dinner-table talk. Her uncle was at his headquarters and she had no chance of comparing notes with him. She was not sure in any case whether she should.

His visit to the apartment was entirely unexpected. As never before he looked like a military automaton with set face, though she knew he was nothing of the sort. She kissed him and regretted that her mother was out.

"Yes, Zia. I waited until she was. You remember Karel Kren?"

So the curtain had risen and she was on stage. She had never spoken to him of Kren or the party at the Polish Embassy in London.

"Of course I do."

"He is flying to Brussels early on Saturday, May twenty-first. Can you find an excuse for being at the airport when he arrives?"

"No. But I can be in Vienna on business. I could ask if I might have a few days off in the mountains and then fly to Brussels with nobody any the wiser."

"Vienna — that's useful! Your mother chaperoned you when you rode in the dressage there."

"Should she go with me? She has a valid visa."

"Perhaps later, if it's advisable. Now yours is a very simple assignment. I'll tell you what is wanted from you and as little about the reasons as I can."

"The club's business?"

"He used that word?"

"Kren? Yes."

"Well, it sounds better than that nasty name of Military Junta."

The general told her that Karel Kren had a genuine, unquestionable excuse for going to Brussels on business, but the real object of his journey was a quick visit to England. He believed that he might be already under grave suspicion and dared not buy a ticket to London because it would be at once reported that he had. He hoped to be able to get his ticket at the Brussels airport, taking the first available flight out and returning the same day.

"Suppose there is someone to meet him at Brussels?"

"That's the point, Zia. I wish I had you on my staff. There is no reason why he should be met. He never is, and he hasn't asked for it. He's a plain businessman and he normally goes straight to his hotel. And so if there is a car from the Embassy with a secretary — a very special sort of

35

secretary — to meet him, we shall know that he is in trouble."

"From his own government?"

"Worse. From their masters as well."

Her uncle emphasized that she could not be compromised. Neither Czechs nor Russians were likely to recognize her. She was nobody's secret agent and not engaged in any plot. She had only to watch the arrival of the passengers from Kren's flight and see that he obtained his ticket to London and passed back immediately into the departure lounge. After leaving the airport for town she was to telegraph an address in Budapest under any name she liked, saying *Returning today* if Kren was safely in the air and *Not returning till tomorrow* if he had been met at the airport and driven away.

"Shouldn't I have a way of reporting what actually happened?"

"If you can disguise it somehow. Obviously he cannot be forcibly detained at the airport of a foreign country. And assuming he is suspected they'll want him alive and well for interrogation. So it is almost certain they will pick him up peacefully and he'll thank them for the courtesy. Any attempt to break away then and there would only make matters worse."

"And you, uncle?"

He was too honest a man to have all the discretion of a conspirator.

"Don't worry, my dear! I'm in no danger yet. Lukash knew nothing. Poor Lukash!"

"This Lukash is dead?"

"I hope so. Forget it! Forget it! That was not his real name in any case. I'll put it this way. Something vital has been settled. On the other side they can count on it, but our channel of communication has been closed down. Everything destroyed in time! Kren has found another channel — old-fashioned but damned ingenious. I think it's completely safe, but he is not."

Zia made the necessary arrangements with her usual calmness, a little astonished at herself although the run-up to action was familiar to her. In competition on horseback or with foil in hand she was never nervous. She sized up the opposition; she did her best; and then all that mattered was the excitement of the contest, lost or won. Luck seemed to be attracted by such indifference.

In this new sport, too, luck did not fail her. Head Office had no objection to her leaving Vienna for a holiday in the mountains. She could take a fortnight if she liked. She had intended to specify Innsbruck, but before she could do so her boss suggested Switzerland and the inspection of a promising hotel with which they had had some correspondence. That partially solved the only problem which was bothering her. Her passport, if ever examined by hostile eyes, would have shown a visit to Belgium when she should have been enjoying herself in Austria. If, however, she were combining holiday with work in Switzerland she could reasonably claim to have traveled up the Rhine and on to the Belgian Ardennes for fun.

She reached Brussels by train from Basel, arriving the night before Kren was due. Next morning at the airport it was easy to remain inconspicuous, mixing in a drift of package-tour travelers off to the Mediterranean and purchasing from the airport shop a straw sun hat which she pulled well down over her forehead. Not many passengers came through into the concourse from Kren's flight and he was not among them. At last she spotted him at the Sabena desk. Evidently he had managed to slip out by the wrong gate and was now buying a ticket for the London flight.

But other eyes were more practiced than hers. As he was hurrying toward the departure lounge with his briefcase, he was accosted by a uniformed chauffeur and a companion. He greeted them with a convincing show of surprise and pleasure as if he had not a care in the world and was looking forward to a successful business trip. His position was now deadly. He would have to explain the ticket to London in his pocket.

Zia for once was shaken. She had her first experience of the immense and ruthless power which was removing Karel Kren from ordinary life without any fuss and bother. He should, she thought, have bolted for the departure lounge, but then activities only suspected would be proved. Presumably he intended to bluff until his opponents disclosed their hand.

She bought a drink and sat at a table wondering what she ought to do. The alcohol gave no answer except that she should not sit there like a dummy. Whether or not there was anything more to see or hear she should be on the spot like a newspaper reporter. She jumped up and took a taxi to the Czech Embassy.

After changing hats and making such simple alterations to her appearance as she could, she stopped the taxi short of the Embassy and walked past it to a café in the same street where she had a distant view of the front door. From her table she could watch — possibly nothing, possibly Kren being driven away to his hotel after a quick interview in which his explanations had been accepted, possibly his arrival at the Embassy if he had interrupted the journey on the excuse of doing some shopping in order to find out how closely he was guarded.

Something of the kind must indeed have happened, for she was not too late to see a black car drive up. The chauffeur opened the rear door. Karel Kren got out. The other man followed, carrying the briefcase, and as he lowered his head in the doorway Kren delivered a smashing uppercut. He either dodged or used his knee on the chauffeur — she could not see which — and was away with his case in his hand. He walked fast without running. The car slowly followed, the man in the back seat holding a handkerchief to his face. Fugitive and pursuers were careful to avoid any public curiosity. Nobody in the distant café seemed to have observed the incident, and at the moment of the attack nobody was on the pavement in front of the Embassy. Kren must have noticed that and made up his mind on the spur of the moment.

Within yards of the café tables he hailed a taxi and she heard him say, "To the station." The taxi drove off with the black car following. Shortly afterward a second car shot away from the Embassy with two more men in it.

Zia too left for the station — risky since it would be the third time she had shown herself in the proximity of Kren, but she was confident that she could never have been picked out among the package tourists at the airport. Though her orders had only been to watch and report, it was too tame to give the warning of Kren's detention without also mentioning that he had escaped and that his journey to England was still possible.

Both cars were parked outside the station, which meant that all four men were trying to spot Kren among the waiting passengers and what his destination was. Zia thought it a fair bet that he would have jumped on board the first train leaving for anywhere at all. There was one for Lille and one for Ostend. Ostend and the crossing to Dover seemed the more likely; but passing quickly from platform to platform, Zia recognized the two men from the second car. Their air of purpose as they hurried down the length of the Lille train gave them away. She had time to pass them closely and memorize their faces. Kren, she realized, had never had a chance to do so. They entered the train just before it pulled out.

She could do no more and it was time to wire Budapest. She gave much thought to the wording of her telegram; if the KGB in satellite countries were already informed of the escape of Kren, so confirming suspicion, every telegram from Brussels could be examined for hidden meanings before it was delivered. She decided to pay her bill, travel over the frontier into France and wire from there. The delay would be less than a couple of hours.

Zia got off the train at Valenciennes, having composed her message on the journey:

NOT RETURNING TILL TOMORROW. MY RUDOLF HAS RUN AWAY AND I DONT KNOW WHERE HE IS DO NOT TELL CHILDREN YET LOVE MARISHKA.

Once that was sent she was suddenly aware of being tired and hungry. Opposite the station was an old-fashioned hotel which promised a stolid, nineteenth-century welcome more appealing to a woman drained of energy than lounges and pillars, eyes, lifts and uniforms. She went in and was ushered by Madame and an aged porter to just the sort of room she expected, of unplanned comfort and with bathroom separated from bedroom by a red velvet curtain.

She had every intention of leaving for Switzerland next day as if she had completed her short tour of the Ardennes; but when next day came and she was considering railway connections over excellent rolls and coffee she was vaguely aware that precipitate action had caused a problem. That situation was very familiar to her. The problem could usually be identified once it had been firmly placed under the microscope.

Her passport, of course! It would show that she had entered Belgium via Luxembourg on May 20th and left Belgium on May 21st, crossing the frontier a hundred and twenty miles away. What had she been doing meanwhile?

Well, there was no evidence to prove she had ever been in Brussels. So how about this? Stayed the night of the 20th at Namur, a reasonable stopover if touring the Ardennes. Met a charming Frenchman who offered a lift in his car to Valenciennes. Stayed the weekend there before returning to Basel. You can check with the hotel.

As an amateur she was pleased with this decision. She was foreseeing an unlikely but possible danger and planning like a true professional to meet it. The future appeared delightfully secure. She spent Sunday familiarizing herself with Valenciennes and the restaurants where her charming Frenchman might have taken her. His imaginary company helped to arouse some interest in a boring town.

The following morning, Monday, May 23rd, with time to waste before her train, she skimmed through the local paper. There, in three short paragraphs on the second page, was the fate of Karel Kren. Zia was appalled, both by his death and the demonstration of her own inexperience. She was, her uncle had assured her, not compromised, not engaged in any plot, a mere reporter of Kren's movements;

and so it might have been if she hadn't rushed her fences. Here she was, pretending that fantasy was security when in fact she was untrained, ignorant of the rules and pitted against an adversary who knew every trick of defense. She wished to God that Kren or the unknown Lukash was sitting on the bed to give her some guidance, but what they would say she knew: catch that train to Basel at once! Or would they? It looked as if this Georges Rivac held the key to that new channel of communication which Kren had been trying to open. They might say: keep out of trouble but get us the facts.

Zia telephoned Rivac's office and was told by his secretary that he was in London on business and expected back next day. One day made little difference. She decided to wait where she was and then go over to Lille, only thirty miles away.

Stuck for hour after empty hour in that provincial town, she had nothing to occupy her thoughts but Kren and Rivac. That was as well, for by the afternoon she had come to the conclusion that it was folly to visit Lille. There could be little doubt that the two men who had followed Kren onto the Lille train were in some way responsible for his suicide. They too would have read the same paper and discovered — possibly for the first time — that this Rivac was involved; so his office might be watched and he himself in danger. The right game was to have patience for still another day, look up his home number and call him on Tuesday evening.

Over the telephone Rivac seemed to be an uncomplicated, rather flustered businessman, and yet he knew the name of Lukash and where Kren was going in England. Could it be that Kren, spotting that he was closely shadowed and unable to shake off his followers, remembered in desperation the Intertatry agent and passed over whatever compromising document he carried in his briefcase, persuading him on some excuse to deliver it?

She threw in a mention of Brussels but he did not respond. Instead he announced that he was off to Prague — proof to her that he was of vital interest and that any knowledge he had would be mercilessly extracted from him. The result might be deadly to this club which played with unreliable soldiers. There was nothing for it but to claim that she herself worked for Bridge Holdings and to tempt this innocent — almost certainly innocent — into returning to England in her company. She and she alone could explain to this Mr. Spring, the club's agent or correspondent in England, all that Rivac had either muddled or did not know.

III

Rɪᴠᴀᴄ ʜᴀᴅ ʜᴏᴘᴇᴅ ᴛʜᴀᴛ his quick interview with the captain of the cross–Channel ferry would be the end of the matter; but no such luck. On arrival at Dover, Harbor Police came aboard and neatly segregated the witnesses while allowing the rest of the passengers to leave. A passport on the larger segment of the deceased had established that his name was Rippmann and his nationality East German. He had traveled from Brussels.

The lady who had seen Miss Fodor slide into Rippmann was quickly dismissed and Miss Fodor herself, who very frankly admitted the momentary contact, was at once exonerated after the First Officer had pointed out that considering the height of the rail no mere bump could have sent the man overboard. If he had not in some way been lifted, he must have leaned far out and overbalanced — perhaps indeed reaching to catch his dentures.

When it came to Rivac's turn to give evidence, the point which most interested the superintendent who questioned him was whether he and Miss Fodor had known each other before sailing; to that he could honestly reply that they had not. Then the interrogation kept pegging away at where he had stood when he saw Rippmann still at the rail and what his own movements were thereafter. He had the impression that his questioner reserved judgment on the steward's statement and was more interested in the time of his arrival

44

on deck — just before or long before. The two Yorkshire drunks, red-faced and belligerent when confronted by police, had turned on each other, one backing Rivac and the other the barman.

Could it have been suicide, he was asked. That seemed to imply that the police accepted him, barman or not, as a truthful witness. He jumped at the way of escape, saying that the passenger had looked extremely ill and that in such a crossing one became indifferent to death or at least to the normal precautions necessary to keep alive. He knew at once that he had overdone it there. The superintendent pressed more severely for the time of his arrival on deck, and Rivac remembered the captain's rather pointed question: "So you were all alone with this man for a moment?" He was told that it might be necessary to get in touch with him again and was asked for his address in England. He replied that he did not yet know it and presented his Lille business card.

When Harbor Police had finished with him he joined Miss Fodor in the entrance hall ashore. Passport Control gave them no trouble. He was surprised to see her pass through the channel for aliens. In spite of her slight and appealing accent he had unreasonably expected her to possess British nationality, probably as a child refugee from Hungary in 1956. It seemed odd that a Hungarian should be employed by any firm so unmistakably British as Bridge Holdings.

Having missed the boat train they arrived in London three hours late — too late, she said, to catch Mr. Thompson at the office. She refused to have dinner with Rivac on the grounds that she needed a long rest at home to recover from her ordeal, and arranged to call for him at the Gros-

45

venor Hotel next morning at half past nine. Naturally enough she was not her calm, collected self.

Rivac slept well, having nothing on his conscience but a white lie and looking forward to at least a morning with this most attractive and sensible sprig of Europe. He hoped that by then she would have recovered her poise. He felt — and was ashamed of it — some resentment against the late Rippmann for managing to fall overboard, thus exposing Miss Fodor to slight unpleasantness and himself to a shade of suspicion besides delaying their departure from Dover and making his evening session with this Mr. Thompson impossible. He also blamed the deceased for not knowing his way around. It was pointless to travel from Brussels to London by sea when he had an airport handy. Rivac vaguely wondered why he had.

Miss Fodor turned up soon after half past nine, exploiting her good looks, he thought, a little blatantly. He preferred his windswept companion of the boat; but, after all, this was London and a young woman had to be what business-men expected of her.

"All ready?" he asked.

"All ready. And when the taxi drops us at Lower Belgrave Street you should ask for Mr. Spring again and then we'll go up to Mr. Thompson afterward."

Rivac was puzzled. The office of Bridge Holdings was not more than two minutes' walk from the hotel, and as she worked there she must know it. He had only the lightest of hand baggage and she had none, so why the taxi? He ran through in his mind their telephone conversation of Tuesday evening but couldn't exactly analyze what was bothering him. He sat down again in the hotel lounge and she joined him with a pretty flounce of the skirt.

"Miss Fodor, excuse me asking — but do you really work at Bridge Holdings?"

"Well, Mr. Thompson has a lot to do with them."

"Then surely we should go directly to him?"

"I don't think that after all he's going to be much good."

"He does of course exist?"

She hesitated while Rivac nervously expected to be snubbed, and then answered with a smile in which there was no shade of shame:

"No, he doesn't."

"Then may I ask how you knew about my visit to Bridge Holdings?" Rivac demanded with as much severity as he could manage toward such an entrancing young liar.

"You told me yourself," she retorted. "I said to you that English friends knew Karel Kren as Lukash and you answered: 'Damn it, they didn't!'"

"Please explain this Lukash."

"If Mr. Kren told you to show the brochures to Herbert Spring at Bridge Holdings and mention the name of Lukash it must be familiar to them."

"But if Mr. Thompson doesn't exist, who does employ you, Miss Fodor?"

"Nobody. At least not this week."

"Well, frankly, I am not going to Bridge Holdings to make a fool of myself again."

"You would rather have gone to Prague?"

"Of course. I am sorry, but I shall return to Lille at once."

"Do you know what will happen to you if you accept the invitation to Prague? You will be interrogated by the KGB until they find out why Kren called on you, what he wanted you to do and what your relations with him were."

"But I haven't any!"

"All the worse for you! When they get nothing out of you because you have nothing to say they will put it down to your courage, Mr. Rivac, not your innocence. And after being treated for courage they couldn't allow you to return to Lille in that state, so you might be regrettably run over by a bus like Karel Kren."

"Nonsense! My dear Miss Fodor, you're making this up! Karel Kren was a trusted member of the Party."

"Which makes it far worse."

"And nobody at all pushed him under a bus," Rivac went on. "If it wasn't an accident it was suicide. He told me that he had an ulcer and couldn't stand pain."

"He had no ulcer, Mr. Rivac. And you too — if you knew what was coming to you — might commit suicide when you were terribly afraid you would talk under torture."

That was impressive. Rivac did not in the least want to be mixed up in any such melodrama, whether all invented or with a grain of truth in it. He said so, and added sternly: "Now, where do you live in London?"

"I don't. I found a hotel last night."

"But where do you come in on all this?"

"It was my job to see that Kren got safely through to London and to report if he didn't. That's all. I lost him in Brussels and then I read how he died in Lille."

"You are . . . you are somebody's agent?"

"I was thinking to myself last night that a stupid security policeman would probably file me as a beautiful spy."

Rivac, calming down, courteously remarked that he'd certainly be half right.

"Thank you, Mr. Rivac."

She made a little bow and held the compliment between

finger and thumb as if to examine it. She had the grace of a ballerina. He remembered how erectly she had carried herself dancing down the deck, the toss of her skirt as she sat down at the beginning of this awkward interview and now this humorous gesture of head and hand. Beautiful? That was too monumental a word for her. Pretty? Of course. Debonair? Decidedly, holding herself as if she owed a duty to the world to walk through it with grace.

"Then who the devil are you working for?"

"Call it our Europe. I think that's true."

"Miss Fodor," he replied, refusing the bait, "you're on your own. I am not going to accompany you to Bridge Holdings."

"I thought all French were gallant."

"I was brought up in England."

"I thought all English were sports."

"What's Europe got to do with it anyway?"

"I can't tell you that."

"*Merde, alors!*"

"*D'accord, Monsieur Rivac. Il y en a beaucoup!*"

"Tell me why the hell I should take you to Bridge Holdings!"

"Because they must know about Lukash."

"But it's just a holding company for export businesses."

"Suppose that's cover for something else?" she suggested.

"Then we'll both end up in jail as two foreigners fiddling with state secrets. And we'll be lucky if they don't put us through the hoops again over the late Mr. Rippmann."

"I don't mind. If they must, they must."

Wide-open eyes expressed her surrender to cruel necessity.

"Well, let's hope Harbor Police have enough," he said, getting up to accompany her and, he felt, leaving common sense behind in the empty chair.

They walked around to Lower Belgrave Street and Rivac rang the front doorbell. As before he was asked by the panel to state his business. He said weakly that he was afraid it was Mr. Rivac again to see Mr. Spring.

Upstairs the door was opened by the same clerk or manservant. Mr. Spring popped out of his office in the same way.

"Come in, come in, Mr. Rivac! And this is?"

"Miss Fodor, a foreign friend — well — er — a Hungarian."

Rivac observed that this time the retainer had accompanied them into the room and that neither of them had so far been asked to sit down. Mr. Spring, though as genial as ever, appeared a person of more authority: the Managing Director himself rather than the Public Relations man whom Rivac had conjectured.

"Now, I was favorably impressed by you on your first visit, Mr. Rivac, and we agreed there must have been some mistake. What brings you back again?"

"It's still this Lukash. He's probably a friend of Karel Kren, not Kren himself. And this lady confirms it."

"But I still do not know Karel Kren."

"I just couldn't make her believe it," Rivac said.

"Where are you staying, Miss Fodor?"

"Nowhere. I shall go back today."

"To Hungary?"

"To Switzerland."

"And what was the purpose of your visit?"

"I was sure you would be interested in Lukash and the message which Kren was trying to deliver."

Her hands apologized for having taken such a leap in the dark, while a tilt of the head suggested that even so they would land safely on the other side. Mr. Spring was unimpressed.

"I have already told Mr. Rivac that we are not. Rivac, how did she get you into this?"

"She thought she could explain to you better than I."

"Did you know this Kren, Miss Fodor?"

"Yes. I think his message was somehow in the Intertatry brochure of their new engine because he could not send it through Lukash. And then he was trapped and committed suicide."

"I see. Merely a case for psychiatry perhaps. But I had better warn you, Miss Fodor — if you are quite innocent — that little games of this sort are liable to be investigated by Security. Now, Mr. Rivac, I can appreciate that Iron Curtain contracts offer — well, all kinds of attractions. But my advice as one plain businessman to another is to leave them severely alone and stick to your profitable small agencies. I am sorry that I cannot help you. I have no knowledge of this Kren or any Lukash."

The manservant — on second thought he looked too physically fit to be a clerk — saw them all the way down to the street and out.

Rivac walked aimlessly up Buckingham Palace Road with a silent Zia at his side. He felt utterly useless and ,frustrated. What he had expected from Herbert Spring he could not exactly say, but certainly some relief from the labyrinth of futilities into which this damned girl had led him. No, not damned girl. A bit intimidating and too sure of herself. As the secretary he had first thought her, she'd drive her boss to drink. But, well . . . luminous and impertinent as a star in a storm sky.

"Kren got the name wrong, Miss Fodor," he said.

"You're sure of Bridge Holdings?"

"Absolutely."

She too was lost in intangibles. Her experience of Western offices and business methods was too limited.

"What did you think of them?" she asked.

"I don't know. In England a holding company can have quite a small place as its registered office. Bridge Holdings — I think they might have very wide interests and official backing."

"Kren was not the sort of man to make a mistake. Lukash must have told him to go there."

"Who the devil *is* Lukash?"

It was obvious to her that Lukash, before he was caught, had controlled in some way the channel of communication, but even so the facts did not fit together. If he was in a position to give the London address where Kren should deliver his message he could equally well have advised the British organization to send a courier to Brussels. Kren could then have passed over his information and avoided the risk of flying to London.

She was about to answer that she did not know; but on second thought this agent from Lille, nervous and full of good will, deserved more generous treatment than that.

"Lukash has been arrested and is probably dead."

"But look here, Miss Fodor! People are dying all over the place! This is absurd. Nothing's worth it. The sooner we get out of here, the better."

"If we can."

"Of course we can. Victoria station over the way, or Heathrow airport in half an hour."

"Do you still want to visit Prague?"

"I want to go back to Lille and drop the whole thing. But tell me the truth and I might see that I can't drop it."

"It's not fair to you."

"It is! If the KGB are going to pull out my toenails in any case I might as well know why."

"I'll tell you as much as I was told by Kren: that the armies of the Warsaw Pact are the greatest guarantee of peace."

"Same old story! I've heard that one, Miss Fodor. Just for home defense against the wicked West. No threat to us at all!"

"Mr. Rivac, they are the greatest guarantee of peace because in time of war they might go over to the enemy. I think Kren had a list of the commanders who were prepared to defect and the units they were sure of carrying with them."

"The Kremlin would stick at nothing to discover that," Rivac said and then realized that his cheerful comment was a cold statement of fact. "Good God! And we —"

"And we! Suppose the list was in the brochures which Kren made you take to London?"

"They don't do it that way. Secret dispatches belong to the time of Napoleon. They do it by radio. Transceiver under the floorboards. That sort of thing."

Exactly! Zia, remembering her uncle's guarded explanation, saw it at once. They had to close down their transmitter in a hurry. That left them with no channel of communication except by hand and without a reliable agent.

So Karel Kren, able to travel at will and still with no more than a question mark against his name, decided to go in person.

"You didn't see anything out of the ordinary in the brochures?" she asked.

"Not a thing. Anyway they would have been printed by the thousand."

Having gone so far, Zia told him everything she knew, leaving out any mention of her uncle, and all her movements from Basel to Valenciennes.

"Well, that explains Lukash," Rivac said. "He was the radio operator. 'Lukash calling' perhaps he used to say. He didn't know what he was sending because it was in code. All he could confess when they got him was who gave him the messages. That would have been a nameless member of the cell or just a drop at a post box. But Kren came under grave suspicion as the link between Lukash and what you call the club."

"How do you know so much?"

"Because my father ran the secret radio in Lille. I only heard all about it after the war, as soon as I was old enough to understand."

"Kren was left free too long."

"Oh, no! Cat and mouse act until he gave himself away. And he did."

Cat and mouse act, yes. It occurred to Rivac that it would not be difficult for any experienced agent to have followed him all the way from Lille to Bridge Holdings to Buckingham Palace Road. He looked quickly behind him and realized that for all he knew the whole blasted KGB could be on his trail.

"Those two men you saw getting on the same train as Kren — would you recognize them again?" he asked.

"Yes. Yes, I was sure. I couldn't have made a mistake! I couldn't have!"

Zia had turned pale and was shaking all over. By now they were close to St. James's Park. He took her arm and led her to the nearest seat.

"Courage! There is no danger. If they try anything on we have only to inform the police."

He threw out his hand toward a policeman proceeding along Birdcage Walk and doing nothing at all with a proper air of stateliness.

"No! No! I can't bear it anymore. Don't you know I killed him?"

"*Doucement, doucement, ma petite!* It was an accident."

"I hadn't any doubt. Tell me I hadn't any doubt!"

"About whom?"

"Him on the boat. He was one of the two on Kren's train. He must have followed you from Lille. And there was I talking to you. If he reported that we were together . . ."

"But you haven't the strength. Imagination!"

"Look! Touch!"

Her forearms, bare to the elbow, shot out from the slits in the green cloak. They were feminine enough but slightly out of proportion. Under his diffident fingers she deliberately hardened the sleek muscle developed by the reins and the épée.

"The deck was empty. So I bumped into him to see what would happen. And then my cloak blew over us . . . oh, it was all in an instant like the crack of a whip. I heaved on the belt around his coat."

55

"But that woman?"

"I never saw her. She was all shapeless under a rug."

Only ten minutes earlier, Rivac exclaimed to himself, he would have called that policeman. But no, he wouldn't! Never! Well, why not? Poor girl! Poor? She could heave him right over the bench if she wanted to. Pink piece, good God, in the bottom of a lifeboat! But lucky they didn't pick him up alive. What do you mean — lucky? Think of papa and maman! Yes, but then there was a war. And what's this, if not? Say something to her, you fool!

"I am most grateful to you, Miss Fodor," he stammered very formally as if she had just picked up his hat which had blown away. "Between comrades . . ."

"You understand?"

"Desperation! Spur of the moment! I mean, not as if you were used to it."

"Is anybody?"

"That thug — we can be sure he was. Got what was coming to him! I don't wonder you wouldn't dine with me last night. Couldn't face it. But all alone much worse!"

Zia had got the crying and shaking under control. That was not due to any effort of hers and she knew it. The mere fact of having confessed her guilt to this very odd companion had done the trick. He reminded her of some half-tamed animal, leaping away and circling and then with unexpected intelligence returning.

"What do we do now? Suppose that Spring man tells the police we are in some shady business together?"

"Stick to our story."

"But the publicity!"

Any publicity would be deadly to the general since the connection between uncle and niece could not be missed.

She could only hope that the club had been able to cover its tracks after receipt of her telegram.

"Spring fired us out, and that's that," Rivac said. "And if you are thinking of Rippmann — well, individuals must often be drowned without getting into the news. He followed me onto the boat and that's the end of him. He can't report on either of us, thanks to you."

"But the East German consulate or someone will make inquiries."

"And just hear he fell overboard. It isn't as if there was a case for the magistrates or the coroner. You're clear anyway. Harbor Police hardly questioned you. You're just a name on a file with a dozen others. I may not have heard the last of it. Serves me right for jumping in when I needn't have done. What we must do now is to find the right place and they'll get us out of trouble."

"What right place?"

"The place where Kren ought to have gone. Somebody gave him the wrong address. Wrong something. I don't know."

"How can we find it in all this?" — she pointed to the imposing remnants of Empire massed along Whitehall — "And if we could we haven't the brochures."

"I think they were just an excuse to make me call on Bridge Holdings. All straightforward they were. And Kren would never have risked secret ink when they were sure to test for it. But I can get the damned things. I've only to telephone my secretary. And you must fly back to Switzerland."

"No, I'll wait. I can get away with it somehow. There is always that charming Frenchman."

"Yes, he wouldn't let you go in a hurry, Miss Fodor. Well

then, you and I might have a weekend in the country."

Zia had not expected this. Mr. Rivac seemed to alternate between treating her as his commanding officer or his younger sister. But beautiful spies could not take offense at the drearier duties of the profession. She had to be tactful.

"Mightn't it be embarrassing for you, Mr. Rivac? We have to remember that you told the captain we were only casual acquaintances. And if they do keep an eye on me . . ."

"*Nom de Dieu,* I did not mean . . . that is to say, it would be an honor, Miss Fodor. But never entered my head. No, I assure you. Just somewhere to stay quietly till the brochures arrive. Out of reach of all inquiries, you see. It is possible that I have not told you I was brought up in England. The village — I should be welcome there. And for you, not far away, is a choice of small hotels. When we meet it will be as strangers. And to my secretary I shall give the address of a post office."

They decided it was wise to separate at once before the British or other police had a chance to suspect any connection between them. Before Rivac left her he called his office in Lille asking his secretary to send to him at Poste Restante, Thame, the two new brochures of the Intertatry engine which were in the drawer of his desk. She was not to give away the address, saying that he was only in England for a few days and she did not know where he was staying. There had been, she told him, no inquiries except from the Intertatry manager who had invited him to Prague. Mr. Appinger had seemed surprised to hear that he had been called away to England.

"You can trust her?" Zia asked.

"Suzi is a dragon, my dear! But very conscientious. I pay her, therefore she obeys me — quite often."

"And asks no questions?"

"Naturally she asks questions, but sometimes I myself do not know the answers. It is the essence of a good businessman to be alive to his intimations. So she is accustomed to not understanding. 'But why, Monsieur Rivac, are you going to Paris?' she will say. 'I have an idea, Suzi,' I reply. That is true, and as often as not I return with a new agency which is not the one I thought I intended. Then she sniffs and asks to what account she is to debit my traveling expenses. On this occasion what shall I say to her? Services to Mr. Lukash?"

"What is your Christian name, Mr. Rivac?"

"Georges. Why do you ask?"

"Because my charming Frenchman has come to life. And I am Zia."

They agreed to rendezvous at one o'clock the following day in the churchyard of the little town of Thame, not far from the village of Alderton where Rivac was brought up. By then he would have found accommodation for her and made sure that he had not been followed. He explained to her precisely how to take train and bus and recommended that she should pack the green cloak and cap instead of wearing them.

"You will recognize me without them?"

"We have known each other for twenty-four hours. It is quite enough."

"Enough?" she asked mischievously.

She had expected Georges Rivac to stammer his way out of that one; but he was used now to the way her mind as well as body took off on impudent wings and settled serenely.

"Enough to be aware of the attractions of which Mr.

Spring was good enough to warn me," he replied with pretended gravity.

Rivac left London at once before any organization — sure to be wildly exaggerated because unknown — could pick up his trail. He carried only his overnight bag, never intending to stay more than a day in England, and chose to walk the few miles from Thame to Alderton, rejoicing in his second country and the scent and snow of the hawthorn dividing field from field and field from lane over the low-lying land.

It was twenty-one years since he had left the village for France, thereafter returning only at intervals to see his grandmother until her death in 1965. He found that Alderton had changed little except for a couple of housing estates where he remembered the cottages of agricultural workers, picturesque outside and inside foul and damp as the mud of winter. At least the neatness of color-washed bungalows, mostly with cars parked outside, was in keeping with affluent Europe however foreign to the stone and rosy brick of the village street. The manor which long before his time had descended the social scale into nothing more than an elaborate farmhouse had been tarted up and proudly exhibited its seventeenth-century architecture, lawns mown, shrubberies disciplined, a brood mare and a hunter in the white-railed paddock.

Daisy Taylor, who had presided over his youth as his grandmother's cook and companion, received him at her cottage gate, at first shyly and then with tears as he gathered her waistless rotundity into his arms.

"Well, well, Master Georges! Who would 'a thought it? And there's a rabbit pie in the oven what you used to be that fond of and I only 'ope you don't want them red Spanish bangers in it what your dear grandmother used to buy whenever she could get 'er 'ands on 'em. And your room's nearly ready if you'll give me a minute to get them sheets ironed, for it's no time ago that Mrs. Stone slipped over to say as 'ow you'd telephoned her to give me a message."

Yes, it would be the same welcome in France but different, and different in Spain but the same, and equally familiar to Czechs and Poles exiled from their Europe, not to mention butterflying Hungarians! He sat down in the kitchen while Daisy ironed the sheets and chattered of lives and marriages and the scandals "which weren't really, Master Georges, scandals no longer. Twins it was, and it weren't 'im that wouldn't marry she but 'er that wouldn't marry 'e. And our Mr. Longwill as you used to catch hares with not to mention that there deer which would 'ave brought you up before the beaks if the sergeant 'adn't been a particular friend of mine — he's made a lot of money in London and done the place up a treat. Got a bit above 'imself but there's nothing 'e won't do for you if you can put up with the way he carries on."

"Married?" Rivac asked.

"One and a 'alf times. 'Ussies, both of 'em! Not that 'e's no better 'imself. Ah, I wouldn't mind being young agin in these days, what with them pills and all."

"Daisy!"

"There! You 'aven't changed much, Master Georges! Still talkin' to 'em over the gate and then 'opping it, I bet!"

Rivac explained his visit by saying that he had business in London and longed to see the old place at the beginning of summer. He did not mention Zia, intending that they should meet accidentally once he was convinced that it was

61

safe to be seen together. Such caution seemed ridiculous; it was impossible that he could be traced and unbelievable that the leafy peace of Alderton could be invaded by barbarities. Still, one must forget that Kren had been obliterated without disturbing any diplomatic niceties, and he himself could be just as badly wanted.

He brought up with Daisy the question of nearby inns where a guest would find reasonable comfort. She flatly refused to let him stay anywhere but under her roof and was easily led on to speak with contempt of neighboring innkeepers. There wasn't one, she said, with an idea beyond the bar takings except the White Hart at Alderton Abbas, which took a few summer visitors; if they had a full house she used to go over herself to cook the dinners.

After Daisy's high tea — a triumph of variegated starches which even a Frenchman, he thought, would admire provided he didn't have to eat it oftener than once a month — he strolled out into the field behind the garden with two hours of the pastel evening light of May to enjoy and took the path to his grandmother's home, snugly tucked away in a loamy bottom between trees. It was up for sale again with an air of being unloved and gloomy. He had gathered from Daisy that the last owners had used it as a weekend retreat from London and after one disastrous Sunday when the septic tank had leaked into the well — a surprise for them which Daisy found richly comic — had run from it as if the devil was after them. From there, after a sad glance, he took the bridle way to the Manor Farm. White gates opened and shut as easily as hotel doors. He remembered that in former days it was simpler to climb them than to wrestle with old Longwill's chains and pins, giving a heave which always loosened the pivot and stopping to replace the lot.

The south side of the house facing open country was worthy of a picture postcard. Brick, moldings and gables had returned to the era of high farming when they were new. He found that the broad, flagstoned terrace which had been hidden behind a straggling hedge of wych elm swallowed up by bramble was now in full view over newly planted yew. He could imagine squire and parson, bewigged and flushed with port, damning his eyes for impertinence as he watched them lurching up and down the terrace. What he did in fact watch was Paul Longwill sitting alone with a book and a bottle of claret, contentedly rid of one wife and a half. The velvet jacket, the dark hair thick over the ears and beautifully groomed, the cushioned and comfortable wrought-iron chair and the general air of exquisite leisure were intimidating. Rivac reproached himself for shyness and gently called: "Er — Paul!" As evidently he was not heard, he tried again vulgarly loud.

Paul Longwill jumped and rose with dignity. When he saw who it was his public manner changed at once to private affection.

"Georges, come around by the gate! Georges, how good to see you!"

For ten minutes they laughed over memories of early youth. Then Paul got up to fetch another bottle and Georges was free to marvel at the admirable taste with which the house had been restored.

"I don't remember that coat of arms over the door," he said when his glass had been refilled. "Did it turn up during the repairs?"

"It could have done. It could have done. And the College of Heralds — for a consideration — agreed that I might quarter the arms of Longueville."

63

"We always thought the name came down from an ancestor of yours called Long Willy because he had one."

"Certainly a village tradition to be proud of, but I'm afraid that is all it is. There can be no doubt that we are descended from Longueville who came over with William the Conqueror."

"What happened? A win on the pools?"

"Pools are grease for the dreams of the proletariat, Georges. I just used the little capital father left me and mortgaged the place as well. No money in pigs, they all said. So they sold and I bought. Two years later shortage of pigs and market strong. So I sold. I put that lot into property and secondary banking and had the luck to get out at the top before both collapsed. That makes me a coming City man with an office in the West End."

"And you're making a profit out of farming?"

"At any rate I am not making a loss. An estate and some horses is the in thing and I can ask anybody, absolutely anybody, to come down for a night or two. Now, tell me what has brought you over to England?"

"I had some business. Small stuff, you know. Just another agency."

Longwill kindly remarked that the foreign agent was the backbone of trade: the invaluable sergeants, one might say, without whom the high command of industry was helpless.

"Mere money is always up for grabs," he added. "But to grab it one must know the right people."

The right people, yes. It occurred to Rivac that his old and much changed friend might know the right people. Much changed? Well, he sounded the biggest damned snob in the country; on the other hand he was not at all uncertain of himself like, say, some building contractor buying a flashy way into the jet set. Ever since that peasant Long Willy — who must have done a bit of boasting too — his roots had been firmly set in his countryside. And Daisy had said that he would do anything for a friend.

"I came over to see a firm called Bridge Holdings, Paul. I don't quite know what their business is. They may be just a holding company or have something to do with government buying and selling, especially import."

"You came over without knowing who they are? How extraordinary!"

"I don't like missing chances."

"You talk like a peddler, my dear chap! Tomorrow I will find out for you who Bridge Holdings are. We have a directors' lunch. Lord Bamborough will be there. They say his daughter is attracting attention in the highest quarters. Useful! He can't be such a fool as he looks. And let me see! I don't like the sound of your Bridge Holdings. I'll give our accountants a call. They know a different kind of everybody. Come around and see me on Saturday morning! I won't be home tomorrow."

Rivac next morning called at the White Hart to inspect it and book a room for Zia. He thought it best that she should not produce a Hungarian passport in signing the hotel register; there might be other investigations into the Rippmann incident besides those of Harbor Police and, to judge by her story, she had no excuse for visiting England. So he christened her Mrs. Fanshawe, mentioning that she was French and married to — he was about to say Colonel Fanshawe, but Paul had reminded him that the English bourgeoisie loved to be impressed. The colonel was promoted.

"The wife of Major-General Fanshawe, commanding the Armored Brigade in Germany, you know."

The proprietor of course appeared to know and asked if he himself was serving in Germany. Rivac, whose military knowledge was limited — his service as a conscript being largely confined to trapping hares for his platoon — decided that he was on the civilian staff of the Commission. It was unnecessary to say what commission.

That done, he set out for the rendezvous with Mrs. Fanshawe. She was late and he paced uneasily around Thame's noble church, assuring himself that she could not be expected to be punctual after an intricate journey in a foreign land, yet more and more certain that she was already in a police cell or unconscious and on a plane to Hungary.

"And that leaves me, Georges Rivac, the other secret agent badly wanted by the KGB," he remarked to the outspread wings of an incredulous marble angel.

Incredulous. Quite right! But it could be true. He was shocked that it could be. One does not, he admitted, readily recognize oneself as a character from news or fiction. Examples of nonrecognition, Georges? Well, what about some hot-tempered woman who occasionally throws a plate at her husband or lays into him with the poker? How horrified she would be if suddenly she were to identify herself as the wife with a rolling pin in the common cartoon.

Denys James Scott K.C.M.G. Born 1829. At Rest in the Lord 1900 with a severely consular granite slab. Governor of New Guinea.

There's another of them — a chap who represented his country in desert or forest or among a stone-age tribe. How can he fail to interest his fellows by all they do not know and can hardly imagine? And then one day Sir Denys, with too fierce a hangover for his age, asks himself: what are you? Answer: the club bore.

So there it is, Georges! You are a secret agent and must accept it. Sunday School 10 A.M. The meeting of the Parish Council will take place on Tuesday. Miss Zia Fodor is having her toenails pulled out. What a shame! They must be pretty toenails. Where the hell is she?

When she passed through the lych gate he did not immediately recognize her. Green tweed, cap, red boots had all gone. She was bareheaded, wearing a neat summer frock of printed linen — he knew it was linen because he represented a small Belfast firm — and easily swinging her suitcase instead of leaving it at the bus station.

"Thank God you've made it!"

"Were you worried? I went shopping this morning — that's why I'm late. Have you found me a nice place to stay and do I have to register with the police?"

"No. You are British by marriage."

He explained her new identity and the story he had made up for her.

"Won't they know my accent isn't French?"

"They will not, Zia. In the English countryside all foreign accents are assumed to be French unless obviously German. They recognize that from war films."

"And I look too young for a general's wife."

"I know. But your parents thought he was a good catch and you submitted to their wishes. Anyway the general is charming and his mustache exciting."

"What's happened to you, Georges?" she asked. "Today you're full of mischief."

"I'm on holiday, you see, till tomorrow."

"Tomorrow?"

"Tomorrow we should hear from Suzi. And I have been in touch with a friend called Paul Longwill. He has become a financier or thinks he is, and he's finding out for me what the City knows about Bridge Holdings."

He sent her off to the White Hart at once, regretfully watching the taxi drive away. But it was essential that if the trail of one was picked up it should not lead to the other.

Saturday was still holiday. When he called at Thame Post Office for the expected letter from Lille there was nothing for him; so he had to wait till Monday for those damned brochures in which he only half-believed. It was astonishing that only a week had passed since the plausible Karel Kren had called at his office and lured him into this intrigue or trusted him to see it through. Trusted. That was better.

At eleven he called on Paul Longwill. A lumpy, pretty girl was bouncing around the paddock on a bay mare watched by Paul and a young man who could have passed for a male model of weekend wear if he had not been so rotund — a smoothness exaggerated by the watchchain stretching from pocket to pocket across his check waistcoat. Rivac, still dressed for Lille, felt as if he were calling for orders.

Paul introduced him, vaguely explaining that Rivac kept an eye on things for him during the week. Tact or snobbery? It was hard to decide.

"Necessary bores who can wait for us, dear Georges," Paul commented as he carried him off to his study. "They are opening a night club where it will be useful to be seen until they go bust. I have been able to find them a backer."

Settled down with a decanter of Madeira — which, Paul had to say, was specially selected by his wine merchant for a few connoisseurs — he was as good as his word and gave him an outline of what was known of Bridge Holdings.

"Export agents with a network of representatives abroad. They hardly ever import, so I am told. You are wrong there. I think they might be interested in your languages. How did they hear of you?"

"Through a friend. I do some business with Eastern Europe. Very minor stuff," Rivac added apologetically, "fountain pens, embroidery and things. But I do have a sale in the North of France for excellent little Czech gas engines."

"Perhaps they think that you could sell British engines in Czechoslovakia instead."

"But I don't know the country and don't speak Czech."

"They must have interests there. The manager, Herbert Spring, is a rather mysterious fellow, always very well informed. It's known that some of the best newspapers refer to him and it wouldn't surprise me if the government asks questions too."

"You mean — well, secretly?"

"Oh, I shouldn't go so far as that. But our accountants say you would be perfectly safe in taking any agency he offers you."

"He reminds me of a terrier," Georges muttered with distaste.

"What on earth do you mean?"

"Oh, you know. Small and wiry and mustached and ready to use his teeth on anybody if he's suspicious."

"I shouldn't be surprised, Georges, if it's his duty to be suspicious."

On Sunday, still avoiding Zia except for a telephone call to see that she was content, he took Daisy over to Oxford by bus and gave her lunch. She was far more impressed by the setting than the food and disguised her merry local accent. The waiters were particularly polite to such old-fashioned dignity, taking her, he guessed, for a provincial lady, comfortably off, entertained by a rather shabby nephew with expectations. The grapevine had already provided her with working notes on the new guest at the White Hart, a pretty young Frenchwoman and the wife of a general.

"She must be lonely, my dear. You should go over and have a couple in the bar. It would do her good, it would, to have a chat in her own language."

"What's she doing there?" he asked, for it was a point to which he had not paid enough attention.

"Looking round to see if she likes the district. The general will soon be 'ome and wants a place with a bit of 'unting and shooting."

Trust Zia! The only possible awkwardness would be if Daisy discovered that it was Master Georges who had booked the room for the pretty Mrs. Fanshawe; but they would not be staying long enough for that. Meanwhile they had successfully covered their tracks pending the next move. That must depend on what he heard from Suzi in Lille and perhaps on Paul Longwill.

On Monday morning there were two letters waiting for him at Thame Post Office. He sat down on a bench outside the Corn Market and opened the envelopes. One letter, posted on Thursday, contained the brochures. In the other, posted on Saturday, Suzi told him that Mr. Appinger had called again the day before and left a present for him: the latest Intertatry calculator. And a *sergent de ville* had come to see him with an inquiry from British police who wanted to confirm his Lille address. If he was still in England they would like a statement from him, if in France a sworn affidavit. Apparently he had been a witness to a fatal accident in crossing to Dover. She had given his address at Thame Post Office and hoped she had done right. It always paid to be cooperative with the police.

However closely he examined the brochures, they appeared just as innocent and practical as when they had been handed over by Kren. Code breakers might of course discover some secret but he, as an experienced agent for the engines, could find nothing out of place or irrelevant. He could only assure Zia, herself incapable of judging, that the brochures were a straightforward commercial job.

He telephoned the White Hart and arranged to meet her in Alderton Wood, exactly describing the footpath she should take which for the last half mile was sheltered by hedge and covert from the observation of the curious. She would then see ahead of her the long grassy glade which divided the wood, and there she should enter the trees and wait. His caution was not due to any fear that she might be followed but to a mixture of motives, all of them sound: Daisy, village gossip and the continuing necessity to protect her.

He had still another reason for his choice of rendezvous — instinctive rather than formulated, like the business journeys when he returned to Lille with an agency quite different from that which he had vaguely contemplated when he started out. He wanted to show her the place, for of England she knew only London. He also wanted to see her there. A stream ran through the great wood, and in the depths of it, far from any footpath, ancient hawthorns curved over the water seeking light in the gap between forest trees. It was like a miniature green cloister with half the vaulted roof fallen away. The floor was sandy and always dry when the stream was low. Around the shadows were dotted clumps of purple Honesty which would be in flower under the snow sprays of the hawthorn.

Arriving well before Zia, Rivac found this sanctuary of youth much as he had left it except that the canopy of thorn was taller and barer at the bottom. Then he sat on an oak stump near the edge of the glade to watch the path by which she would come, ready to show himself and direct her if she was in doubt. On the other side of the glade, not far from the road to Thame, the persistent call of a jay broke the silence of the trees in the mild midday warmth. A sparrowhawk swooping over the birds huddled under outlying bushes which dotted the grass on his side probably accounted for the jay's alarm though he was surprised that it should fuss over attempted murder in, as it were, the next street. Rivac was momentarily back in his happy English boyhood and reproached himself for infidelity to sweet France. He smiled at the absurdity of that. The loves were one.

Zia gaily entered the wood, adding Hungary to his affection, and he led her to his treasured shelter. The Honesty was a bit of a disappointment, she herself being too subtle for such vivid purple. But there was the usual bonus. The shifting arrows of sunlight within the flowered darkness of the truncated vault sparkled now on the water, now on her.

"So you don't think there's anything in it?" she asked.

"No. But the somebody who knew Lukash must see for himself — if you can wait till we find him."

She said she thought she could spend another week by pleading illness or something. She was evidently enjoying the role of Mrs. Fanshawe and was full of laughter at the inane conversations in the bar of the White Hart.

"And what else did your Suzi tell you? Is she selling the stock over the counter?"

"She says she had to give my address to the police on Saturday. A nuisance, but it won't affect you. And that on Friday the visiting manager of Intertatry called again and left a present of their latest calculator for me."

"Does Intertatry manufacture calculators?"

"No. At least they never have. This must be a prototype."

"Georges!"

"What's the matter?"

"Don't you see what the calculator may be?"

"It multiplies. Suzi doesn't need it. But it may be a hint for me."

"Where did she put it?"

"On my desk, she says."

"Bugging — isn't that what it's called in English?"

"The telephone?"

"No, no! A little device left anywhere. At home — well, ordinary people don't have to bother. But anyone who wants to discuss a subject which the government should not hear is careful to do it out-of-doors."

"I don't see that it matters. They can listen to Suzi all day if they like. I have to."

"Think! That calculator was on your desk when Suzi gave your address to the police. You must leave here at once."

"But where to? I can't go back to Lille. I can't go anywhere. I can't spend my whole life in hiding because these people believe I know all the secrets of their blasted mutinous armies. I have to get advice from someone who knows what's what. I have to talk to Paul. I have to —"

"Georges, you are excited!"

"Of course I'm damned well excited."

"You must go underground for the moment."

"I *am* underground. What about you?"

"They don't know of my existence yet. And even if you were followed from Thame you didn't go to the White Hart. I shall be all right for a day or two as Mrs. Fanshawe. Now let's separate!"

"Stay here for a while, Zia!"

She was very ready to stay. The combination of Georges and his private sanctuary, this exquisite, unchangeable refuge among flowers, delighted her. His explanation of why he wanted her to stay was disappointing.

"If anyone followed me from Thame he must be on the other side of the glade. I know every yard of this place. I shall show myself crossing the open. Then he'll stay in that half of the wood and you can safely follow your path back to Alderton Abbas."

"Do you think you were tailed?"

"No. But I did hear a jay call when she shouldn't. I used to do a bit of poaching once, you see."

"Georges, you amaze me! Very well, I'll do what I'm told. And telephone me this evening between seven and eight to let me know where you are. Then I'll join you."

After leaving Zia Georges was thoroughly ashamed of his nervousness and jumped to the other extreme, skeptical of all that appeared to be happening to him. It was possible that this calculator was transmitting all conversations in his Lille office, possible that his address at Poste Restante, Thame, had been discovered, but both were very unlikely. In any case the KGB — Czech or Russian or straight up from bloody hell — could not know that he had been brought up in the village of Alderton and had no way of guessing where he was actually to be found.

Under observation all the way from Thame? He was not looking behind him and he could have been — but only by a man on foot after careful study of the map. And that was absurd. Wait a minute! Those chaps had had the Thame address since Saturday and time to organize. What had he been up to on Sunday? Lunch with Daisy. Got a lift from the village to Thame. Bus to Oxford and back. Then a taxi home from Thame bus station to Alderton.

Say they watched the bus station, for it was a very small town and on Sunday there was not much else to watch but church and the main street. Say they spotted the late Kren's agent taking the taxi. They need not follow it and risk giving themselves away; they had only to hire it for a short journey immediately it returned and get into conversation with the talkative driver. All this assumed that they were able to recognize Georges Rivac. Only Appinger, the bogus Intertatry manager, could do so. Then he must have flown over on Saturday, reported to his chiefs in London and collected some kind of local team. Team. A very nasty thought, that!

He considered whether or not to report to the police and ask for protection; but they were not likely to believe him, especially as he himself was far from convinced. Also there was no way of leaving Zia out of his story, and left out she had to be. If ever some connection between them were suspected, his eyewitness account of the accident to Rippmann would become even more dubious than it was. No, for the time being and until he was in touch with some department of Intelligence which recognized the name of Lukash, police must be avoided.

He was on his guard all the way back to Alderton, wishing that he was as small as when he had returned from minor criminalities as a boy. But hedge and ditch remained familiar enough and when he reached Daisy's garden gate he was quite certain that anyone who had tried to follow him was lost. The brochures now. There could be no doubt that Appinger and his team — if it existed — were sure that he had received and had not yet delivered some message of outstanding importance. It might be wise not to carry them on his person. In the narrow gap between Daisy's boundary hedge and hen house was a pile of broken bricks, gutters, wire and rusty paraffin cans. He took the brochures out of Suzi's envelope and pushed them into a length of pipe, then hid the pipe among the rubble.

Returning to the cottage and Daisy, he told her that he had received a letter which made it essential for him to go back to France that evening, and promised to visit her whenever he was in England which in future would be more often. That seemed quite possible. Whatever happened to his business, Lille could be unhealthy until such time as Kren's unclean spirits were convinced he was a worthless catch.

No taxi this time and no Thame! He took a shortcut to the main road where he could pick up a bus to Oxford. The timetable showed him that he had twenty minutes to wait. This annoyed him and he started to fuss. There was no convenient cover from which he could see the bus approaching and he had to remain exposed on the roadside. His walk had been along lanes and could have been observed. He ought to have gone north and taken a train or hired a car at

Bicester. Hadn't enough money on him anyway. He ought to have done anything but what he had. He wished some kind person would see him waiting and offer him a lift. Fortunately in another five minutes there was such a kind person, and he did.

IV

THERE WAS NO CALL from Georges Rivac between seven and eight. Mrs. Fanshawe was not yet alarmed. She was by now accustomed to the plunges of her excitable companion like those of a nervous thoroughbred. His rider could not always detect what he shied at and why the high-pitched neigh, but the plunges seemed as a rule to have reason. He might have decided that the White Hart was not as secure as they thought.

When on Tuesday morning there was still nothing, she decided to go and see that Daisy Taylor of his. For that she had to have a solid excuse within the normal pattern of the village, good enough to deceive Daisy, who evidently was no fool. House-hunting at last provided it. Remembering that Georges had said that Daisy sometimes cooked for the inn, she told her host that she was attracted by the peace of Alderton and had found a house for sale which needed a lot done to it. She understood that a housekeeper, who had lived there for years, had a cottage in the village. She would much like to meet her and ask a few questions.

"Our Daisy! Yes, she'll tell you all about it if she takes to you. Now, I'll be going through Alderton this afternoon and I'll drop you there."

Mrs. Fanshawe thanked him warmly and added that she must really hire a car.

Daisy at once reminded her of the adored, bustling peas-

78

ant grandmother she had known as a child. The information came pouring out.

"You buy it, Mrs. Fanshawe. It would like you, it would."

"Didn't it like the last people?" she asked.

"Ar-r, they 'ad some surprises comin' out of the taps, but nowt our local builder couldn't put right for 'ee."

Zia baited the hook, saying that they often had the same trouble in France, but all the same she preferred well water.

"Gives 'ee the woollies to think of all them chemicals they puts in the mains," Daisy agreed. "And may I ask where you comes from in France, Mrs. Fanshawe?"

"My family lives in Valenciennes — near Lille, you know."

"I suppose you didn't happen in with a business gentleman called Georges Rivac?"

"No. But everyone has heard of his father."

"Well, if it ain't a small world! Would 'ee believe that 'is son was staying 'ere up to yesterday?"

It was not difficult to extract reminiscences of Georges's youth. She understood more fully the solid base which underlay the sensitively swaying little businessman. Little? Why had she thought of him as little? He was slightly built and a bit hatchet-faced but well above average height.

She let Daisy talk herself out before starting to ask questions. Yes, Mr. Georges had left soon after lunch. He had to return to Lille.

"I could 'ave got him a lift into Thame, but 'e was always one for causing nobody no trouble and don't care whether 'e walks one mile or twenty. So 'e sets off to catch the bus to Oxford on the road."

That was to be expected. Zia was sure that the one place Georges would not go was Thame.

79

"And bless me if I don't 'ave the coppers askin' for 'im while I was just clearin' up me tea. Not that 'e's done nothing wrong. Just saw some poor man fall overboard and they wanted a statement from 'im. Only a German 'e was though they tells me they're just as good as the rest of us in these days. And did 'e 'ave a girlfriend, they asks. Never was one for girlfriends, I says, but what 'e may be up to in them foreign parts I don't know, I says. 'E didn't speak of a Miss Tessa Forder or some such name, they asks. Not to me, I says. Then they wants to know 'ow well I knows 'im. Since 'e was three, the lamb, I tells 'em, and if you wants another opinion like them doctors do what can't find it in the book when you tell 'em what's wrong with you, you go and ask Mr. Longwill at the Manor Farm, I says."

"And did they?"

"They did, because 'e comes round to me last night with a bottle of cherry brandy though 'e give me one last Christmas and it was layin' it on a bit as 'e always does and 'what's young Georges been up to?' 'e asks. Young Georges! I like that from 'im when there ain't more 'n a month or two between 'em! 'Well, 'e may 'ave taken up with a 'Ungarian,' 'e says, 'and if I'm any judge,' 'e says, ''e's been tellin' a packet of lies.'"

Zia was not much afraid of the line the police had taken. She agreed with Georges that there was no case for magistrates or coroner. But if Harbor Police were not satisfied with statements taken on the boat they could well be fishing for any connection between Georges Rivac and Terezia Fodor in case one was protecting the other.

"Georges don't tell lies," Daisy went on, "not unless it's just kindness like, and if it was I'd still buy a secondhand car from 'im as they say. As for 'Ungarians, 'e never did care where anybody came from. The farther, the better, you might say. It wouldn't surprise me if 'e was to take up with a pair of Siamese twins, Mrs. Fanshawe. 'E's not experienced like you and me."

Zia came away more worried than ever. Georges had started off according to plan and it now seemed certain that he had been trapped or could not easily reach a telephone. This was far worse than her impulsive visit to Valenciennes. Then at least she was in touch with possible futures, friendly or hostile. Here she was utterly alone with a false name in a foreign land and unable to imagine even tomorrow's future. She was tormented by guilt for having seduced Georges into what was none of his business and rather less tormented by the memory of Rippmann — though in the absence of any moral support that too was becoming intolerable. On top of it all was the crushing load of responsibility to her uncle and his club.

It couldn't go on. This Paul Longwill had to be seen. Georges, casually mentioning their meeting, had found him in some way comic, but at least they were fond of each other and apparently loyal to boyhood friendship. She'd have to play it by ear, giving nothing away until she was sure what, if anything, he had to offer.

She prowled about the Manor Farm, trying to make up her mind. She saw Paul Longwill arrive in a white Jaguar, immaculately dressed for what they called the City, so he was at home. The combination of farm and finance was unfamiliar to her. The lovely old house was obviously a *kastély*, too luxurious for a private farmer, too small for an old-time landowner. In her own country she would have guessed that it was one of the perquisites of an important government servant.

Where the footpath skirted the paddock she leaned on the white rails, casting an expert eye over the bay mare — powerful quarters, good hack, could probably jump — and a gray gelding which looked very spruce, in keeping with its surroundings and nothing more. Both came up to her, the mare a little distrustful, the gelding greedy and affectionate. She noticed a small coil of rusty wire rather too close to the rails; it was unlikely that wind could carry it into the paddock but it should not be there. As she bent down to throw it farther away she realized that there in her hand was her introduction. She swung herself over the rail, gentled the mare, made her lift the off fore, slipped the coil around it and was back on the footpath, praying that nobody had seen her from a window.

Zia rang the bell of the front door. Mr. Longwill himself appeared, now very much the country gentleman, having had time to change into a yellow polo-neck sweater and beautifully cut check trousers.

"I am so sorry to bother you," she said, "but I was passing the paddock and saw that your mare was in trouble. She has got one foot tangled up in a coil of wire."

"How very kind of you, Mrs. . . . er . . ."

"Fanshawe."

"Ah, yes! The general's wife staying at the White Hart. Not good enough for you, I'm afraid. But worthy people, worthy people! Now let's have a look at the mare!"

The mare was panicking — another strain on Zia's conscience — and it was obvious to her that Mr. Longwill had no intention whatever of removing the wire. He looked helplessly around.

"I fear my man has knocked off."

"Oh, I expect I can do it. My husband and I still keep up the cavalry traditions."

"You will be careful?"

"I am always careful," she replied, giving him her most dazzling smile.

It was not all that simple to bring the suspicious mare to her, but that done the removal of the wire was no problem. Paul Longwill immediately invited her to come in and have a drink, saying that two people would be there.

"In fact I think I have just heard their car arrive. Lady Jane Thistleton-Thorner I expect you know, and Sir Humphrey Baylis is one of the sheriffs."

A sheriff sounded sinister though she had a vague memory that sheriffs in England gave dinners and no longer caught Robin Hoods. As for Lady Jane, Zia could only hope that she had never mixed in army circles.

They seemed harmless enough, both of them in their late forties, and courteous. Longwill introduced her as Mrs. Fanshawe.

"Her husband holds an important command in Germany. And here is his very *belle alliance* with France."

Nobody asked about General Fanshawe. Knowing Longwill, they probably reckoned that he was a mere colonel and one couldn't be expected to know them all. But worse was to come.

"Good Lord, I thought she was Zia Fodor!" Lady Jane exclaimed. "What an extraordinary likeness!"

"Who is she?" Zia forced herself to ask.

"She rides for Hungary. Won the President's Cup at Vienna. A certainty for the Olympics if those bloody communists would only buy her some decent horses."

"All you women look the same in a riding hat," Paul Longwill said.

She did not dare meet his eyes and show her gratitude. An hour of acting dragged out, acting and calling up all her Magyar gaiety to help her. When Longwill's distinguished guests at last got up to go — the sheriff full of compliments to his host's champagne and the general's French wife — she herself followed.

"I'll run you back, Mrs. Fanshawe," Longwill said.

He stopped well outside the village. His eyes were keen and severe, but the lines of the mouth could not quite keep up with them.

"And now, Miss Fodor?"

"It's a long story."

"He went back to Lille very suddenly without saying good-bye. Not like Georges at all. When did you last see him?"

"On Monday morning. He had just had news from his office. We met in Alderton Wood. There was a place where he was sure we should not be seen. Under some bushes by a stream."

"I know it. A charming spot and his own. He must be very fond of you to take you there."

"Business, not romance, Mr. Longwill. He has no reason at all to be fond of me. But we must not be seen together and we have to meet. Often."

"The police?"

"Partly. But it's more important than that."

"Anything to do with Bridge Holdings?"

"I have a confession to make. I put on that wire myself."

"Oh, I guessed that when the old girl recognized you."

"Will she talk?"

"She won't bother to look up the army list; there's probably a Fanshawe of some sort anyway. She'll snort that you're just one of Paul's attractive women. Now, tell me why you had to see me."

"Do you know anything about the British Secret Service?"

"No more than the revelations of newspapers — which are far too many if it's supposed to be secret."

How much should she tell him? She dared not plunge and yet she had to convince. Secrets, secrets. It was intolerable to know so much. Nothing in her active life had trained her for this. Protection of the club, of Georges, of herself was balanced against the duty to pass on at least some dark shadow of the facts, omitting the detailed outline of reality.

"Georges came over here with information — military information — which must be of value to somebody. I made him come. He was told that Bridge Holdings would understand, but they couldn't and would have nothing to do with us. Perhaps they thought we were *agents provocateurs.* Two men have been killed already, Mr. Longwill — a Czech called Karel Kren and somebody nicknamed Lukash whom we don't know. And now I am worried about Georges."

"Then you must go to the police at once."

"But they wouldn't pay much attention to two foreigners with a story that doesn't hold together. They would wonder what our game was, like Herbert Spring. And Kren's death — it would take them a week to check and they'd only find that he was run over by a bus in Lille."

"At least I can get you a hearing, Miss — Mrs. Fanshawe. Discreetly. Only last week I was dining with the Chief Constable."

"I don't think you should. You see, another man has died too."

"You mean — well, you and Georges were involved?"

"We were witnesses. And we don't want to talk. Not yet."

"When will you talk?"

"When you find the right person to listen."

"In my position I cannot afford to be compromised, Mrs. Fanshawe."

"But you know so many people. You're in — what was it Georges said? Oh, yes — the corridors of power."

Georges had actually said that Paul liked to think he was, but clearly she was on target.

"Near them perhaps," he answered complacently. "Whom do you want me to approach?"

"I don't know. People who are interested in the military strength of the Warsaw Pact."

"The Ministry of Defense. But forgive me — they have professionals reporting on that sort of thing."

"I know. But sometimes an amateur, without wanting it at all, can give them more than they dream."

Paul Longwill's manner changed completely. It was as if he had suddenly got her into perspective and appreciated her problem. He began to speak from experience without any of his tiresome affectations.

"Security. I don't know anything much about it, but I can tell you what I have noticed. Where secrecy is vitally important, security is often overdone. Let's say I'm working on something that mustn't get out. Think of me at the center of a circle and around the circumference I have placed my personal barbed wire — guards, diversions, prohibitions — to prevent a leak. Very effective. But suppose somebody like you or Georges wants to come in with valuable information? Way blocked. No thoroughfare. If security is to prevent anything going out, it must also prevent anyone coming in."

Zia was impressed. The man's pretense of worldly wisdom seemed to be merely an unnecessary decoration on the real thing.

"Mr. Longwill, you are so wise."

"Kind of you, but I doubt it. I can find my way through some wire fences but not that one."

"Perhaps you could if you were to go and see Herbert Spring yourself."

"I will for your sake, if you can give me something simple and sane to tell him."

"You told Georges that Bridge Holdings had interests in Prague, so they must have an agent there. Ask Mr. Spring if the agent knew Karel Kren of Intertatry and if he ever gave him the name of Bridge Holdings. If Spring answers that he doesn't know, then someone should go to Prague and talk to the agent. It would be very dangerous to write or telephone. And leave me out of it altogether! Explain that you were brought up with Georges and you're doing it for him. You don't know of my existence. He'll talk to you about me and tell you that I'm an adventuress and a crook. But he liked Georges."

"You'll be here for a few days more and all right?"

"I'll be here till I know what has happened to Georges."

"Good! I'll pass the word around that the general has asked me to look after you."

"At Eton together?"

"Do you want to walk home?"

"If you'll walk with me."

"Zia, you are adorable. Count on me!"

He dropped her at the White Hart and drove away after a genial and squirely word with the proprietor. Zia made for the lounge which provided for RESIDENTS ONLY four comfortable chairs and a table with its own serving hatch. A man standing at the bar politely intercepted her and asked:

"Mrs. Fanshawe?"

"Yes?"

He was wrinkled by the sun with gray stubble on a rugged, badly shaven face and black, wavy hair turning gray over the temples. Already used to judging English types in a country bar, she decided that he was neither farmer nor farmhand nor one of the bolder spirits out of fast cars who were inclined to approach her and offer a drink. He could be police; he could be worse. But neither was likely as yet to have spotted the connection between Mrs. Fanshawe and Georges Rivac.

With his back to the bar he asked in a low voice where he could speak to her. His accent was markedly foreign, probably Latin. She led him out to a garden table between wallflowers and tulips where they could be seen from bar and kitchen windows but not overheard.

"I come with a message from a man you know."

"Oh, thank God!"

"Wait! No thank God. Not for him. He asked me to tell you that you are quite safe. They know nothing of you."

"Who is they?"

"Those who have him, Mrs. Fanshawe. I don't like it here. We can be seen from the road."

A difficult problem. She could hardly ask a stranger up to her bedroom without arousing curiosity nor could they talk in RESIDENTS ONLY where every word could be heard through the hatch. When she hesitated he said:

"I came to sell you a motorcycle, Mrs. Fanshawe. You answered my advertisement. It is in the garage. I did not want to leave it outside. My name is Diego Irata, at your service."

Evidently a quick-witted and experienced operator. The garage was deserted. Mr. Irata ran the engine of his Triumph as if showing it off.

"Mrs. Fanshawe, I do not ask what you are. I take a risk for you and hope you will take one for me. I will tell you frankly about myself. I am a Spaniard and a communist, the servant of an Englishman very distinguished. He too is a member of the Party, secretly, for many years. He is not one of their *policía*. He is bigger than that, an intelligencer. But they were in a hurry and desperate and could find no one else, I think, with the facilities. He had to obey.

"And why are you, Diego Irata, a traitor, you will ask. I will explain. At last I can go home, if I can get there."

She could see that Irata was prepared to go on justifying himself indefinitely and firmly switched the conversation to Georges, putting on the manner of a professional interrogator — or as much of it as she could remember — friendly but with a hint of powers in reserve. Irata freely accepted that she had a right to question, but his answers led only to growing despair. No reason to thank God was right.

Georges was held in the house of a Mr. Fyster-Holmes, apparently an imposing specimen of the governing class who had retired early from the Foreign Office and was now in his early fifties. Irata did not know the name of the prisoner nor his importance. The house was on the right bank of the Thames upriver from Moulsford, with its garden running down to a patch of marsh in which was a small muddy creek and a landing stage. It was approached from the main road by a lane and partly hidden by a belt of trees. Georges was to be embarked on a motor cruiser that very night and taken down to the estuary for transshipment. Irata himself was to go with him.

"That is why I am here, Mrs. Fanshawe. I shall be taken to the East and never allowed to return home. Not to go home to Spain when now at last I can? That I do not accept!"

Zia ordered him to accompany her at once to the police. Whatever the cost to her family and herself, it seemed the only hope. Irata refused, saying she must go by herself.

"But it will be useless. I tell you this man has served his country abroad with distinction. Think! You say you are told by his Spanish servant that he is a spy and always has been. They will laugh at you. Then perhaps you tell them who is the prisoner and what interest you have. That is more serious. They may take you to higher authority who will give you a nice cup of tea and start inquiries. And while you are waiting and repeating your story to sergeants and colonels and generals of police the boat will have passed out to sea and Fyster-Holmes will deny any knowledge of it, swearing that it was all invented by the communist Irata."

"Have they hurt him?"

"I never heard him scream so I do not think so. Out of respect for Fyster-Holmes they would not risk a scandal. He is frightened enough already. It's bad luck for him that he has so quiet a house by the river."

"Who is in the house besides your boss?"

"Only one. A Czech."

"No wife?"

"No."

"His tastes?"

"As you imagine. But do not mistake our relationship! I was only his servant, both of us at the orders of the Party."

"When did you speak to my friend?"

"This morning. I was on guard outside the door and forbidden to talk to him. But he heard me cursing in my own language because I had dreamed of returning to my hills above the sea and now knew I never could. A man may serve the world, *señora,* but still be sick with longing for one little spot in it. He overheard me and spoke to me in Spanish. 'Do me a favor, *compañero!*' he said and gave me the message for you. It was then I decided I would run. It seemed to me you might be a friend. I had need of one."

"Mr. Irata, you will take me at once to the house on the back of your motorcycle."

"Not I!"

"Then you'll get no help. It will take time to get your permission to return to Spain. An exiled communist must visit the consulate and register his name and I don't know what else. These people will trace you and kill you. Or the English may put you in jail as a spy."

"It is true I do not know where to stay safely or how to travel," Irata answered resignedly.

"I will do it all for you if you will drop me at the lane which leads to the house. Then you are to go straight to Alderton, which is near here. Down the road you will see the signpost. Find the Manor Farm — it is the biggest house — and give a note to Mr. Longwill. Wait here for me while I write it!"

She dashed to her room and scribbled:

Dear Paul: Please take this man on as your new Spanish valet. Keep him out of sight. I know where Georges is and am going after him. No time for police, but perhaps I can help.

She quickly changed into a sweater and slacks and racked her brains for an excuse to give the landlord for suddenly disappearing on the back of a stranger's motorbike. She wanted to buy one of Mr. Longwill's horses, she said, and had asked her husband's farrier to vet it for her. He was free this evening, so she was going to run out to Alderton with him. A weak story even for a vague woman explaining in a hurry, but it would have to do.

The sun had gone down when she set off on Irata's pillion, and the land no longer smiled at her. Irata chugged briskly along narrow roads just below a range of wooded hills with flattish country to the right, sometimes invisible behind the rampant green of May, sometimes mazed with tree and hedge and disappearing into a formless distance. She was disturbed by this journey into nowhere without any mental map or any of Georges's confidence to reassure her.

In less than half an hour Irata crossed a stone bridge, ran through a country town with a flickering of lights and a drawing of curtains and then turned left between the river and another range of hills. So that was the famous Thames which she had only known in London where it possessed a certain dignity like a raddled and incontinent old duchess in attendance on the court. Up here it was the duchess in youth, pretty but undistinguished. What a closed country this England was, without any great river, lake or mountain! The inhabitants perceived its singularities with pride, though to the foreigner it was all the same and mysterious in its sameness. And here she, a Hungarian, rode behind an unknown Spaniard launching herself into an obscurity of night and geography. The only comfort was that Appinger might find it no less foreign. To this Fyster-Holmes, however, there would be no mysteries and Irata too seemed quite at home.

"How long have you been in England?" she asked him.

"Five years."

"And before that?"

"Mexico."

"You have liked it here?"

"In everything except that it is not Spain. Look! I have read history. England like Spain has lost an empire. We sank very low. So could England. The hope for both is to be part of something greater than ourselves."

That in a way was what had accounted for the sympathy between Kren and Rivac; the mirage of a unity less rigid than that of communism. It reminded her that she had a creed to support her; she was not just a foolish woman adventuring in a void.

Irata pulled up.

"Around the next corner is the lane to the house " he said. "I shall go straight past, stopping for an instant to let you get off. Take cover in the trees, and God be with you if there is one!"

"Is the house guarded?"

"No. Now that I have gone, only the boss and the Czech will be there. But the boat may bring others. How much am I to tell this Longwill?"

"Nothing yet. If I am free I will telephone him. If I disappear, tell him all your story."

She slid off and into the trees at the entrance to the lane. The noise of the motorbike faded away. The road was fairly busy, headlights streaming past the inconspicuous way to the house; yet the house itself had a quiet and natural privacy protecting comings and goings without any need for special security. No wonder Fyster-Holmes was nervous at the sudden intrusion of violence! Here by the river he could relax, certain that his home had never been under suspicion and had never given reason for it.

It was now dark enough to sneak cautiously along the shoulder of the lane. Though Irata had assured her there were no guards she was alarmed by every patch of darkness and once suffered from a shivering which could not be put down to the chill of evening. As soon as she could make out the outline of the house she was calmer. It was an elegant rectangle with a circular gravel drive to the left and to the right what looked like lawns and flower beds. A few dim lights were showing.

She followed the scanty cover to the right and discovered that the garden was terraced. That was fine. By keeping low she could work her way along the south side of the house and see before she was seen. Then the river, black and silent, came into view. The east side faced it across an indeterminate distance which had to be the marsh. The creek was hard to distinguish. Eventually she found that it was not in that direction at all but below the garden on the south side. Steps led down through two low terraces to a wooden landing stage above a black pool. That must be where the motor launch would arrive. The water, still and unbroken, looked deep enough.

Zia decided that it was pointless to close in on the house. The only useful action was to await the boat; at least she could take note of its name, size and color and describe it to the police. Looking for cover from which to watch she explored the bank of the creek, revetted with planks and still a little boggy from spring floods which had come up as far as the lowest terrace. Beyond the landing stage the pool ended in hummocks of black mud with slimy water glistening between them in the scanty light of a waning moon and clusters of rushes from which half the length of a punt was sticking out. Even if one could get into the reeds without sinking it would be impossible to escape without a noisy, squelching struggle.

The only possible hiding place was in a tangle of twigs and rushes where the main branch of a leaning willow had fallen into the water and was carrying on its own amphibious life. The punt too was tempting if it could be reached; lying down in it she would be covered from the landing stage but probably in full view of the boat as it came up the creek. The punt on closer inspection proved not to be moored to anything at all. The visible timber was clean and polished, so it was not derelict. It must have been given an impatient shove into the reeds to make room for the expected craft without bothering how it was to be recovered. There was other evidence of haste, now that she had time to think about it. On the edge of a flower bed she had passed a wheelbarrow half full of weeds or plants with a garden fork leaning up against it. Somebody had stopped work in a hurry and had been too occupied ever since to finish and put tools away — perhaps when Georges arrived or Irata left.

Traffic had died away. The night was silent except for the humming of an occasional car on the main road. For the first hour Zia was continually looking at her watch and finding that her estimate of time had to be divided by three. The house was all quiet innocence without a sign of life save the darkening of one ground-floor window. As another hour dragged on she was tempted to take some action — any action. She insisted that an enterprising burglar would long ago have been in through the window and had to remind herself that the burglar was unlikely ever to reappear. To fill up time she reconnoitered the quickest way to the lane, nearer than she thought, and established to her satisfaction that she was quite alone in the garden.

She was beginning to wonder how she had allowed herself to be taken in by Irata and his story when the white boat with no lights showing came drifting out of the night as silently as a swan, with barely enough steerage-way to reach the stage. Caught in the open between terraces, she dropped flat in a flower bed. She could just make out a man outlined against the sky as he stepped ashore and moored his craft. He then came up the steps of the two terraces, passing her closely, and she heard him crunching over the gravel of the drive as he approached the front door. Shortly afterward all lights in the house were extinguished.

On board the boat was neither light nor a sound. It seemed safe to take a closer, cautious look. It was a motor cruiser with a saloon amidships and a skylight in the bow, probably over a cabin where Georges could safely be confined during the voyage down river. Her experience was only of Danube navigation, but the boat appeared easily capable of that much and ought to be good enough for the open sea. Nobody was left on board unless asleep which was unlikely. Its name was *Amanda*.

They must have emerged from a french window opening onto the lawn for there was no crunch of gravel to warn her. The first she heard of them was a murmur of low voices. Escape under cover of the terrace was still easy but she was determined to observe. In a minute there was not going to be anything more, ever, to observe. The only game was to delay, leaving them with darkness, a mystery, a mess. She cast off the cruiser's painter, lay down and pushed, with her back against the bollard, legs against the bow. The cruiser drifted away into midstream and she had just time to creep out into the marsh along the fallen willow branch.

Four figures were approaching the landing stage, one leading the way with a pool of light on the ground ahead of him and another man immediately following. Behind him were Georges and a companion. The leader, who sounded as Fyster-Holmes ought to sound, exclaimed:

"My God! You didn't moor her properly!"

"Of course I did. She's still moving. Someone has just done it."

"Irata! He must be in the marsh."

"I'll reach her while you get him. Is the pole in the punt?"

"Yes."

The second speaker ran down over the grass and landing stage and jumped, just making the stern of the punt and tumbling forward into the bottom. Pushing the punt clear of the mud, he drifted down on the cruiser and started the engines.

V

GEORGES RIVAC ENTERED THE car which had so courteously stopped for him. Asked if he was bound for Oxford, he replied that he was. The driver said that he himself was going to Oxford, but on the way wanted to see about some business at Waterperry which wouldn't take a minute. Georges knew the little village and took it for granted that the business was with its horticultural station since there was nothing much else. The driver seemed reluctant to discuss horticulture, switching the conversation to his passenger on the excuse that he appeared familiar with the district. On that point Georges was careful to give nothing away and took refuge in an unlikely story of a broken-down car. Only then did it occur to him that he was on his guard against trusting anybody with his past but had impatiently trusted with his present the first person who came along.

By this time they had turned off the main road through the village of Waterstock and into a lane which was hardly more than a field track. Georges pointed out that they could not get to Waterperry that way, but the driver kept going with confidence. Bumping across ruts he turned a sharp bend.

"Ah, there he is!" he exclaimed and pulled up behind a plain black van parked on the shoulder.

He got out, leaving the door open. Simultaneously Appinger, that hospitable Intertatry manager last seen at Lille, swooped from the back of the van. Georges promptly obeyed the order to change from car to van, for the barrel of an automatic was only a foot from his head. The van started as soon as the door slammed. The whole operation had not taken more than twenty seconds.

He was thankful to be alive; he could just as well have been popped into the van as a corpse. It had been so smooth and easy a kidnapping that he was ashamed of himself. Surely it should have been possible to resist, to run, to yell? But one needed experience. Criminals, secret agents, policemen, they knew what to do. Probably had a practice ground somewhere. And he might have had the sense to remember that they wanted him alive and wouldn't shoot.

Of course! That jay this morning had been right. Somebody had followed him from Thame, lost him in the wood where he met Zia, picked him up as he was meant to do when he left, lost him before he entered Alderton — he was sure of that — and waited till he reappeared on his way to the main road. Then a quick phone call, and out came the car in the hope of collecting him.

The choice of the deserted track was excellent and the journey too short for him to start thinking and become suspicious. Appinger and his service must have quickly recruited an assistant who knew the country well and lived not far off. No telling where. The van was windowless with a partition between him and the front seats, and he could not distinguish the direction in which it was heading. So far as he could judge there was a short spell of main road, a long spell of secondary roads, then through a town and a steady run. Thirty-five minutes in all. Say, twenty miles from Waterstock.

When the van stopped, the Czech slipped through the back door still with his pistol. And no arguing with that, Georges, even if they do want you alive. May not be pleasant. Well, damned if I commit suicide like Kren. With a sack pulled over his head and shoulders he was led across a gravel drive, through the ground floor of a house, up three flights of stairs and into a room. When the door was locked he took off the sack as nobody seemed present to object. He found he was in a little suite of bedroom and bathroom, windows facing west onto trees with a hint of downland beyond them. A guest room, probably, in a mature house which might be anywhere.

As soon as he had sat down and drawn breath Appinger came in, giving him no time to think. He was not armed — or not visibly — but taking no chances. Before the door shut Georges caught a glimpse of a stocky fellow on guard outside.

"Now what is this?" he exclaimed. "What have I done? What has Intertatry got against me?"

Absolute ignorance was, he reckoned, the best and simplest game to play: to throw himself back to six days ago and to know no more than he did then. It was not likely that he would be believed, but at least the questions might show him how much they suspected.

"What a pity that you did not come to Prague with me and avoid all this embarrassment!" the Czech replied in his harsh French.

"But I was coming! *Voyons,* Monsieur Appinger! I just had to visit England first on business."

"And what was the business?"

"But you know already! Karel Kren wanted me to call on some government importers who had been making inquiries

100

about the new model of the engine. He said he had not time to go himself."

"Why you?"

"I understood it was because I had been doing some promising business for Intertatry and I spoke good English. I was very surprised. His visit was entirely unexpected."

"There had been no such inquiries, Monsieur Rivac."

"So I was told. I couldn't make sense of it."

"Whom did you call on?"

"But I told you in Lille. The Ministry of Defense. A Mr. Lester."

Georges again omitted Bridge Holdings. Going by Paul Longwill's description of the firm and its reputation for collecting information, it could be suspect.

"What message did you give them from Kren?"

"No message. I did my sales talk and answered questions. I think they are going to give you a trial order."

Appinger spread out the contents of Rivac's case on the table: pajamas, toilet necessaries, passport, traveler's checks and the large envelope he had received that morning. He opened it and pulled out Suzi's two letters.

"You see, Monsieur Appinger! Only on Friday, three days ago, you left a present for me from Intertatry. This change of attitude is incredible," Georges protested.

"We are always generous, Monsieur Rivac."

Appinger glanced casually through the letters and put them back in their envelope.

"Why did you ask for these brochures?"

"Because I had left them behind."

"But on your first visit to England you had them with you."

One of Georges's intuitions suddenly sparked and flared.

"But, Monsieur le Directeur, that is just what I did not. On my first journey I did not bother to take any sales literature, understanding from Monsieur Kren that they had it all. I found that they did not. They needed details of the improved engine and the quite revolutionary exhaust to prevent fumes in any workshop. Well, I could have sent them copies of the new brochure by mail, but you were so polite, so grateful for my services to Monsieur Kren that I thought the least I could do was to go over again and deliver them in person. But that was hard to fit in. I had engagements. I was flustered and in a hurry. And when I opened my case in London what did I find? That inexcusably I had packed the brochures for the older model. Both, you must admit, are much alike, both covers pale blue and showing the size of our little engine compared with a liter mug of pilsner. So at once I telephoned my secretary to send me the right ones."

Though such inefficiency was not in Georges's character, the gush of nervous excuses was. He almost convinced himself that the mistake had really happened, but his interrogator offered neither sympathy nor comment and disconcertingly changed the subject.

"What are you doing at this village of Alderton?"

"I am there because I knew it as a boy. I have an old friend whom I like to revisit when I can — my grandmother's housekeeper."

"And who else?"

"Nobody. So many years have passed."

"Who was the man you met in the wood this morning?"

"I met no one. I was taking a walk. Very natural, is it not, to revisit scenes of one's youth, Monsieur Appinger? I do not know what you can have got into your head. This is an outrage!"

"An outrage, Rivac? Then explain this second letter from your secretary! You were witness to a fatal accident."

"Unfortunately yes."

"Can you tell me what happened?"

"A man fell overboard. The captain said his name was Rippmann."

"I am aware of that. Perhaps you will tell me how you recognized him?"

"I didn't recognize him. How should I?"

"Then I will put it this way. How did you know he was to report your movements?"

"But why should anyone report my movements? I still do not understand."

"Enough fooling, Rivac! Do you expect me to believe it was a coincidence that you just happened to witness the death of a man whom you wanted to get rid of?"

"But I didn't want to get rid of him. I knew nothing of him."

"Rippmann had a colleague with him on the ship, Rivac."

A lie! The colleague would have reported the presence and involvement of Zia.

"Well, if he'd got any eyes he could tell you what happened. The sea was very rough. This Rippmann was puking over the side. He had forgotten to take out his dentures and overbalanced trying to catch them when they fell."

"With a little help from you. It is not customary for agents to commit murder, Monsieur Rivac."

It seemed more and more certain that they knew nothing of Zia. That was quite possible if Harbor Police had taken no action and merely filed the doubtful case. And Appinger had not pressed the question of a meeting in the wood, seeming to accept his explanation. Perhaps when off duty his own heart — if he had one — was among the mushrooms of some Russian birch wood.

"For the love of God, I am nobody's agent."

"I do not think you are, or you wouldn't be here. How much did Kren pay you?"

"Nothing. Why should he?"

"What message did he trust you with?"

"I repeat — apart from business, none! At least tell me what it is supposed to be about!"

"Monsieur Rivac, you are rather cleverer than I expected. I fear that you will have to come with me to Prague after all. Think it over!"

He was left to think it over. What was it Zia had told him? "They will put it down to your courage, not your innocence." Courage, hell! He'd hand them those bloody brochures with pleasure if he had them. Or would he? It would be interesting to find out. A worse problem was Zia. His perfectly simple story might well be accepted provided he was free to explain Zia's part in it. The French are gallant, she said. And so, by God, we are! What about the plaque on the wall of the Rue Feidherbe? Damn the little love!

When Appinger brought him a tray of supper he was accompanied by a masked man, tall, middle-aged and of some distinction, to judge by clothes and bearing, who examined him with interest but did not open his mouth. He could well be the owner of this very civilized house, taking special care that his face should never be recognized. Georges was then left alone for the night.

Escape was impossible. The stout door was locked. The

window had been very recently nailed up. He found a clothes brush marked with a silver F-H which had evidently been overlooked, for everything else which might give a clue to identity had been removed. The brush and warm water provided an occupation in trying to improve the state of his Lille business suit. Longwill and his masked host had made him conscious of rumpled shabbiness. He wondered whether he had been taken for a small, provincial business-man ready to accept anybody's money or whether secret agents normally tried to look insignificant.

At first light he at last fell asleep so soundly that he was woken up by Appinger with breakfast.

"Have you thought it over, Monsieur Rivac?"

"A thousand times! But still I do not know what you have against me. Kren called on me, good! But why shouldn't he? In any case he was a member of the Party."

The moment he had said it he knew it was a disastrous mistake. The technique of keeping him sweet and amenable and then encouraging conversation when he was in a comfortable bed and half-awake had worked.

"So you are aware that Kren was a traitor!"

"Traitor? To what?"

"Come, come, Rivac! If your dealings with Kren were purely commercial what does it matter whether he was or was not a member of the Party?"

"Well, I can see you believe he was up to something political."

"Why?"

"Look at the trouble you have taken to find me! I cannot imagine how you did it."

"As soon as you realize that there is little we do not know, the better for you."

105

"Then, Monsieur Appinger, I will put a question myself if you allow it. Why the devil should I push this Rippmann overboard?"

"Yesterday I asked you how you recognized him. It is one of the points which will have the attention of my colleagues in Prague."

"Of Intertatry?"

"Rivac, you are overdoing your part of an innocent. You know very well by now that I am not employed by Intertatry. So shall we assume that your first visit to London was to establish contact and your second visit to deliver — what?"

"The brochures which I forgot. I have told you already."

"As yet Intertatry have never ordered any new brochures to be printed."

Georges was silent. There at last was proof that the brochures did indeed contain Kren's message. His only hope was to hand them over; then the truth — that he had believed Kren and quite naturally obeyed his instructions — stood a chance of being accepted. The time for any other defense of himself had passed. And in any case what was there to defend?

"Where are those brochures now?" Appinger asked.

To his dismay Georges heard himself answering:

"But naturally I mailed them at once to Mr. Lester at the Ministry of Defense."

"You mailed nothing this morning. You never entered Alderton. You opened the envelope in the main square of Thame, read the contents and left at once to revisit scenes of your youth."

"And found them charming, Monsieur Appinger."

"Then I will leave you with another charming thought to

occupy your morning. If you disappear, your friends in Lille will believe you are in England and your friends in England will believe you have returned to Lille. You are such a traveler, and always it seems at short notice. It will be some time before anyone discovers where you are or may be. Now enjoy your breakfast! It will be your last meal today."

He left. Georges considered possible reasons why he should be left hungry and arrived at the alarming theory that during the move he would be put out of action by some drug which must be administered on an empty stomach.

The only comfort was that they knew nothing whatever of Zia's existence. He paced the room, muttering excitedly to himself until he realized that the walls might be bugged. About midday he heard someone else complaining to himself with a rich selection of Spanish expletives, presumably the guard outside the door. All that could be guessed was that he had received some order which he was not going to obey.

"What part of Spain is your home, *compañero?*" Georges asked.

There was silence. It might be due to the guard's surprise at being addressed in his own language or because he was forbidden to speak to the prisoner.

"Vizcaya. And you?"

"Also the north, but from León."

"What have you done?"

"They say I am a British agent."

"That cannot be true. You would have been protected."

"It is human to err."

"*Joder!* Then you could help me!"

Close to the door in a voice that hardly carried the guard told his troubles. He had been ordered to accompany the

prisoner on board a boat which would take them out to a
rendezvous at sea. He did not want to go. He was a communist, yes, but he longed to return from exile to his Vizcaya now that the Spanish government allowed it. The KGB
would see that he didn't. He knew too much.

"And so this afternoon before it is too late I shall bolt.
Where to I do not know. They will kill me if they can find
me."

"Take me with you!"

"I cannot. It will be hard enough to get away myself. But
I will give a message if it can be done secretly."

"To the police?"

"They will not come in time. They will hesitate, for the
man who owns this house is above suspicion. But I will give
a message to your chief if I can reach him. At least I can
say where you are and how you will leave. And then for me
he might find a place of safety and a way of travel."

The man sounded honest and desperate. If only Georges
had in fact been a British agent delivery would have been
in sight, but whom was he to approach? Zia and Paul Longwill were the only possibles but neither could undertake a
rescue operation at short notice.

"Can you open the door?"

"No. The Czech has the key."

So there could be no meeting to judge the man eye to
eye; his plausible story and his voice must suffice. He
sounded sincere and desperate, prepared to take the chance
that his prisoner — if it would do him any good — might
report his intention to Appinger. There was a risk in sending him to Zia, but it could be accepted since the true identity of Mrs. Fanshawe was not easily discoverable and her

involvement in the Kren affair quite unknown. Assured of that, she could return to Hungary.

"Do you know the country east of Oxford?" he asked.

"Well enough. I ride a motorcycle when I am free. For two years I have been the manservant here. I look after the house while he is in London and sometimes I report on his visitors."

"Go from Thame to Alderton Abbas. At an inn called the White Hart ask for Mrs. Fanshawe. She is the French wife of a British general and has the contacts which could help us. Tell her first that these people know nothing of her or her movements. For the present she is quite safe. Then tell her where I am and what they mean to do with me. *De acuerdo?*"

"Never fear! I cannot hope that we shall meet again. But if we do I am Diego Irata at your service. *Salud, compañero!*"

From then on there was the usual silence, emphasized by the line of trees stirring in a light breeze without a sound. Above the treetops the strip of sunlit downland offered the sanity of freedom. He heard a car or two drive up and quickly leave, probably delivering mail or supplies. In how many secluded country houses was there, he wondered, a guest unknown to police or neighbors or to the normal services of daily life?

In the afternoon a motorcycle drove away at unusually high speed. That could be Irata. For the first time he heard an excited voice loudly calling from the house below him. Alarmed they would certainly be until, after thinking it over, they could be pretty sure that Irata would not return with police. What was a Spanish manservant's improbable story against the utmost respectability and a room by then tidied up without a trace of a captive? And was Irata likely to proclaim himself a defected agent of the KGB when all he wanted was to go home to Spain in peace without any police record?

Georges waited for Appinger to come in with the syringe or an apparently harmless drink. Without Irata to hold him down there might be a chance of resistance unless that superior fellow, his host, lent a hand. Till now it had hardly occurred to the peaceable Georges that he himself might turn to violence — not that he had much chance of success in a free-for-all if Appinger used that automatic of his. It was possible that no one else was in the house besides those two, for the van had driven away after unloading him. The driver who had offered him that fatal lift could be there, but Georges came to the conclusion that he was on the outside sales staff rather than an executive of the firm. He had looked startled and shocked when Appinger swooped from the door of the van.

A boat, Irata had said. Well, the house could not be anywhere near the sea but could be on or near the Thames. He knew little about the river but presumed it was easy to borrow or hire some roomy, seaworthy craft for a week. And who would disturb a sleeping passenger down below? Dear old Rivac — or whatever name they chose to give him — drunk as usual!

Night fell and still nothing happened nor was likely to happen till the complete darkness after midnight. He was far from forgotten, however, for when he pressed the switch no light followed. He stared out of the window, his only communication with the world, night sight growing keener until he could just distinguish the bare skyline: a strip of black between the faintly moonlit sky and the darker black of treetops.

At last Appinger came in accompanied by a physically powerful partner whose face might be that of any European nation. He was probably English since Appinger had to communicate with him in his own scrappy version of the language.

"I'll hold him down," the newcomer said.

"Later. On boat. Not want carry him."

Georges was efficiently gagged and ordered to clasp his hands behind his head. It was no use to resist. Appinger was weighing the automatic in his hand, showing rather than pointing it. Georges was reasonably certain that he would not be killed until Prague had got what it wanted from him, but there could be no objection to disabling him, if necessary, by a bullet through arm or leg.

He was taken downstairs through the dark hall and out into a gravel drive. The presumed owner of the house was waiting with his back to them and led the way down through two terraces to a landing stage, keeping the pool of light from his torch on the ground so that the captive should have no chance of recognizing his surroundings. Apparently the boat should have been waiting but it was not. They decided excitedly that Irata had returned and cast off the mooring. They were sure of that though it seemed to Georges highly unlikely in view of what Irata had said to him; but the motives and intentions of all concerned were as impenetrable as the pool of black water among reeds.

A white cabin cruiser was slowly drifting in midstream. The beam of the torch played over the banks of the pool, revealing nothing at all but mud, rushes and the stern of a punt among them. The big man who had brought the boat from the Thames into this puddle — for it was he who denied that he had moored her carelessly — wasted no time. He launched himself in a running long jump onto the punt, poled it to the cruiser and gave her a touch of power, going astern and then maneuvering to come alongside again.

Meanwhile Irata's employer had rushed along the bank in the hope of spotting him hidden among the reeds. He must have decided either that it was hopeless in the dark or that Irata was safely stuck in the mud, for he turned back almost immediately. As soon as he had done so, something splashed into the water behind him.

"Here!" he shouted.

Georges could faintly discern the lower twigs of a willow shaking. Appinger too must have seen the movement and fired two shots, one above and one on the level of the branch. The reports woke Georges from his helplessly disinterested observation of what the hell was going on. Appinger was alone with him and his gun was pointing away. The punt drifted in the pool broadside on. He dived from the stage and came up on the far side of it.

A respite, but little hope. He was hidden from the two on the bank but in full view of the man on the cruiser. He drew a long breath, ducked under the punt and swimming on his back with his arms against the bottom propelled the punt back into the rushes. When it was aground forward and the mud began to catch at his legs he knew a moment of panic — black night, black wood against his forehead, black slime to breathe, jammed under the punt until he suffocated. But it was not as bad as that. His head easily came clear and in the cover of the reeds he could safely put one hand on the side of the punt and remove the gag with the other.

The cruiser could get in no further and reversed out. Appinger, however, was not a man to be beaten. He had lost a prisoner through a moment of carelessness and was open to reprimand for failing to prevent the disappearance of a useful Spanish underling. Perhaps pride and patriotism also counted. At any rate he decided that if Rivac could reach the punt so could he. He flung off his coat and plunged in; but the punt was now firmly aground and he could only approach it by walking or froglike squirming. He chose to wade; and that, till he could pull out a leg, was the end of his advance.

Georges meanwhile was hauling himself through the mud by the stems of rushes, using the long punt pole as horizontal support. A clump of stems pulled out under the tug of his hands with several pounds of black sludge attached to the roots. It was too good a chance to miss. He whirled the clump around his head and let fly. It caught Appinger full in the face just as he was hauling himself into the punt.

"This way, Georges!"

The voice was not Irata's but, amazingly, Zia's. Then he distinguished her outline crouched on hands and knees between the shoots of a willow branch which had dropped into the water. His recent host, the only man left on the bank, also saw her and managed to grab her ankle with both hands. He was leaning forward at full stretch and the left side of his throat was exposed. Georges, encouraged by his magnificent piece of slapstick which had spattered and momentarily blinded Appinger, went over to the attack. With his feet now on a firm clump of roots he gathered up the heavy punt pole like a lance and lunged with such force that he himself fell forward. The little brass crescent at the end of the pole took the man in that inviting throat and whirled him against the hard bank. Georges climbed out and looked at the mangled mess of gullet and muscle and the fast stream of blood.

"Good God! I'm afraid I've hurt him!" he exclaimed.

The ludicrous understatement released Zia's tension. Her nerves had been stretched to the limit by the risk she had taken in creating a diversion, by a bullet which had gone through her hair and the final loss of hope when Fyster-Holmes grabbed. She burst into a peal of half-hysterical laughter, quickly swallowed.

There was no doubt that Fyster-Holmes was dead or rapidly dying. Whichever it was, they had only seconds to get clear. The boatman had thrown a rope to Appinger and hauled him on board. The cruiser was already nosing the landing stage.

Georges was slow off the mark, his clothes a flapping mass of mud — but so were Appinger's. Zia by now knew the layout of the garden. She led the way straight up the lane, across the road and over a gate into a field of young potatoes. Georges signaled to her to drop down and lie flat in a furrow. In the darkness they were indistinguishable from clods of earth.

Their two pursuers could faintly be heard searching the belt of trees which bordered the road. They soon gave up. They might have picked up the black trail which showed that the fugitives had crossed the road and were hopelessly lost in the night. After that there was silence.

"Do you know where we are?" Georges whispered.

"More or less. We went over a bridge at a place called Wallingford."

"Who's we?"

"The Spaniard who came with your message. I made him bring me here on the back of his motorbike and sent him back to Paul Longwill with my compliments."

"He knows who you are?"

She told him her part of the story, assuring him that Paul would help if anybody could.

"We have only to get back."

"I can't. Look at me!"

She could hardly recognize him as human till he sat up.

"Someone will give us a lift. We'll say you fell in the river."

"And when he is found, when his — er — body is found? The chap who gives us a lift will go straight to the police. Hopeless! Hopeless! Accused of murder! I shall give myself up."

"Georges, patience! You have only to tell your story."

"This chap you call Fyster-Holmes — Irata said he was above suspicion. I've no proof. I'm a bloody burglar from Lille. Or one of Fyster-Holmes's boyfriends. Tried to rape me. Sloshed him with the punt pole. But I ought to have let him, so the judge says. Hell!"

"Georges, your imagination! Come back to earth! They'll think it was Irata. They quarreled. Irata killed him and ran away."

"That's worse still. Poor Irata! And they won't think it long. Fingerprints on the punt and the pole. There must be some when the mud dries in the sun."

"What happened to your case?"

"Appinger has got it. And a lot of good it will be to him!"

In the distance they heard the slow beat of a marine engine and the change to full power as the boat reached open water.

"Gone!" Zia said. "But you can describe the boat. There must be evidence that there really was a boat."

"Fifty like it on the river. They wouldn't choose anything out of the ordinary. Scrubbed clean by morning and moored where it always is. *Amanda* — hell! *Amanda* — *je m'en fous!* Painted on a strip and stuck on! I could see it when the bow came close, and they would have fixed the stern too."

"Then Appinger. He can be traced."

"Appinger was only the name he gave me in Lille. It won't be on his passport. And he'll be out of the country tomorrow."

"He will not, Georges. Not without you, if he knows what's good for him."

"Well, he won't catch me again. Not till I come up before the beaks and he knows where to find me."

"What's beaks?"

"Judges of First Instance. I'm a secret agent, Your Worship. Who for? Don't know. What for? Thought I could be of use. To this country? To Europe. Remanded in custody for medical examination."

"*Nous sommes des espions. Des espions! Plon, plon!*" Zia chanted.

"*Cachons! Cachons! Entre les pommes de terre!*" he joined in.

"*Patati! Patata!*

"Not so loud! You're so good for me, dear Zia. Now then, down to earth! If we keep moving away from the river we shall come to downs and find a place to lie up. At dawn I can probably tell you where we are."

"You haven't told me yet what they wanted from you. The brochures?"

"Those, yes. And how I recognized Rippmann."

"You?"

"There was no reason to tell the truth."

"Georges, I don't deserve such loyalty."

"You do. You and Kren and your uncle. What you are serving I serve now."

There was no way out of the field but the gate which they had climbed, so they had to follow the road until they came to a lane running uphill to the west. The night had become overcast without a star or any moon to show the points of the compass, and it was now Zia's turn to feel lost and apprehensive. In Georges, however, there was still enough of his English upbringing to recognize when he felt it the southwest wind blowing clear over downland; and feel it he did, muttering that the equally cold and mud-soaked Appinger — God damn his eyes! — had a cabin and a drink. A track faced them where it was certain there would be no traffic in the small hours. Thankfully they followed it, but landed in a farmyard where dogs barked furiously and a bedroom light went on. The only quick and obvious way out was over the low roof of a range of pig-sties. They dropped into a field and kept going up a steep hillside until they were in thin, wild woodland.

It was her turn to ask if he knew where they were.

"No. But the light is growing. I can find out before anyone else is awake. You stay here."

He made a circuit of the farm and regained the lane which they had taken. Higher up it joined a main road and a second lane came out at nearly the same point. All were well signposted, forming an unmistakable rendezvous which could be overlooked from the hillside.

On returning to Zia he proposed that she should go down

to the nearest village, which must be Streatley, and telephone Paul Longwill to come out with some clothes. After
that they could consider the next move.

"I'd better not hang about so close," she said. "Suppose
the police find out that there was a woman involved. What
is the nearest big town?"

"Reading, I think. And there must be buses going there
from eight o'clock on."

"Then I'll aim for the road and the river and catch one.
And we had better have fixed times for the rendezvous.
They can't be on the lookout for us all day. Shall we make
it at twelve, at two and then every two hours till dark?"

"And you are sure of the rendezvous?"

"Main road from Streatley to Blewbury. At the junction
of lanes to Moulsford and Cholsey," she repeated.

He went with her for a mile in and out of the shelter of
trees and left her on the edge of open country where a track
led east toward the unseen river and she could not miss her
way. Then he returned by the same route to the hillside
where they had been at dawn.

The view was extensive but there was not much cover.
When he had taken off his clothes and spread them out to
dry he felt in more danger of arrest for indecent exposure
than for murder. Even if clues in and around the marsh
ruled out Irata there was no evidence leading to M. Rivac
of Lille.

The calm early morning passed with no near visitors but
rabbits. By eleven his clothes were nearly dry though still
filthy enough to arouse suspicion. The lack of a clothes
brush absurdly brought home to him his state of absolute
destitution — no passport, no possessions, no money except
for a damp pound note and some small change in his trou-

sers pocket. His earlier confidence, sparkling as deceptively as the vanished dew, was fatuous. He could not appeal to the police without risking arrest for double murder unless he involved Zia in Rippmann's death and allowed Irata to be arrested for the killing of Fyster-Holmes, both of which were unthinkable. Only perhaps in Lille could he ask for police protection on condition that they believed his unbelievable motives.

What was in those brochures must be of vital importance, and Appinger seemed certain that they had not been delivered and that Kren's agent knew what was in them. Evidently there had not been the time or the facilities for more than a summary interrogation. That awaited him elsewhere until he was mercifully and discreetly killed — a nightmare that he must always keep in the back of his mind wherever he walked or slept. One had only to consider the speed and efficiency of organization. On Friday they had learned his address. On Monday he had been trapped and all was ready for Tuesday night. Apparently the only slight risk they were compelled to accept was the enlistment of Fyster-Holmes and his hidden mud pool. No doubt the poor devil had protested but he had to obey.

Georges dressed and explored his immediate surroundings to find somewhere to lie up and watch the road junction where Zia and Paul were to wait for him. A patch of young gorse out on the open hillside was the best. Showing only his head he could see the cool peace of the Berkshire Downs and the wooded Chilterns on the other side of the Goring Gap. A very pleasant plot of Europe — but he wished to God he was back on the pavements of industrial Lille, preferably returning from his office with no more thought of Cold War than the forced headlines of the morning paper when there were neither fires nor murders nor political scandals to arouse the righteous indignation of the reader.

Returning? He never could. Good-bye, Zia! He called up picture after picture of her. How had he not realized till parting with her at this lonely sunrise on the downs that she was his life if he had any? A fine time to be dreaming of past and future when the line of the desperate present might continue indefinitely. His only duty was to ensure that she could safely take all that grace and laughter back to Budapest.

The distant farmer over whose pigsties they had climbed seemed to be holding a party; to judge by the scatter of cars someone had died or a daughter was getting married. As he watched, a van drove up and unloaded two dogs. One would have thought that the farm had enough damned dogs already. But that was a uniformed policeman on the other end of the leashes. Hills, Zia, Lille were all blotted out simultaneously by mental images of the banks of the creek, a punt pole, the trail of mud to the potato field, the distance between himself and those police dogs. What tracks had Zia left? She was wearing low-heeled shoes. She had never been into the mud, and it was probable that on grass, lane or dry farmyard she had left no tracks at all — or none that the police would find until they had time for a more exhaustive investigation of Fyster-Holmes's garden. The dogs would presumably know that they were on the trail of two persons, not one. But dogs could not talk.

Dogs couldn't talk. That went around and around in his head until between absurdity and terror he almost laughed. Except on his tour of exploration at first light he and Zia had never been more than a yard or two from each other till they separated. By now she should be far away in some kind of public transport. With luck her scent rather than his might be followed.

The dogs, their handler and two constables started at a smart pace up the hill, twice checking where his single track crossed the double line of escape from the farmyard. The check allowed him to get away ahead of them unseen, following his own path exactly — so far as stumbling panic allowed — back to the copse and the spot where he and Zia had rested. The dogs had now clearly decided that the double scent was correct and their duty was to follow it. That was worth knowing. If they were to track Zia traveling alone it would be against their better judgment. The eyes of the handler must be persuaded to overrule those more perceptive noses which couldn't talk. He had seen that happen when he and Paul used to follow the Bicester hounds on foot, seen the huntsman lift them at a check and put them on the wrong line. Once they had been so close to the fox that Paul swore it had winked at them.

He was obsessed by a hollow ash, struck by lightning and thickly draped with ivy, on the edge of the woodland near the point where Zia had left him and taken to the downs. A hollow tree would not be the slightest use as a hiding place, but it was an objective — typically vague and changeable on impulse. When he reached it he had lost his lead; but still the hounds, glimpsed during one of his dashes across the open, must be minutes behind and there was time to place a bet on eyes taking over from noses.

He looked inside the tree. The blackened interior was wide enough for a man to climb up — if he could use knees and elbows like a mountaineer — and hide himself among the ivy. Well, they might think he had been fool enough to do it and then lost his nerve. It made a convincing police picture.

He took off his coat. Bought in Paris and without any name inside the collar, it would not be much of a clue to identity. Dashing out on Zia's track, he threw it down in long grass, not too easy to see but impossible to miss. Then he returned to the blackened ash and left a maze of tracks for the dogs to puzzle out. A hundred yards away and upwind of them he allowed them to pass. Then frozen with terror and blankly trying to think of a story in case his gamble completely failed, he left the ground altogether by way of a low beech branch.

The dogs went straight for the hollow tree.

"Come out, Irata!" the handler shouted. "We've got you!"

No answer. It was not surprising that the police should take the missing Irata as the first and obvious suspect. The two constables looked up into the ivy from all angles, but only a nesting thrush at last lost her nerve and flew out with a squawk.

The dogs started to work the maze he had left. The two constables strolled into the open, spotted the coat, still warm, and yelled. Down to the coat, hot on the fresh, straight trail, went the dogs. They were then faced with Zia's single track and wanted to go back, but to their handler the story was plain. Irata had tried the hollow tree, realized that it was useless, dashed about in panic searching for some other hiding place and had then decided to run for it, panting, desperate and discarding his coat. From a fork halfway up his beech Georges could watch the men's enthusiasm and the dogs' reluctance. But the handler cast forward and they obeyed, intelligent eyes looking up at him. "If half of what we were chasing is what you want," they implied, "half you shall have."

Off they went over the grass on Zia's track. Georges, still trembling, stayed in his tree, undecided what to do. It was ten to one that when the party reached the road in Streatley it would give up. On the other hand this direct hunt was only the opening move of the police, so fast and unexpected that it nearly succeeded. Subsequent moves would be routine and calm. That bit of Europe which had seemed so friendly was going to be searched with international efficiency. There might also be road checks. The rendezvous with Zia was impossible.

So long as he could get safely out of the district he could go where he liked — up to a point. The description of the wanted man would be that of Irata, short, stocky, dark-haired, speaking with a foreign accent; but the jacket picked up by the police could not possibly fit Irata though it obviously belonged — even before laboratory analysis of the mud — to someone present at the death of Fyster-Holmes.

He was very hungry after all that exercise and nothing to eat for thirty-six hours. Worse still, he had a raging thirst and had not discovered a single stream in the smooth, dry valleys. Thirst decided what he must do. Risk or no risk, he must mix with his fellow men and find a tap.

It was wise to assume that the party with the dogs had by now come to the tentative conclusion that two men were concerned and that Irata had escaped in time while the other had very nearly been caught. This accomplice was coatless — nothing exceptional about that — of medium height, slim build and possibly French nationality. But before that description was broadcast, surely there must be a conference, a report, even an argument? Hurry, then, hurry!

He came down from his tree and ran to the edge of the woodland. The hunters had crossed the dry valley below and were near the skyline on the other side, still going hard on Zia's track. They came into sight again going west on a green road across the downs. Lord only knew what the girl had done! She had turned away from Streatley, buses and the river into the emptiness of the grass. Well, they could not possibly catch up with her unless she had kept walking to nowhere for the last five hours. Meanwhile the way into Streatley was clear. He drank at the outside lavatory of a pub, thus leaving no memory of himself at the bar, and boldly crossed the bridge over the Thames. He found a police car waiting on the other side, but there was no turning back. He was not questioned. He did not fit the description of Irata and there could not have been time, as he had foreseen, for news of the possible accomplice to come through.

England, he hoped, was now all his except for Thame and Alderton where he must on no account be seen. He had only to telephone Paul Longwill, arrange for money and a change of clothes and find out whether Mrs. Fanshawe was safely back at the White Hart. Irata was the main problem; he had somehow to be kept on ice. If he was arrested, his evidence of Fyster-Holmes's true allegiance with details of his visitors was going to bear out Rivac's own story. But then what of Zia? And what of himself after a juicy court case of spies and cross–Channel ferries and punt poles fully reported? Any future depended on convincing the right person that this Lukash had existed — if he had — and that the Intertatry brochures were indeed as vitally important as the enemy believed.

VI

❧

Zia was intoxicated by success. In those first days at Brussels and Valenciennes she had been only an observer, taking on responsibility beyond her orders, but still an observer. Now defense had changed into attack for the sake of Georges, her uncle and his unrevealable club. The impulsive drowning of Rippmann, a terrified reaction of which she had been ashamed, could pass conscience as a justifiable act of war. As for Fyster-Holmes, there was nothing else Georges could have done — Georges with his lance and the dragon. The dragon might not have deserved it as richly as Appinger but one way or another had it coming to him. Lucky the traitor didn't live in more decisive times when he could be cut down while still alive and his private parts burnt before his eyes!

Dear Georges, what unhesitating loyalty! If he had told the truth about the death of Rippmann they might have believed him as innocent as he was. Dear Georges, so wise in the country ways he had learned as a boy, and now so modest and unpredictable in action though his instinct usually turned out to be right! Such a gallant man and so lovable as well! And what, my little Zia, is this? I wonder if the thought has ever occurred to him at all or if his admiration is just for a girl in trouble.

The sun was warm. Larks sprang up in front of her and

sang like very distant shepherd's pipes in Transylvania with a tune of the meeting of air and earth which defied the solidity of human music. The sky was as wide as on the plains of Hungary with smaller and more playful clouds. The grass beckoned her, daydreaming, on and on over the waves of the land, their tops breaking into the dark green foam of little woods and clumps of trees. It would be lovelier still on a horse, putting up larks and small blue butterflies with every beat of the canter. A bridle path crossed her green track. An incongruous signpost (how overcivilized they sometimes were!) announced that it went to East Ilsley. The name of the village was familiar. She must be on the edge of the famous gallops of the Berkshire Downs. Wonder if Georges can ride? I must teach him. Light hands he would have, but too gentle. Very gentle. Oh shut up, Zia! And where the hell is the Thames? I ought to be there by now.

After another mile she came on a tractor, brilliantly red and yellow, with a trailer behind it. Tractors were always eyesores instead of being camouflaged to suit their countryside. But the man standing still on the empty trailer and looking out over the rolling splendor of his home was evidently enjoying a moment of unity between himself and the land. He said good-morning in a cheerful, hearty voice and she asked him if he could tell her where she was.

"Well, that'll depend where you want to go, Miss. You're on the Ridgeway and behind you is the river and ahead of you nothing much till you come to Wantage."

"And Reading?"

"Reading is about twelve mile away over there."

"Oh! I think I must have lost myself."

"Where's your car?"

"I haven't got a car. I'm walking."

"Just the day for it! Where have you come from then?"

That was difficult; it might be unwise to tell the truth. But the names of such towns as she knew were all too far away. She plunged for Wallingford. It seemed to be acceptable. He highly approved of going from Wallingford to Reading the longest way around.

"But I reckon you must have borne right instead of left," he said. "Now, I'm going down to East Ilsley and if you don't mind jumping on the trailer I can take you there. Then you can get a bus to Reading."

She accepted gratefully. Time was getting on. The midday rendezvous was impossible, and the two o'clock unlikely.

Turning around in his seat, he carried on conversation over the rattle of the tractor.

"French, aren't you, if you don't mind my asking?"

"Yes, but my husband is British."

"Ah, all the same you women are wherever you come from."

"Well, not quite."

"Take my wife, for instance! Clever woman she is! Don't know what I'd do without her. But when she means left, she says right. And if there ain't no weathercock handy she don't know bloody north from bloody south."

"What about the women who sail round the world alone?" Zia yelled back indignantly.

"Well, you can do it east or west but you come home to the same place in the end so it don't matter" — he waved a hand at the horizon. "Now there's a soft job I wouldn't mind!"

Her eyes followed the hand to the Ridgeway. Three uniformed policemen and two dogs in leash were striding out over the high ground. It seemed unlikely that they could have anything to do with the death of Fyster-Holmes so soon — it might not yet have been discovered — and they were miles away from the wood where she had left Georges.

"Do you think they are after a criminal?" she asked.

"No! Aren't none up here except the racehorse trainers and that's only in the way of business. Exercising the dogs, I reckon. Any time there's a fine day you send a man ahead with a kipper on a string and have a good walk to the nearest pub. It makes a nice change from chasing teenagers up the back streets."

He dropped her in East Ilsley, recommended the best pub to get a snack at the bar and went on his way. Zia at once called up Paul Longwill. He was at home. She felt that now the luck was running her way.

"I was afraid you would be in the City."

"And how could I be in the City, Mrs. Fanshawe, when you send me —"

"Presents, Mr. Longwill."

"Presents without a word of explanation. Are you all right?"

"Yes. But our friend is in trouble."

"Where are you?"

"A place called East Ilsley. It's somewhere between the Thames and Newbury. Can you pick me up there? Now! Urgently! How long will it take you?"

"About an hour if it's where I think it is."

"I'll wait for you by the church."

She had a hearty snack at the pub and ordered sandwiches to take with her to the rendezvous, remembering that Georges must be even hungrier than she had been. At

128

half past two Paul Longwill picked her up. He was more reserved than when they had parted the evening before.

"You have been thinking that you believed me too easily, Paul. A mad Hungarian, no?"

"I have been thinking that you told me as little as you possibly could. But about Georges you were really worried."

"And now I am more worried. I couldn't tell you all about Irata. Is he safe?"

"Not as my valet. Impossible! Valets are for merchant bankers when they're in luck and homosexuals when they aren't."

"What have you done with him? What did he say?"

"As little as possible, like you. His motorbike is in my garage and Irata is at Georges's grandmother's empty house — by courtesy of Daisy. I told her that Georges wanted him kept away from the law."

"And she didn't mind?"

"Not Daisy! She still thinks of Georges as her boy and as likely as ever to get into trouble — especially as the police were asking for his address."

"I know. About Rippmann."

"Rippmann?"

"A man who fell overboard from the Channel ferry we were on."

"Did he have any help in falling overboard?"

"I don't know. He might have done."

"We'll leave that for now. Where is Georges?"

While they drove down to the river and on by the valley road Zia told her story: the kidnapping, the marsh, the boat, Appinger and the end.

"And you are telling me Georges killed him?" he asked skeptically.

"He didn't mean to. Oh, think! Can you stand in a bog and strike at a man with a long punt pole and be sure where it will hit?"

"Show me the house when we pass it."

When they came to the lane there was a constable on guard at the turning and they could see cars at the other end of the drive. The solid, unmistakable fact of an investigation in process appeared to convince Longwill at last that the rest of her story was true.

"Fyster-Holmes — I know a little of him," he said. "Highly esteemed but unlucky. That may be why he did not get the usual knighthood. Wherever he was posted he ran into riot and revolution. I suppose it never occurred to anyone that he might have had a finger in it himself. By God, you've got courage, Zia!"

"Or conceit."

"None of us can live without some conceit, my dear. Well, there's no proof of Georges Rivac's presence at all if we keep quiet about it. But if the police pull in Irata, Georges has to come out with the whole story and he can't do that without involving you."

"Then he must."

"But your family! And hadn't you better tell me the truth about the man who fell overboard?"

"He had followed Karel Kren and was after Georges."

"Great God! And nobody saw?"

"There was a doubt."

They arrived at the meeting of the two lanes for the four o'clock rendezvous. Zia pointed out the wood where they had rested at dawn and the patch of gorse on the hillside from which Georges ought to be watching. If he was there he could make out the arrival of Paul's white Jaguar but he did not appear.

"Shall I go up and see?" she asked.

"Better not. I believe criminals are expected to return to the scene of the crime. Sounds old-fashioned but it may be true."

He drove back to the river where they walked along the bank and lay down on warm grass. The meadows were golden with buttercups — a landscape innocently Utopian like that of any European river not too far from a provincial town, with a few fishermen sitting patiently by their rods and the occasional couple with or without the children and the dog. Silence was awkward though partly covered by the charm of the flowing water so black and sinister the night before. Zia could not altogether place him, but the fact remained that he was undoubtedly discreet and the only person in the world able to help if only by giving some recognizable shape to formless and impending disaster.

"You are quite right, Paul. I have not told you enough."

She gave him the preface to the happenings of the night: herself, the club, her deception of Georges Rivac, the arrival of the brochures at Thame Post Office. He listened without interruption, judging her integrity, she guessed, as well as her story. At the end he said:

"It would be useful if I knew more about this Karel Kren. I am not clear why he chose Georges."

"Because he was desperate. He took the first train out of Brussels, the Lille train. When he arrived he spotted that he was followed. I don't know why he did not go to the police and ask for protection — no time and no police except busy traffic police, perhaps. Or he saw that if the police were to believe him he would have to give too much away. He was just a factory director and a patriot, you see, not a trained agent. But he knew all the KGB methods. If he didn't make some quick decision, he would be found dead or unconscious with his briefcase gone. And then he remembered the Intertatry agent with his talk of Europe which had so impressed him. He managed to dodge into Georges's building, handed over the brochures of the new engine and gave him the address of Bridge Holdings. When Kren came out of the office they must have got him, perhaps on the staircase. It's all conjecture and nobody will ever know the details. What is certain is that he couldn't escape but did see a chance of killing himself."

"Where are the brochures now, Zia?"

"Georges told me this morning that he had stuck them in a drain pipe in Daisy's garden. He can't see anything wrong with them himself."

"Well, he shouldn't be able to. Nobody should be able to until the brochures are back in Prague. Then find out who printed them at Kren's order and how many. One couldn't plant a code in the real brochure, printed and distributed by the thousand, without confusing the customers. So the KGB has only to compare the fake with the genuine, and Bob's your uncle."

"They will shoot my uncle."

"Then we have to see that they shoot Bob instead. I think it's time to go if we are to be at the rendezvous at six."

As soon as they reached the road junction it was only too obvious that Georges would no longer be on the hillside. A couple of civilians were walking down it accompanied by something superior — to judge by his uniform — in the hierarchy of the police. There were three cars parked on the shoulder of the lane, one of them a police car in which an inspector was reading an evening paper. Longwill stopped alongside him and leaned out of the window, country gentleman all over.

"An accident, Inspector? Can I help at all?"

"A criminal investigation, sir."

"Good Lord! Nothing wrong at the farm, I hope?"

"A Mr. Fyster-Holmes has been found dead under suspicious circumstances. You may know him."

"By name, yes."

The inspector folded up the paper with a slight air of disdain and handed it over.

"You can read about it there, sir. For once they have got it nearly right."

Paul thanked him, hoped they'd catch the bastard and drove on until they could read the report in privacy. There was not much beyond a short obituary of Fyster-Holmes with a veiled suggestion that he might have made enemies abroad in the course of his distinguished career. His Spanish servant, Diego Irata, was wanted to help police with their inquiries. He had disappeared and it was believed he had been accompanied by a woman. The number of his motorcycle was quoted.

"And must be hidden immediately," Paul Longwill said, turning for home. "Did the woman leave anything behind up there?"

"No. But detectives couldn't miss my footprints on the bank of the creek when they got down to a thorough search."

"Then we should not be seen together till I find somewhere safer for the motorcycle. I'll drop you off not too far from the White Hart."

The precaution was probably right and the walk was only a mile, but she resented it. She was dead tired and dragging herself home to the inn was almost the hardest effort of the day. After a large brandy and soda in the bar she went up to her room and lay down, longing for a bath but afraid to have one lest she should be called to the telephone. That was as well, for the call came through within a quarter of an hour of her arrival. Either Georges's voice or the brandy at once returned strength.

"I couldn't get hold of either of you," he said. "But I didn't expect to till after six. All well?"

"Yes. And you? And you?"

"Tell Paul I need food, clothes and money. I'm on the A428 close to the turning to Nuffield. What about our foreign friend?"

"At your grandmother's house."

"The cellar?"

"Paul didn't say. Shall I come out with him?"

"Of course, but don't go near Alderton."

She passed the message to Paul and set out again on the weary walk to the spot where he had dropped her. Her movements must be puzzling them at the inn, but that could not be helped. Still another lie would have to be invented. The presence of Irata had complicated everything; without him she and Paul would have been able to carry on ordinary social intercourse with no risk at all. She was inclined to sulk till she reminded herself sharply that without Irata Georges would now be sleeping peacefully as *Amanda* ran under the London bridges on her way to the open sea.

The roads were fairly clear in the still evening, and Paul made the rendezvous in half an hour. When Georges Rivac appeared from the bushes Zia was shocked by his appearance. He looked a fugitive, a dear fugitive, mud-stained, drawn, unshaved and new. This was a man of spirit, though near the end of it, and no longer the slightly shabby, indeterminate agent from Lille.

"The best I could do for you at short notice," Paul said. "It's all going to hang a bit loose but I've brought safety pins for the trousers and the windbreaker doesn't matter. You could be carrying toothbrush and spare socks inside it. I'll take your revolting shirt and trousers and have them cleaned."

"I'll have to get a shave somehow."

"A razor, Georges, seemed to me even more important than clothes. Bristles are unpardonable except on Sunday morning when they seem to be considered a sign of virility. And I'll drain some hot water off the radiator. Driving mirror and all mod. cons. Tell us what happened and we'll know what to do."

"We'll never know that."

"Well, what not to do."

Georges took up the story from Zía's departure. When he came to the dogs on his trail she exclaimed:

"But I saw them!"

"Where?"

"On the skyline. Not far from a place called East Ilsley."

"What on earth were you doing there?"

"Thinking."

"They didn't catch up with you?"

"No. I got a ride with a farmer behind his tractor. Oh God! And I told him too much — that I was French and married to a British officer. They'll know exactly where he picked me up. How long before they trace him?"

"They should have done it already and have a description

135

of you," Paul replied. "But there's no reason why they should hit on Mrs. Fanshawe and the White Hart unless someone noticed the number of Irata's bloody motorbike."

"What have you done with it?"

"Under some hay for the moment. We will now invade the nearest hotel, have an excellent dinner and panic afterward if we feel like it. Georges, you look tired, but my suede jacket is so obviously expensive that you will be welcome anywhere. What would you say, Zia? An overworked doctor getting the surgery out of his lungs?"

He could be, Zia thought, but getting a punt pole out of his memory. She was relieved when after a vast steak and some glasses of Burgundy he began to crow in his high laughter at the thought of Daisy and Irata.

"In the cellar, of course!" he exclaimed. "Did you tell Daisy about it?"

"I had to. But she was in the secret all along and never said a word to your grandmother."

"Didn't your grandmother know the house had a cellar?" Zia asked. "What did you use it for?"

"Nothing much. To small boys existence is what matters, not use."

"And Irata is down there?"

"Yes. Now, I have been thinking, like Zia," Paul said. "Georges can't be run in — not known to exist and untraceable. But his life is and always will be at risk from Appinger's organization. Zia is in deadly danger from Thames Valley Police and none whatever from the KGB, who haven't a clue beyond what they read in the paper."

"She must never go back to the White Hart."

"The police can't work as fast as that, Georges. What we must avoid is the White Hart mentioning her suspicious movements. The landlord must be curious already. Get on the telephone at once! Say you are General Fanshawe and sound military, but not too military! I'd do it myself but they might recognize my voice. Ask them to give her a message when she comes in. That implies that the General knows where she is and what she is doing. Ah yes, and we'll give them a bit of romance to jump at. The message is that she is to report to Defense Security in Oxford at ten A.M. Then order a taxi to be at the White Hart at nine."

"Not from Thame."

"Make it Bicester. I know the chap. Very reliable and with all the right ideas. Calls himself the Shire Transport Company when all he has is an old Cortina and a cattle truck. Now, tomorrow? Yes, tomorrow! You haven't given me a chance to see Bridge Holdings. That must be done at once. Georges, you're all right here or anywhere. Zia, you can be traced from the White Hart to Oxford, so you mustn't stay there. You should go straight to London, I think. Put up at the Regency Hotel with another false name and address. It's not far from my West End office."

Zia said that she was afraid of not remembering a new story and giving herself away. Always she had to account for the foreign accent.

"I'm going to stay Mrs. Fanshawe, Paul. I know her so well, her parents and all. I can even do the army wife stuff. I imagine General Fanshawe as just like my uncle."

"Well, if you'd rather. It will only be for a day or two. Georges, you were shivering when you came in and you are finished. You think you aren't, but that's the Burgundy. No traveling tomorrow. No worries. A deck chair in the garden if the weather holds and a second long night to follow."

"I can go up to London tomorrow and join Zia."

"No, you can't. What will you use for money? When one has an identity it's up for grabs. When one hasn't, one can't get at it. Zia will need everything in my wallet which leaves it empty. I have to leave home early and be in London all day tomorrow. I must fit in your business between the Exchange Control Commission, a directors' meeting and then a dinner at the National Farmers Union where I hope to meet the Minister before he's sacked. The only solution is to mail you a couple of hundred in cash, and you can't leave here till you receive it."

"I hope you can afford it."

"I have an overdraft and a reputation, Georges, like everyone else who matters. If your possessions are ever returned you can send me a check from Siberia. Buy yourself some clothes in Henley, pay your bill and meet me at the Regency about six the day after tomorrow."

"What about Irata?"

"I'll have a long talk with him tonight so that he doesn't feel he is forgotten. Daisy will have been over there anyway."

Paul Longwill left for home, taking Zia with him, and dropped her — since it was now dark — rather nearer to the White Hart. When she returned, again on foot, she could feel curiosity as thick as bar smoke; but no questions were asked and the General's message duly passed to her. At last and thankfully she enjoyed the much needed bath and sleep.

In the morning when the taxi was at the door and the landlord and his wife had said good-bye to her, he whispered mysteriously:

"If we can be of use to the General, Mrs. Fanshawe, don't

hesitate to call on us! We know the district as well as any-one."

That sounded as if he had swallowed the bait. She gave him her sweetest smile and said she had always doubted if she could take him in with her excuse of house-hunting.

"But don't spread it around," she added, "in case my husband wants to use me again."

She hoped that would stop him putting two and two together and taking the initiative in passing on his suspicions; but if the police questioned him of their own accord it would not be long before her night's absence was found to coincide with the death of Fyster-Holmes and fingerprints were proved to be identical with those on Mrs. Fanshawe's dressing table. She remembered holding on tightly to the rail of the trailer.

Paul had instructed her how to cover her tracks when the taxi dropped her at the Oxford railway station. She was to tell the driver she was traveling to Birmingham. As soon as he had safely driven away she was to walk to the bus station and take the first bus to London. All that went very smoothly and probably would not go so smoothly for detectives on her track.

She felt lonely without Georges and — yes, of course — Paul Longwill. She was on her own again and no longer had that spurious sense of adventure which had supported her at Brussels and Valenciennes. She had a wild and miserable dream that if she burned her passport she could be tried and sentenced in England without any mention of Georges and without her true identity and nationality ever coming out. Morale needed a lift. After booking in at the Regency she visited the downstairs salon and had her hair done.

A day and a half had somehow to be passed, and somehow must be dragged out without continual thought of Budapest, Alderton, the future and the mess in which she had landed the dear and defenseless Georges. The streets of London were dangerous, so full of foreign tourists and among them Hungarians for some of whom she herself had arranged flights and accommodation. So she stayed in her hotel for the afternoon of Thursday, June 2nd, and decided to spend the following day between a cinema and a park in the suburbs. The only familiar name was Wimbledon, and it turned out to fit the requirements.

She sat anxiously in the hotel lounge until Georges arrived at teatime and took a room in the hotel — still another Georges, dressed more as a farmer up for the day who couldn't be bothered with greater formality than that of the weekly market. He was rested and seemed at ease with himself for the first time since she had met him, noticing and boldly approving the new arrangement of her hair.

Paul Longwill appeared an hour later — also a new Paul, for he had not his usual condescending air.

"I've had the hell of a time," he said. "Deflated, and how!"

He ordered drinks to be sent up to Zia's room and, glass in hand, half-sitting on the window sill where he could look down on his audience, recovered his poise.

"I got Bamborough to arrange an appointment with your Bridge Holdings for yesterday afternoon. Spring must have spent the rest of the morning making inquiries about me and discounting the answers. He was not at all impressed by his lordship. I threw the Export Credits Department at him. He said they were well-meaning and kept his head on one side like that terrier you called him waiting for a ball. I realized I might as well be persuading Saint Peter to open the gate by saying I had once had a gin and tonic with the Archbishop of Canterbury.

"So straight to the point: that a certain Georges Rivac had been a close friend of mine since childhood. He merely replied that you had called on him twice. I noticed that he said nothing of Zia, waiting for me to bring up that lovely and awkward question myself. Then there was nothing for it but to stumble along into your story. I think now that it was just as well I laid off my image and gave him a chance to judge the very raw me."

"How much did you tell him?" Zia asked anxiously.

"Just that somebody must have advised Karel Kren — now deceased and I told him how — to get in touch with Bridge Holdings and that the somebody was very likely to be his Prague agent. He made no comment, so I asked him what he thought of you both. Zia was an obvious Hungarian adventuress, he said, and Georges would make a good bank clerk in a foreign branch. That gave me an opening and I replied that bank clerks required absolute integrity.

"He wuffed at that, so I drove it home, saying that cosmopolitan integrity, classless but not characterless, was worth listening to. He admitted that he had thought so the first time he met Georges, but Zia and unexplained accidents on Channel ferries were a bit much. I pretended to know nothing about Channel ferries and asked him what he meant. He told me that he had thought it best to check — privately — Rivac's antecedents and journeys and learned that a rather questionable character had fallen overboard. Statements given by Rivac and Miss Fodor were equally questionable, and did I know where the lady was?"

" 'Not if it's a case of annoying a defenseless little foreigner' — that's you, Zia — 'on no evidence,' I said.

"He assured me there was no risk of that. The coroner had no interest, nor had Passport Control. Harbor Police only wanted more exact statements for their files."

"So he was coming around," Georges said.

"Not till I read him my lecture on security: that if you keep everybody out you sometimes prevent the most valuable person coming in. He was good enough to say it was not confined to the City. I then put it to him that he should send somebody out to Prague at once to ask his agent — out-of-doors — if he had had any dealings with Karel Kren and what they were. He refused, and so I offered to pay full expenses as proof of good faith. All over again he wanted to know what the point of it was.

" 'The point is,' I said, 'that when Kren's channel of communication was shut down he believed your agent could help him. I don't ask why he should have thought so, but I want to know if he did. Then we may be able to find out where these two innocents ought to have gone with their information.'

"He laughed quite pleasantly at my calling you two innocents and added that on the question of ultra-security I had impressed him. I snapped back that I was going to impress him some more, and I gave him all that happened in Lille, including the bugging of Georges's office and as much as I thought proper of your kidnaping and escape. He decided to go out to Prague himself by an early plane today and hopes to be back tonight. He has a visa and seems to be able to travel anywhere with government contracts in his pocket."

"And he'll do the follow-up?" Georges asked.

"I think he'll try. If anybody can find his way among all

these MI fives and sixes and the odds and sods who don't belong to MI at all, I suspect that he can."

"Did you mention Irata? He needs help too."

"I certainly did not! I had a talk with Irata the night before last when I got home. He's restless. Who am I working for and what are my intentions? Good Lord, I wouldn't mind spending a couple of days down there with Daisy's cold pies and some bottles. What suspicious blokes communists are, Zia!"

"They'd better be. Does he know he is wanted for the murder of Fyster-Holmes?"

"Not yet. What he wants is reassuring. Daisy does her best. But he is waiting for someone — preferably in uniform with a few medals and a gun — to say: 'Diego Irata, arise from your tomb!' Well, I must be off. About time I had a silent night in the country. Spring has my number if he wants me. And you two juvenile delinquents had better remain here where I can get hold of you quickly."

Zia and Georges went out to dinner. It was the first time they had been alone together under anything like peaceful conditions. She wished she had something more alluring to wear than the summer print he had already seen on her arrival at Thame. His eyes showed an interest, which was satisfactory, but conversation remained on a comradely plane, each of them searching for details of that unknown past before Karel Kren had brought them together. His manner remained very chivalrous and attentive — so much so that she was faintly exasperated until she realized that it was not specially assumed for her but his normal attitude to the opposite sex.

"And no girlfriend?" she asked.

"They try, you know. The mothers, I mean. But I'm not much of a catch. And they are all so pink and white. The daughters, I mean."

"Haven't they any ideas but marriage?"

She really implied that hadn't he.

"I daresay. I daresay. But between business all day and customers and cafés in the evening one never seems to have any time."

"So there has never been anybody?"

"Well, there was a Spanish girl once."

"Tell me about her!"

"Nothing to tell. A secretary and learning French. I was inclined to be — well — attracted. But h'm . . ."

Georges's embarrassment was plain. In fact the lady in question had been a frequent attendant at a *maison de rendezvous* — allowing slightly more illusion than a brothel though presents did pass and, Georges remembered, plenty of them. He had been infatuated with his firm-fleshed, flamboyant beauty until she left to try out her secretarial and off-duty accomplishments in Barcelona.

"What was she like? Very Spanish?"

"On the surface. New international model. All much the same except you."

And that was no idle compliment. He had spoken as if it was unquestionable that she was different from all other women.

"What's so special about me?"

"I don't know. You're very lovely and very brave. And you're Zia."

And *your* Zia, she said to herself, but that would be much too frank for him.

"You don't find a Magyar very foreign?"

"Foreign? Heart of Europe!"

"Daisy told me she wouldn't be surprised if you turned up with Siamese twins."

"Daisy! Daisy has a sexpot mind, Zia, and is a darling. All old ladies in English villages have either got religion or sexpot minds and frequently both. She always hoped I'd start rolling in the hay with some other fourteen-year-old. As a matter of fact I was in love with the pretty teacher at the Infants' School, but that was my secret."

"Do you always keep it secret when you fall in love?"

"If it's hopeless."

"How do you know when it's hopeless?"

"Well, wrong. Leading nowhere. One has no right to take advantage of circumstance . . . defenseless . . . er . . ."

Intolerable man! Old-fashioned, overchivalrous bourgeois morality! Dominant male overcoming scruples of unprotected female! Well, it could be played his way, if that was what he wanted. She still was not at all sure how far she should go. He simply would not take a hint. Returning to the hotel in a taxi, she arranged some casual physical contact but all she got was a brotherly arm around her shoulders. One might as well try to seduce some charming and sensitive homosexual. An attempt to slide his good-night peck accidentally onto her lips failed miserably.

She woke up as determined as Appinger to get to work on him. Words, distant allusions, eyes downcast or conveying the message directly into his, he nobly resisted the lot. Perhaps it was due to the dull sameness of her appearance last night. A more primitive approach was needed, like that of his nasty, coarse Spaniard. Well, there was certainly nothing sisterly about her strawberry bedjacket with its neckline plunging to the belt. If that didn't work, she thought while touching up lips and eyes, Georges Rivac deserved to have coffee and rolls by himself for the rest of his life and good luck to him! She called him on the internal telephone, saying she had slept very badly and was worried. Would he come and have breakfast with her?

When he came in she was carefully posed at the little round bedroom table with another chair next to her own. He was shaken all right. He exclaimed "Zia!" and quickly added:

"I am sorry you had a bad night."

"I'm so much alone."

"Yes, it's hard. Well, thanks to Paul, here's a day more when we can be together. A pity I'm too young to pass as General Fanshawe!"

"I could always pretend you are."

"Splendid! Keep it in mind the next time you can't sleep!"

"I don't think it would help."

"Wouldn't it? Then dream of your mother and uncle and Budapest. You'll get back, you know, and nobody any the wiser."

The waiter entered and placed the tray of breakfast on the table. Georges moved the chair and sat down. Perhaps the diaphanous proximity of legs had bothered him, but it wouldn't do him any good. The view from the opposite side of the table was far more provocative when she leaned forward to pour coffee.

"You're so good to me," she said, holding out a hand to him.

He kissed it and when it was not withdrawn kissed the whole cool length of the bare arm.

"Zia! Lovely, lovely Zia!"

Another Georges! A Georges flaming with desire, more passionate than she ever imagined he could be. She responded, and then with a desperate effort remembered that for her nervous thoroughbred the mate should be demure and timorous.

"No, Georges, no!"

She held the bedjacket over the other breast which remained to be kissed, but the pretty gesture, the last of gestures it was going to be, was interrupted by the insistent buzzing of the telephone. They fell apart.

"Yes?"

"Paul here. I've been trying to get Georges. It's very urgent. Is he with you?"

She handed him the telephone, tidied herself and sat beside him.

"Paul, I just came in to see if she was all right."

Faintly she could hear the reply:

"Like hell you did."

"Nothing of the sort, Paul! Now what the devil do you want? . . . Spring's office . . . yes, of course I am dressed . . . yes, I can be there in twenty minutes."

He turned to Zia, still as a statue except that she was breathing a little quickly, due he thought — and quite rightly — to his behavior.

"I am sorry. Just as well. I should apologize but I don't. Such a pity when I love you so much."

Georges left his breakfast and took a taxi to Lower Belgrave Street while Zia hurled the empty pillow to the floor and stamped on it. Paul had said that he was not invited; it must be made clear to him later in the day that he had merely called on Zia at her request. He was very angry with Paul and with himself, though muddled as to whether it was because he had overwhelmed his unprotected Zia or because he hadn't. Just ten disastrous days had passed since he met her and seven of those wasted in being too busy to realize what he thought of her. Saturday morning — what right had Herbert Spring to be at the office?

Run off with her — that was the thing to do. Where to? How? All the utter impossibilities came crowding back. This third visit to Bridge Holdings might result in anything at all — protection or arrest for murder or deportation to Lille where he would never be able to visit the office of a new and unknown customer with any confidence that he wouldn't wake up on the wrong side of Europe. His finger did not want to ring the bell. Paul had given away far too much. Rebuking finger for disobedience and dithering, he pressed the button so firmly that the bell was as audible as a burglar alarm.

He murmured his name. The door opened. The usual manservant received him at the door of the apartment and ushered him into Herbert Spring's office. Far from appearing in the passage with his customary cordiality, Spring was sitting at his desk accompanied by a gray-faced, black-coated civil servant in his early fifties — a frightening man with firm mouth and commanding blue eyes. A judge off duty was Georges's first impression. But no! In spite of the sun-starved, paper-bound complexion he looked as if he had once been a soldier.

"Sit down, Mr. Rivac! You will be glad to hear that my visit to Prague proved nothing but was suggestive."

"It was very good of you to go," Georges replied in much

too high a voice and added in too low a one: "May I know what happened?"

"Exactly what your friend Mr. Longwill predicted. Three weeks ago our agent there was approached by a Mr. Karel Kren of Intertatry, who wished to know how to get in touch urgently with what he called the British Secret Service. The natural course would have been to apply to our military attaché but Kren was aware that he might be under surveillance and did not dare go near a Western embassy. Why he should have thought a commercial agent was a good introduction I cannot imagine, but he did. Our man told him to call on me and take it from there. Kren did not mention your Lukash. British Secret Service, you see, is a very vague description of a number of departments. This gentleman represents one of them, which is called MI Five. You may have heard of it."

"Of course! Of course! The British CIA," Georges replied, having read a dozen descriptions of its supposed iniquities by overimaginative French journalists.

"It is not in the least like the CIA. But I am always forgetting you are a Frenchman. MI Five is more or less the French Deuxième Bureau."

The gray-faced man opened fire:

"Now, Mr. Rivac! I have had full reports from the police who know nothing of you unless I choose to tell them. I also have from Mr. Spring as much as your friend reported: that is to say, your action in Lille and that there was an attempt to smuggle you abroad from the house of Mr. Fyster-Holmes. Was it you who killed him?"

"Accidentally. Yes, I'm afraid it was."

"Do you wish to confess the whole story?"

149

"Well, not yet. Later, of course, when somebody understands that I have been forced into all this from a sense of — well, Europe is what I tell myself. I mean . . ."

"We will leave on one side for the moment the whole question of Kren and his engine handbook, Mr. Rivac. We'll cross that bridge if we ever have evidence that yours is not a case for civil police. Meanwhile I want your Mr. Appinger. That is my only interest in you."

"It shouldn't be difficult."

"No? We have only your description of him and I could find you half a dozen people in the street outside who correspond to that. We do not know the name on his passport, where he is staying, when he entered the country and how and where he will leave it."

"You're going to run him in?"

"You sound as if it alarmed you, Mr. Rivac."

"Not in the least. Not in the least. I just wondered."

"About what?"

"About the trial."

"We do not necessarily try these friends from over the way. We sometimes return them in exchange for similar facilities of various sorts. As things stand, you are much more likely to be tried than Appinger."

"But, I say —"

"You must understand, Mr. Rivac, that if I am to compound one certain felony and one probable, I risk going to jail myself. I must be absolutely sure what my duty is. My instinct is to believe you, but the facts are against you. I cannot give you any protection. The best I can do for you is to know nothing — as yet — of you and Miss Fodor. The rest is up to you."

"But Fyster-Holmes! Aren't you going to follow up his connections?"

"My dear fellow, are you really as guileless as you seem? Might it not be convenient if we had no idea that Fyster-Holmes was a traitor and believe that Irata murdered him?"

"But what about Irata then?"

"That is also up to you."

"But do you want these people to kill him for you?"

"What a lot of 'buts,' Mr. Rivac! I fear there always are in Security."

It was blackmail. All that this shady, double-dealing crook offered was a half promise of neutrality if he exposed himself to Appinger and a threat of prosecution if he didn't.

Georges Rivac lost his temper — internally, that is. If he was supposed to take the initiative, he bloody well would. He could attack as satisfactorily as the next man and a nice change it would be from defense. He was tired of being pushed around by the lot of them, of running away, accepting lifts from kind strangers, being chased by dogs, patronized, disbelieved, telephoned before breakfast and threatened by their damned, British, uncompromising respect for Law.

"I shall return to Alderton," he said. "That's enough to bring Appinger on to me."

"I doubt if it will. He'll assume it is a trap. Obviously we can pick up any foreigner in a country district who is not known to the locals."

"It won't be a foreigner who watches my movements. There's that boatman and two drivers and probably others. You tell me the brochures don't matter. Well, they matter to Appinger. He's got to have them. If you are not convinced, I am. And he knows they are almost certainly in Alderton."

"You could have delivered them already."

"No. I received them in Monday's mail. All my movements on Monday morning were reported, and he read the covering letter from my secretary in Lille. He will expect me to return to Alderton."

"It won't work."

"It will if he doesn't know I *have* returned."

"But he must know if, as you believe, his organization is keeping an eye on the place."

"No, he won't."

"Why not?"

"That's my business. If you refuse me protection, I'll protect myself. I'll set up my own organization. And meanwhile you find out from some other department who Lukash is! Here's you and here's Mr. Spring and I can guess you're in the same game the way one is in accounts and the other in sales and you don't get together till there's a row up top. So between you, you ought to be able to find out."

Setting up his own organization sounded fine. But Zia must on no account be involved. So the only members were Daisy and Irata with Paul watching from the sidelines, which was all that could be expected of him. It was not an impressive cell.

That crook from MI5 didn't think so either.

"I must warn you, Mr. Rivac, that if your village cronies — I suppose you have something of the sort in mind — so much as mention Fyster-Holmes the Law must take its course."

"They won't. If I told you where Miss Fodor is, could you slip her back into Hungary?"

"I could not. And the last thing I want to know is where she is. Would you like to tell me how a certain Rippmann fell overboard?"

"Certainly. Very heavy sea and reaching for his false teeth."

"Was Appinger content with that explanation?"

"He was not."

"I'd love to have heard that interrogation. He took you seriously?"

"He took Kren's brochures very seriously indeed."

"Then for God's sake be careful, man! A bit of British caution in the French élan! By the way, some colleagues of mine have told me about your father. I am sorry I had to greet his son so formally. But I hope you understand."

The gray face became human. It smiled. It rose to its feet and shook his hand. So, to his astonishment, did Herbert Spring. Georges felt more charitable. Crook? Well, in that job what else ought he to be?

He returned to the hotel and went up to Zia's room. The door was open; the housemaids were busy, and he could not see her bag. His first thought was that she had been so disturbed by his behavior that she had decided to leave; his second — now that he had time, too much time, to think about it — was that her resistance had been far from determined; his third that her reason for leaving in a hurry had nothing to do with breakfast.

He did not ask at the desk if she had gone, since the less evidence there was of a Rivac-Fanshawe connection the better. All he could do was to wait anxiously in his room for her to telephone. Eventually he heard her voice.

"Georges, this is Mary. I hear they have managed to trace your sister."

He nearly replied, "Where are you?" but followed the example of her discretion.

"Good Lord, Mary, how exciting! I am sure she shouldn't be in London."

"That's what I thought too. How did the interview go?"

"Very well. I'll tell you all about it some time."

"Will you be at your aunt's?"

"I'm going to import wine for a bit."

The reference to the cellar beat her for a moment.

"Spanish wine," he said.

"Oh, I see. Will you have a job for me?"

"No. No, certainly not."

"So long as I know where you are. Good-bye for now, my darling, darling, darling Georges."

He was about to respond without any discretion at all, to say that nothing mattered and he had to be with her; but she must have foreseen what was coming, for she had promptly cut him off. And how right! There was no reason why the waiter that morning should have known the number of his room and his name, but they had been together in the lounge the day before and if the hotel telephone operator had a good memory for internal calls she could confirm that they knew each other.

It must be Paul who had let her know that the police were after Mrs. Fanshawe and it was possible that Paul himself was in trouble. Risky or not, he had to have a word with him before going underground with Irata. He had not yet any plan of campaign, though sure that his instinct to return to Alderton was right; but if there was police interest in Mr. Rivac of Lille the game was going to be twice as difficult.

He cleared out of the hotel and took a train to Bicester,

having got rid of the cheap suitcase he had bought for show and substituted a knapsack. If Appinger was not to know that he was back in Alderton, the village had to be reached on foot and after dark. No lifts, thank you very much.

Avoiding all passing cars while he was in the well-known lanes, he took to the fields until he reached the paddock and garden of the Manor Farm. The only light was in Paul's study. Watching from the darkness Georges was impressed by his concentration on vast sheets of accounts, at intervals making notes and doing quick sums on his calculator. That side of Paul was probably familiar to his associates in the City and allowed him to get away with what he called his image: a fashionable playboy on the make.

The fact that he had not bothered to draw the curtains was probably deliberate. Any interested person would see at a glance that he was busy and unworried. Georges threw a small clod of earth at the window without leaving the darkness. Again Paul was at his best. He could not help starting, but then performed an operation on his calculator, entered the result and left the room as casually as if he needed a drink. He came out of the back door and circled the garden until he arrived at Georges's position.

"Trespassing in search of game, Georges?"

"Learning by experience. But not so well as you."

"Wait here till I've shut down the study. Then I'll turn on the bedroom light to show that I have gone to bed and leave the back door open."

"What about servants?"

"Now that I am a bachelor, Georges — permanently, I hope — I refuse to be compassed about by witnesses. I am looked after by the sisters Marlene and Muriel. 'Ussies,

155

Daisy calls them. But they prepare an excellent breakfast, clean the place up and return in the evening only if I have guests."

Georges crept through the darkened house and into the bedroom. Too impatient to sit down or even to reply to Paul's inquiry as to what he wanted to drink, he asked what had happened and why Zia bolted from the Regency.

"I think brandy and soda at this time of night," Paul said. "And try the bed if you don't like chairs. Well, I was having a lie-in this morning after all I've been through the last few days when Spring woke me to say he expected you. Then the police came when I was shaving. Good God, one might as well be in Russia and have a knock on the door at four A.M.! How did the interview go?"

"Never mind that! What about Zia?"

"The fuzz — our latest jargon for coppers, Georges — got on to her very quickly. Someone in the bar noticed the make and part of the number of Irata's motorbike when Zia rode off behind him. He wondered about it but didn't take any action. Like most of us he thought he might be wrong and disliked being one of those busybodies who go to the police just for something to do. But on Friday he did go. The chap at the White Hart made it worse by whispering that Mrs. Fanshawe was employed by her husband on a secret mission. An official of some allied commission in Germany had booked the room for her.

"Police check army Fanshawes, if any, and come to me. I informed them that she had told me her husband was a general, that she was house-hunting and that she wanted to buy one of my horses. The White Hart had said that she came out here on the back of a motorbike, so I had to admit it. The police asserted that they had reason to believe she had stayed the night with me. What a reputation!"

"Look at the way you jump to conclusions about an innocent breakfast!"

"Well, if she looks as sweet in bed as out of it . . ."

"Get on with your story!"

"O.K. It was lucky I didn't fall into their trap and give her an alibi. They knew damn well where she was that night. Fingerprints, I suppose. That meant that they would be checking hotels for a Frenchwoman with no passport. So I called her immediately to clear out of the Regency and keep in touch."

"And has she?"

"Not yet."

"I'm going in with Irata. Don't visit us on any account!"

"Georges, you lay down the law like a boardroom tycoon. What's happened to you?"

"I've got religion."

"But what the hell will you do in the cellar?"

"Wait for something to turn up — with Her Majesty's approval which she will instantly disown if I am wanted by the police."

"Daisy can probably feed both of you. Water is the trouble."

"I can manage that from the house at night."

"If you do you'll get dysentery from what I've heard."

"Nonsense! There's a rainwater butt at the back. What worries me is Irata. He's now a good Eurocommunist, but he won't like betraying hard-line comrades even when they are out to get him. Have you still got his motorbike?"

"I have. Why?"

"Your story about the general's wife and the horse won't stand up. Too many loose ends! We can't rule out a police search of the farm."

"I'll wheel it over to your grandmother's house before dawn. I have a spare key. How can I let you know when Zia surfaces?"

"By Daisy."

"She doesn't know that you and Mrs. Fanshawe are friends."

"All the better if she does."

"I see. Love me, love my dog! Hand in hand on visiting day to see Master Georges in Dartmoor!"

"I'd settle for that if Zia is in the clear with her own people."

"Got religion, did you say? Well, well, I suppose we can call it that while it lasts."

Georges slipped out into the darkness and made his way to his grandmother's empty house, which lay in a shallow bottom out of sight of the village, approached by a narrow lane if you were on wheels and across the fields if you were not. As always the trees on each side of the little valley seemed to close in at night more than in the sunlit day when they formed a private and pleasant boundary to a sheltered human habitation. The Victorian brick house looked damp and unloved, very different from those years in the middle fifties when it had echoed with laughter of friends — unless he and Paul had good reason for silence.

The cellar, as Georges realized only when boyhood was long past, was not a cellar at all but an icehouse excavated centuries before by the owner of some earlier house on the site when winters were harder and the marshes of nearby Otmoor undrained. Between the trees on the ridge and the garden the steep slope had been allowed to go wild and had become an impenetrable thicket of struggling sycamore seedlings, in places close as a stockade, interspersed with stunted elder and trailing briars on which the pale wild roses showed even at night. There Paul and he, cutting their way into the mess — pocket knives for machetes and conspiratorial village cats for jaguars — had come upon a depression and around it a few moss-covered stones which seemed to form a section of an arch or bay. They thought at first it was an old well and treated it with caution; but clearance of the undergrowth showed that it was an entrance into the ridge, blocked up by silt trickling down from above and forming a fertile bed for nettles which over the years had added their topsoil.

The boys — ostensibly after rabbits — had secretly dug their way in, finding half a dozen ruinous steps and a considerable chamber under the hillside so dry that there were still traces of straw. There they hid themselves, plotted and lived out their fantasies whenever they were sure that grandmother and Daisy believed them to be far away and they could safely approach by crawling through the trees on the skyline, then following their zigzag path through the scrub.

Georges on arrival did the same, but the passage was now too easy. He could see that Paul on Tuesday night had been over with a billhook before consigning Irata to the depths. The debris needed to be cunningly replaced. As it was, anyone passing along the crest — especially a small boy — might wonder where the rough pathway led.

The chamber was empty. It had been made habitable with a camp bed, plenty of blankets, candles, a basin and a table and chair. There was an open book upside down —

a treatise on economics with Paul's overstately bookplate in it — and the candle wax was still soft; so Irata must have cleared out as soon as he heard Georges's inevitably noisy approach and was not far off.

Georges called softly in Spanish:

"Don't fear, *compañero!* It is I. We meet again. I see my friends have been looking after you."

Kneeling at the entrance he shone his torch quickly on his own face. Irata appeared from the bushes farther down the slope.

"The devil! So you got away!"

"Thanks to you and Señora Fanshawe."

"So why am I kept here any longer?"

"To protect you."

"Cannot your Secret Service do that?"

"Not yet. None of the men they want is known by sight."

"And Fyster-Holmes?"

"He is dead. According to the police, you killed him."

That seemed the simplest way to keep the impatient Irata out of circulation; but Georges realized at once that he had made a mistake.

"I? I do not commit murder. I would not kill a comrade who trusted me. I am a man of honor. Where is my motorcycle? Give it me back! To hell with you and the police! I will make my own way back to Spain without you."

"Your motorcycle can neither fly nor swim, friend. And under what name will you go?"

"My own."

"And how long will you last when your late friends find you?"

"If the police already know what Fyster-Holmes was, I am not worth killing."

160

"The police do not know. They believe you quarreled with him, cut his throat and ran. It is all in the papers."

"But you can give evidence for me. You know Fyster-Holmes was alive when I left."

"He may have been. But I cannot swear to what happened outside my room."

"How did you escape? Who are you?" Irata asked sullenly.

"Who do you think?"

"I think you are a Spaniard who has lived long out of the country."

"So I too might want to return and take you with me if you trusted me."

Georges felt a twinge of conscience at jumping at the lead Irata had given him. Yet it could be a vision of coming reality. If the gray-faced man wanted to avoid any trial or public inquiry and police were hot on the trail of Rivac and Irata, he must agree to smuggle them abroad.

"When does somebody come here?" he asked.

"Always at dawn — a fat lady who brings food and drink. She is very kind and is not afraid to be alone with the filthy, unwashed *pícaro* that I must appear."

"She sees only what is within a man, friend. And who else?"

"Once the *tío* who brought me here came back. He does not please me. A little capitalist, very proud to own land."

Typically Spanish, that acute and deadly summing up! But superficial. It omitted Paul's loyalty and humor.

"Well, you'll have me for company now. Lend me one of your blankets and as we can't tell spades from clubs in the dark tell me about the home which is so near your heart."

A little later both of them heard a rustling among the

weeds and grass which had overgrown the approach to the house. The night sky was clouded and nothing could be distinguished but a light inside which was quickly flashed on and off. Then there was the click of the front door latch as it was closed. The cautious visitor could only be Paul.

"That was our friend hiding your motorcycle."

"Why should he?"

"The police must not find it in his house."

"What am I to say if they catch me?"

"Just tell them that you left without notice because you so badly wanted to return to Spain. Don't mention Fyster-Holmes's politics or that you too were a communist or that there was a prisoner. Then I promise you have nothing but the KGB to be afraid of. The evidence against you won't stand up."

Georges had fitful intervals of sleep but started to worry at dawn when there was no Daisy. Hour after hour all was still until the church bells of Alderton began to rejoice that it was Sunday and summer. The warm brick of the house below radiated the sun with only butterflies among the nettles to bask in it. Irata was restless and impatient. Georges started an argument over Syndicalism, maintaining that if there were any logic in politics Franco should have been a hero of the Left, not of the Right. That successfully evaded the two topics at which Irata was continually and clumsily hinting: the name of his companion and for whom he was working.

Daisy did not appear till her village world was at Sunday dinner, moving quietly up from the house by some route of her own instead of down from the trees. She greeted Georges with joy and astonishment.

"Well, I guessed you 'adn't never gone back to Lille,

Master Georges, and was in trouble as usual, but I didn't expect to find you 'ere along of this nice Spanish gentleman. Relative of yours, is he?"

"Not exactly, Daisy, but we're in much the same trouble. Does she always do you as well as this?" he asked Irata.

"No complaint," Irata replied, smiling for the first time. "It's the best jail I ever was in."

Daisy's basket held a cottage loaf, butter, cheese, spring onions, a roast loin of pork and two liters of dark wine supplied by Paul, who, she said, had told her that Spaniards could not eat without it. Yes, and Mr. Longwill had had a visit from the police asking about that Mrs. Fanshawe who had been staying at the White Hart. A detective had called on Daisy too. She could only tell him that Mrs. Fanshawe was house-hunting and had been interested in the empty place of which she kept the keys. He said that the lady hadn't got a husband, at least not in the army, and that she had been in the district on some shady business that they'd like to know about.

"Did he mention my name, Daisy?"

"No 'e didn't. Did 'e ought to have done?"

"He didn't ought have done. But if Mrs. Fanshawe ever comes to you for help, please do what you can, Daisy dear."

"Ah, so that's the way it is! Well, if I didn't suspect nowt, no one else won't neither. But what's 'er 'usband going to say, Master Georges?"

"She hasn't got a husband, Daisy. She's keeping quiet like me and this gentleman here. Any inquiry about him?"

"No. Not about Mr. Irata."

"What makes you think that's his name?"

"There ain't that number of runaway Spanishes round 'ere, so I guessed it when I read in the papers that 'e was wanted. But I knew 'e wasn't no murderer or you and Mr. Paul wouldn't 'ave aught to do with 'im. All the same I aren't happy, dear Master Georges, though I was never a one for 'aving faith in me bodings like you were."

"I give you my word that Mr. Irata is quite innocent, Daisy."

"Oh, it ain't that. But I keep 'avin' a feeling that I'm bein' watched. That's why I'm late today. I didn't want to go on leavin' me back gate before sunup when I couldn't give no reason for it. So this morning I takes my cleaning things and puts 'em on top of the basket and comes out 'ere to give the floors a polish which everyone knows as I do to the old place when it needs it. And when all was quiet and I sees it for sure I comes up through the bushes instead of the way as Mr. Paul showed me, and I'll go back down with an armful of dog daisy and crab apple on top of the basket as if I'd been agatherin' of them which is what I was doin' when I first came on your bury and wouldn't 'ave you disturbed no more than a pair of dancin' fox cubs."

If anyone was indeed watching her movements he would be a lot easier to see in daytime than before dawn. Georges asked her to go ahead with her wild-flower picking and take her time over it. He then left Irata with breakfast and wriggled his way cautiously up the slope as in youth. From time to time he could see Daisy's head bobbing about and twigs of crab apple blossom springing back from her hands. Nobody was on the opposite slope, which was fairly open, nobody in the lane or on the field path leading to the house.

In the shelter of the belt of trees he rose to his knees. Daisy could be right. At the far end of the ridge and also just within the trees a man was standing. He had a clear view of one side of the village and of Daisy's back gate and garden. He could have seen her leave and then by changing his position her arrival at the house. It was unlikely that he had ever observed her earlier visits in the half-light, for in that case he could have followed her straight to the cellar and Irata. Why he should have watched her movements this particular morning was a puzzle. It was probable that he had an entirely different objective: to observe Monsieur Rivac when he returned to recover the brochures.

The figure remained intent on the village, so Georges returned to Irata and asked him to come up as quietly as he could. The silent feet of a manservant could not compare with those of a mildly delinquent juvenile trained in the country, but sound was masked by the ridge and the watcher heard nothing. Georges pointed him out.

"Do you know him?"

"I cannot see his face."

Georges imitated the squeal of a rabbit caught by fox or stoat. The man turned around sharply.

"Why do you want to know?" Irata asked.

"Because neither of us wish to go to Russia and he is too close for comfort. Simple!"

"He sold ice cream from a van."

"What was his route?"

"From Oxford down the Thames. Sometimes he called at the house. He may have brought messages. Fyster-Holmes would not allow his telephone to be used on business."

The watcher stayed where he was until Daisy returned to her cottage with flowers on top of her basket and a long, light feather brush for cleaning cobwebs as a pretext for her journey. He then made off to the far end of the village and out of sight.

A devoted agent of the Party presumably, and in the

most innocent of professions. From village to village he drove his ice-cream van, tinkling a tune on his bell to announce his approach to children and their mothers. It was hard to see how at short notice he had been able to change his route from the upper Thames to the farming lowlands east of Oxford, but no doubt Daisy would know.

VII

As soon as she received the warning from Paul Longwill, Zia quickly packed and paid her bill. It must have been a close thing. The desk asked if she had her passport on her. She replied that of course she had not, that she was a British subject by marriage. Another clerk then addressed her in French, very politely inviting her to see the manager for a moment. She answered haltingly in the same language that she infinitely regretted she had a train to catch and no time. He hesitated. Obviously he had been expecting her to be French and was momentarily disconcerted when he recognized from her accent that she was not. Before he could start again she swept out and onto a passing bus.

She got off at the first Underground station that came into view and took a train without knowing or caring where it was bound. As a bunch of fellow passengers changed at Piccadilly Circus she changed with them and returned to the surface at Knightsbridge, feeling reasonably certain that if she herself did not know where she was the police wouldn't either. Harrods, that familiar name, appeared in the distance. It ought to have somewhere comfortable for a fugitive to change her clothes and think out the next move.

The fourth floor presented a panorama of capitalist glamour intimidating even to a traveled Hungarian. Searching through dreamlit hall after hall devoted to the languorous enhancement of beauty, she found at last a cloakroom fit to receive a general's wife in no immediate need of rejuvenation. First she called Georges at the Regency so guardedly that no one listening could guess who she was. It occurred to her that the idiot was quite capable of thinking she had run away from him, so she threw in three passionate darlings and cut him off before he could respond. That done, she sat down in the adjoining café with a glass of Madeira to consider how to dispose of Mrs. Fanshawe.

Georges had said that the interview with Herbert Spring had gone very well. That surely must mean that the enigma of Kren and Lukash was near to being solved and that somewhere must be a secret and powerful ally. If she could hold out for another day or two without the name of Terezia Fodor ever appearing in the English press or Hungarian police files, her uncle and his club would be secure and she could safely return to work.

Hold out — but where in this foreign country and how? She was warned not to visit Georges in his mysterious cellar and it would be wise not to communicate with Paul while his connection with her was being investigated. Yet she must let them know where she was. Hotels were to be avoided. Whatever the efficiency of British police it was impossible that every receptionist could be advised to look out for her, but she would at once be in trouble if her accent or an inadequate story aroused suspicion and she was asked to identify herself.

It was then that Alderton Wood occurred to her. It was so near to Georges that if she was forced by any emergency to get in touch with him she could do it secretly or by way of the Manor Farm. "He must be very fond of you to take you there," Paul had said, and she had coolly replied that it was business, not romance. Yet it was there in the wood only last Monday that she had first realized that she would be far from sorry if business, for at least a mischievous moment, was forgotten.

The first essential was to buy a map. When she spread it out all her movements, including that fatal and dreamy wandering off onto the downs instead of turning left to the river, jumped from vagueness into reality. She remembered from her first journey to Thame that buses stopped wherever there was a village or a turning to one, and made a note where she should get off. It seemed to be more or less where Georges had accepted that disastrous lift, but that did not disturb her. She was not in the least afraid of Appinger and his friends, who only knew that some woman had been present at the death of Fyster-Holmes and had no description of her. The ever-present danger was the police.

She bought a sleeping bag to carry on her back and then returned to the top floor to transfer a few intimate possessions — in mind the thought of her next meeting with Georges — from suitcase to bedroll and changed. She was going to look a bit too formal for one of the determined young hikers on the English roads, but the slacks which she had worn on the night of Georges's rescue were dirty enough to pass and the coat could be rolled up and carried. Leaving her case with the attendant and saying she would pick it up later, she carried out her plan: a train to Aylesbury where the police had no reason to expect her and she could safely wait for dusk. She bought bread, wine, a length of salami, a pound of tomatoes and a torch, and took a late bus to that turning she had marked on the map.

If she was not to lose her way in the darkness she had to pass the White Hart. She managed that by crossing fields while keeping the lit windows of the bar in sight and then picked up the path she knew and the low stars visible down the length of the glade. After several vain plunges into the thicket she at last found the stream and followed it to the bank where she had sat with Georges. There she slept happily under the snow of the hawthorn until awakened by the clamorous dawn chorus of, as it seemed to her, more birds than in all Hungary and most of those in England.

Her problem was to get a message to Georges without showing herself in any nearby village. After staying six nights at the White Hart her face was familiar to too many people. In this district of small and friendly communities everybody seemed to know everybody else or, if not, were able to fit a name to a face. She had to find a person who had perhaps gossiped about her but had no reason to recognize her.

She spent an hour composing a message to Daisy, who would be acute enough to guess that it was meant for Georges in his cellar; it had to be unintelligible but must be plausible. She had learned that many of the older generation in their pretty cottages took a surprising interest in minor details of their countryside — these noisy little birds, for example. But she didn't know enough names of birds. Flowers then. Flowers might do. Georges had made a fuss over this purple thing he called Honesty. After editing various versions it seemed to her she had arrived at a good one.

Would you please tell Mrs. Daisy Taylor that Tessa has found the flower she wants in Alderton Wood and what shall she do about it?

Daisy of course would see no sense in it, but Georges would — especially if he remembered that Tessa was the

English diminutive of Teresa as Zia was in Hungarian. She practiced her message over and over again so that her accent was as strained and correct as in an English class for foreigners.

It was a reasonable morning in early June with the soft mist clearing by eight o'clock and restoring warmth to limbs chilled by an inadequate sleeping bag and a brain wasting heat to work out its puzzle. Stopping to look around her, hurrying on, stopping again in imitation of Georges's movements, she made her way to the road to Alderton. There she leaned on a stile from which she could see approaching traffic and disappear behind the hedge if it was useless to her. She recalled the various vehicles which did the round of the villages, stopping in the main street to serve customers: the baker, the traveling grocer's van, the County Library Service. Some of them ought to pass sooner or later on the road to Alderton and all the drivers would know Daisy. At this hour in the morning there might even be the red Post Office van, though she doubted if it was wise to send a message by the postman. As a government servant he might, for all she knew, make a daily report to police.

None of them passed and very little traffic at all. A distant peal of bells reminded her that it was Sunday. Hell! But it appeared after all that religion did not affect the Sunday dinner. The fried-fish van came along, its chimney polluting the morning with the reek of steaming oil which the English seemed to enjoy. She decided that it would not do, that if Daisy ate fish she would cook it for herself. Shortly afterward the fish-frier was followed by a gaudily painted ice-cream van, ambling along with a red and light green canopy over a white body. Her motives for not stopping it were still vaguer. Surely mothers and children bought ice cream, not comfortable widows? And the Hungarian colors (or Italian for that matter) were unnatural in this empty, pastoral quarter of Oxfordshire.

Ridiculous feminine reasons! She reproached herself for irresolution and determined to stop the next likely person who turned up. This was a man on a rusty black bicycle, in his kindly fifties and probably a prosperous farm laborer; at any rate, bicycle and all, he belonged to the land. Zia popped up and asked him if he was going to Alderton.

"Trying to catch up the fish — that's what I am," he answered.

She said she was sorry. She had wanted to send a message to Alderton.

"Ah, I can do that for you. Who'd it be for?"

"Mrs. Daisy Taylor."

"I knows 'er as who doesn't. But I tell you how it is, young lady. The missus goes off to church and she says to me: Bill, she says, don't you forget to buy a nice piece of cod for dinner, 'cos I won't be out in time 'cos Alice's baby is bein' christened and I just want to see 'ow she can look the vicar in the face, not knowin' who the poor mite's father was or likely to. And blast it if it didn't slip my mind, being busy with the lettuces, so I'll catch the fish up and be back with it fresh as out of the sea, like. And I'll tell 'im to tell Mrs. Daisy. 'E won't forget. Always obliging he is when it comes to taking a parcel or seein' that the cat 'as her little bit."

Zia gave him her message, which he repeated.

"What sort of flower is it you found, Miss?"

That was a question she had not foreseen. Georges's purple thing would have to do, but made to sound as if it was worth reporting to Daisy.

"A pink form of Honesty," she said.

"Want an answer?"

There was no answer Daisy could give, but it was a pity to waste the informal means of communication which had offered itself. So Zia compromised, saying that it didn't really matter unless Mrs. Taylor thought it did.

"Camping, are you?"

"Yes, one or two of us."

"Well, you be here around three o'clock. It's likely the fish will be passing on his way 'ome, but if 'e ain't someone else will."

Zia returned to her sanctuary under the hawthorn and waited, now uneasy at being dependent on an outer world. The stream which flowed past her, rippling out of an unknown source and on into an unknown future, was, she felt, so much in keeping with her desperate life of the last ten days in England. At three she was at her stile again, not too closely hidden and with her map half-open as if she were just considering whether to turn right or left on the road. No passers-by paid any attention to her until the ice-cream van came along and stopped farther up the road. In the front seat were two men: the white-aproned salesman-driver and a companion in a plain business suit who got out and walked back to her.

"Are you the young lady who sent a message to Mrs. Taylor?" he asked.

"Yes, that's me."

"Well, she says you're to dig it up and bring it around tonight to the gate at the back of the garden. I hope it's not a protected species, Miss."

"I don't think so. Just a freak color."

"Must be the cold spring, I reckon."

She thanked him and was about to accompany him back to the van and buy an ice cream, but he did not wait for her and was off.

She returned to the wood comforted but a little puzzled. The fish for some unknown reason had passed the message to the ice cream. If he had forgotten to deliver it or changed his route, that seemed to be in keeping with the helpful tendrils of the village grapevine. But Daisy must have been remarkably quick to understand and to respond so cunningly to the unknown Tessa. Perhaps Georges had been in her cottage at the time and had prompted the reply. "Dig it up" could not mean anything at all and was simply thrown in for verisimilitude.

She was not at all happy at the thought of committing Mrs. Fanshawe to Alderton, even to a back entrance at night. Also she doubted if she could find her way around the village in the dark and whether she could recognize the right gate.

Setting off in the dusk she got as near to the village as she dared before the light failed. She could not see Daisy's cottage though the lane she had taken to it on her single visit was plain enough; so were the open, rolling fields behind it across which she was meant to approach. Georges had said that he went that way if he did not want to be observed. But when darkness came down she realized that she would far rather have looked for a missing tourist in the stews of Marseille than launch herself into dogs, cows, hedges and indistinguishable open spaces which were not open at all when you tried to find your way out of them.

At last she discovered a footpath with several garden gates opening onto it. Only one had a hen house, so that must be Daisy's. No light showed in any of the cottages to reassure her that she was in the midst of human beings. She told herself that anyway the last thing she wanted was to be seen and questioned and that it was perfectly natural for there to be no light. The good people were sitting in their front parlors watching television or mending or both. At the back were only kitchen and bedroom windows. Washing up had finished and bedtime had not yet arrived.

She waited, not knowing whether to go in and knock at Daisy's back door. It seemed imprudent. Instructions stated the garden gate and carefully said nothing about coming in. The village was silent except for the occasional shutting of a door. Down the lane some dogs barked but not with any conviction. Beyond Daisy's hedge she could see nothing but the outlines of the hen house and the cottage. She had to admit that the rendezvous was very well chosen, but Daisy or Georges should by now have been on the lookout for her and appeared. Twice she imagined that she heard them.

A light was quickly shone on her face and switched off.

"Good evening, Madam. I am a police officer and must ask you to accompany me."

"Where to? What for?" Zia asked in panic. "May I see Mrs. Taylor?"

"We are investigating certain activities in and about Alderton. Mrs. Taylor is helping us with our inquiries."

This was appalling. Then they must have picked up Georges too, and everything would come out.

"Where is she?"

"For the moment she is over at the house she looks after up the valley."

She pulled herself together. It wouldn't do much good to fence with police but at least she could parry until they forced her to hang up her foil and come quietly.

"Does she? I didn't know."

"Your full name, please."

"Tessa Fanshawe." She threw in the Tessa because the police must have intercepted her message. It was no good lying when they had only to run her over to the White Hart for identification.

"How did you come to know Mrs. Taylor?"

A catch question. Lunge and let's see the strength of his wrist.

"Oh, she's been friends with my mother for years. And so when she knew I was camping in Alderton Wood she asked me to look out for a flower which she had heard was there."

"How did she know you were in the wood?"

"She told me it was a good place to camp."

"You are not British, Miss Fanshawe. What are you?"

Miss Fanshawe? He could hardly have made a mistake and ought to know very well that she was French or pretending to be.

"I was brought up in Switzerland. Please, sir, this is my first visit to England."

"Our information is that she told you to dig up a flower."

"Yes, but I hadn't got anything to dig it up with."

"Why did she tell you to come here at night with it?"

"I don't know. Somebody said it might be a protected species. Is that possible?"

"Now, now, Miss Fanshawe! You know very well that it was not a flower which she asked you to look for."

Relief, fear and light at last! There were only two places where the brochures could possibly have been hidden when Georges was grabbed—Daisy's cottage or Alderton Wood

— and he could very well have buried them temporarily in the wood if he believed he was in danger. In fact Georges had felt fairly secure; but from their point of view he had been so desperate that he killed Rippmann.

The man was standing back and she could not see his face clearly; nor had she seen the boatman very clearly, but they could be one and the same. Obviously he knew nothing at all about the Mrs. Fanshawe who was badly wanted by the real police and must be wondering whether this commonplace young camper with a pack on her back was or was not the mysterious woman in the marsh at the escape of Georges Rivac. He had not mentioned the name of Rivac, which was promising. She had to convince him that she was just Daisy's innocent stooge.

"But it *was* a flower!" she insisted. "It was a pink form of Honesty."

"What did you find alongside it?"

"Nothing. I hadn't a trowel or anything to dig it up with. I told you."

"We will see what Mrs. Taylor has to say to that. You will kindly come with me."

"Yes, of course, if I'm needed."

It seemed unlikely that Daisy was really at the house. Appinger would hardly dare to detain a respectable old lady for questioning and risk bringing the full force of the police down on his unsuspected organization. To kidnap Rivac, the foreigner without any base except the cottage of an old retainer, was quite a different project and comparatively safe. Should she yell for Daisy and the neighbors? It was a temptation, but she boldly resisted it. She must show herself quite convinced that she was in the hands of police and go with this man like a good citizen. The only other alternative was to run; but that would prove guilt and she could not be sure of getting away.

She walked side by side with the uniformed stranger along the field path to the grandmother's empty house in its melancholy screen of trees. The door was not locked, suggesting that Daisy had opened it and could be inside after all. Her companion never showed a light till he was in the house and then pointed his torch at the floor as they passed down a passage and into the kitchen. Opening out of it was a scullery with a trapdoor thrown back and steps down to a cellar. So it was all up. They had Georges and Irata. Her own story might still be credible unless they searched her and found the Hungarian passport of Fodor, Terezia.

The stranger ordered her — still with the cool politeness of the police — to go down the steps, followed and closed the trap. A lantern was then switched on. Another man, in plain clothes, was standing there. Neither Georges nor Irata was in the cellar and she saw no sign that they ever had been. The place was empty except for a crate of bottles, a box of tattered children's books and some old garden furniture. The cobwebs had not been disturbed. The uneven brick floor was uniformly dusty.

"Where is Mrs. Taylor?" she asked.

The plainclothesman replied that she had been taken to Oxford police station.

"I think this lady is quite innocent," his uniformed companion said, "and there is no more point in detaining her."

The other put a few questions which she easily parried. No, she had not been alone in Alderton Wood. Another girl, a Miss Zwingli, was with her, also on her first visit to

England. She had moved on while Tessa tried to carry out Mrs. Taylor's request — though they both thought it was a bit of nonsense — and they had agreed to meet in Oxford and see the colleges.

"Can you tell us exactly where Mrs. Taylor instructed you to find this pink flower?"

It was all clear now. Her guess had been correct. They had made a sound, logical and utterly wrong deduction from her note to Daisy. Believing that Georges could have hidden the brochures in Alderton Wood, what more natural than that he should have asked Mrs. Taylor to recover them, warning her that she might be watched? The arrival of this girl had presented her with the perfect opportunity.

Zia described the course of the stream, the half arch of hawthorn and the supposed pink Honesty among the purple. There was only one such flower, she said, and it could not be mistaken.

They asked her to follow them upstairs. Simultaneously one shone a light on her face, and the other a light on what was undoubtedly Irata's motorcycle pushed into a deep, narrow larder. She managed to remain expressionless or at least only puzzled, looking from one to the other.

"Have you ever seen this machine before?"

A plain "no" would be too prompt. She examined it carefully.

"I don't think so," she said. "But one doesn't notice all the motorbikes that pass."

"Very well, Miss Fanshawe. I hope you will accept our apologies. We will take you to Oxford and drop you wherever you like."

"At the bus station, if you would be so good," she replied. "My friend will be waiting there."

179

The general air of British police at their best changed abruptly. Someone in the passage whispered urgently:

"Quick! Take her away! I'll stay."

She recognized the hoarse voice as that of the man alongside the driver in the ice-cream van. So that was how they had got hold of her message. The two salesmen, covering the same villages and not competing with each other, would naturally be friends, and fish might have mentioned his strange errand to ice cream among others. It had almost certainly never been passed to Daisy at all and the reply invented.

She was hurried off by the back door and on to the point where the two lines of trees met at the head of the little valley. Beyond them a black van was waiting on an upper road. It did not look like the regular police cars with which she was by now familiar and could well be the van which had carried off Georges. The uniformed man, carrying her pack, got in the back with her where they could not be seen. The other joined the driver in the front.

The pretended cop took off his tunic — which she noticed was much too tight under the arms — and laid it on the locker.

"Now I have to ask you to open your pack," he said and spread it out on the floor.

Unexpected and deadly and no escape possible. As if eager to show her innocence she helped him to undo the zips of the pockets and while he was examining her clothes managed to extract her handbag and slip it under his tunic. It passed through her mind that pocket-picking was really too easy, but of course this scratch organization would not be as experienced in searches as Hungarian police.

When he had finished she rolled up the pack and threw it as if accidentally on top of his tunic.

"Oh, I am so sorry," she exclaimed. "I didn't notice it was there."

She pulled out the tunic carefully, gave it a motherly shake and held it out for him to put on.

"No, no! Thank you very much! One is so glad sometimes to get out of uniform."

He put on a sports coat which went very well with his blue police shirt, and took off his tie. The alteration was enough. If the van was stopped for any reason no one would suspect that he had been impersonating police.

Relations with this shy girl who asked silly questions about criminals remained amicable all the way to the Oxford bus station. Zia gathered up her roll, under it the bag in her hand, and got out. They waited to see her greet her friend. Fortunately there was a girl standing indecisively outside the waiting room. Zia embraced her affectionately and as the van drove away rattled off apologies for mistaking her for somebody else, switching to German when she discovered that the lost loiterer was desolate as only a German or a puppy could be. It was then very difficult to get rid of her, but at least she provided some protective coloring. Two young foreigners in Oxford with packs on their backs were worth only a glance from any passing police car, whereas for one single girl resembling the badly wanted Mrs. Fanshawe the car might pull in to the curb. For the moment she was more worried about Georges than herself. It was likely that either he or Irata was the person whose approach had startled the fake police.

It was nearly midnight and the crowds were thinning.

Action had to be taken quickly. Georges was somewhere unknown and the only possible way to get in touch with him was through Paul Longwill. She still considered it too dangerous to call him at the Manor Farm, so he must be contacted at his London office where telephones were unlikely to be monitored. London was where her German friend wanted to go, so Zia suggested that they should take the last bus out along the London road to the terminus and then try to cadge a lift. As the fraulein appeared afraid of rape, she pointed out that there were two of them and that the English were not in fact so addicted to rape as continental papers supposed.

When the pair had got off the bus and were all alone on the edge of a dark lay-by where it had already started to rain, Zia felt she had been too impulsive, foreseeing that if they got their lift they would arrive in London before dawn and she would have to wait in empty streets, inviting curiosity, until Paul turned up at his office. She did not underestimate the interest of the Law in Mrs. Fanshawe. A well-known retired diplomat had been murdered. Mrs. Fanshawe was strongly suspected of having been present. Worse still, she was known, according to Paul, to have traveled on the pillion of a motorcycle on the night in question, and whose was it if not Irata's?

The luck ran for her. A six-ton truck bound for London Airport stopped at their signal. Her companion, who wanted to take refuge with a friend in some northern suburb, turned it down. Zia insisted, for London Airport would allow her to vanish among faceless people until Paul was available.

When the kindly driver — in fact so chivalrous that Zia gave him a kiss for his own sake — had dropped them off and proceeded to the freight terminal, the pair entered

Terminal 2 and made themselves comfortable alongside a party of students waiting for a chartered flight to leave at first light. It was safe to relax. She fell into the deep sleep of exhaustion, waking to find that the students had gone and so had her German companion — probably mistrustful, now that she had time to think, of Zia's behavior from the Oxford bus station onward.

It was nearly nine and she was all alone — in the sense that no one was within three yards of her. When she got up a man approached and addressed her in French. Though only just awake she had the sense to answer in German and then in heavily accented English. She noticed that he followed her at a discreet distance to the lavatories, unsure of the possible identification. Once inside she washed her tired eyes until they sparkled, and returned without makeup and with her bedroll on her back looking, she hoped, too young and innocent to be Mrs. Fanshawe. He let her pass, apparently intent on a timetable. That was encouraging, showing that the police had never traced her to Harrods and had no description of her present appearance. Even so, when she took the bus to the town terminal she realized that she might still be under observation, since she had deliberately given the impression of waiting for a flight and yet had left the airport.

On arrival at the Cromwell Road she walked straight out and then played her former game of changing from one form of public transport to another regardless of destination. She reverted to her own feet in an unknown part of London where a maze of rotaries, overpasses and road junctions would make it difficult to pick up her trail if anyone had ever been on it. Opposite her was a station called Kew Bridge and a telephone box. Waiting till she was sure that nobody was paying any attention to her she dialed Paul Longwill's office, bypassing an officious secretary by saying she was Mrs. Daisy Taylor.

"It's not Daisy and I am calling from a box."

"Give me the number and stand by."

The standby seemed interminable. She reminded herself that he had to telephone from outside his office. Meanwhile some damned salesman — whose grandmother was a whore — occupied her box and proceeded to pass a sheaf of orders to his headquarters. Eventually it was free and it rang.

"Where is our friend?" she asked.

"All right. I saw him the night before last. Still nothing to implicate him so far as I know. But if they get you or the night rider the game's up."

"And you?"

"The City can always find urgent business in South America."

"Can you get me an interview with the man Georges saw in Lower Belgrave Street?"

"No. But Herbert Spring wants to know where you are. He has found another firm which may be interested."

"Then now! At once!"

"Where can you be found?"

"Here. I'll wait and wait. It's a place called Kew Bridge station."

"Cross the bridge, go into Kew Gardens, feed the ducks on the lake! O.K.?"

Zia had much needed breakfast at a nearby café, collected some extra rolls and followed instructions. Few people were in the gardens on a Monday morning, and the ducks, mysterious over the telephone, became real and demanding. By midday rolls were finished and the ducks had deserted her for mothers with delighted tiny children and an occasional old person scattering crumbs from a bench as a bribe for momentary society. One other visitor caught her eye — tall, thin, loping along like an intent carnivore, though intent, one would say, on past rather than future meals. A soldier, perhaps, occupied by a recent and disappointing love affair rather than military business; a plant collector, perhaps, accustomed to striding studiously from one Himalayan valley to another.

A bold duck approached him, stopping near his feet with head on one side. He began to throw scraps of biscuit ahead of her so that she appeared to be leading him slowly along the lake. When they came past he was talking to her as if she was an old friend.

"Nothing else for you this morning, Zia," he said. "I'm off to the tropical house now."

It was so naturally done that for a moment she thought the use of her name must be coincidence. Then she followed him, keeping well behind until he entered the tropical forest under its immensity of glass. He caught up to her among the bananas and appeared to be continuing a conversation exactly as if she were some young student of botany whom he was showing around.

"And this, my dear, is a most interesting hybrid of the Cavendish and the Breadfruit, supplied to us for further experimentation by my friend Lukash of the Prague Botanical Gardens."

"Oh, thank God!"

"We will now go through to the next hothouse where there is nobody at the moment and we can sit down."

Side by side, pupil and professor, they walked through into more steaming greenery where there was a bench.

"My name is Colonel Mannering, attached rather loosely to the Ministry of Defense and a little more closely to NATO," he said. "You must think we are quite mad, Miss Fodor. How long have you been in England?"

"Twelve days."

"The only comfort is that if we can hide ourselves so well from the other cats we must be pretty good at hiding from the rats. Now, Lukash. We were expecting a most important message from him when he went off the air. Do you know what happened?"

"No — except that he was arrested. But his employers were sure he knew nothing of what he was sending."

"And the message?"

"I don't know what it was. But it is in an Intertatry brochure describing their miniature four-stroke engine, specially printed to look like the real thing."

"Where is it?"

"Georges Rivac hid it in an old drain pipe behind a cottage in Alderton."

"And Rivac himself?"

"I don't know."

"Nor does anybody. The only idea these damned security people came up with was to use him as bait."

"I think it has worked. They are watching Alderton."

Zia brought him up to date with the happenings of the last twenty-four hours.

"Can the security lot act quickly?" she asked.

"Yes, when it isn't a case of passing vital information to the right department. They think it's unprofessional to ask too many questions."

"I believe Appinger's men will dig in Alderton Wood to-day."

"So simple?"

"From their point of view it makes sense."

"For only a handbook describing an engine?"

"Karel Kren killed himself rather than be questioned — and they would be interrogating Georges Rivac now if he hadn't escaped."

"Thanks to you, I hear."

"But can you protect us from the police?"

"Easily — by giving everything away."

"I see."

"Good girl! I thought you would. Do you believe in ghosts?"

"Well — er —"

"Then you'd better because you are one. So is Rivac. The police can't see you. This fellow who calls himself Appinger can't see you. But they know damn well you're tapping and haunting. The first job is to get you safely out of here."

"I don't think I have been followed."

"Perhaps not. But a girl with a pack on her back, dark hair, right dimensions, complexion like a young lioness married to a peach — colonels are often poets at heart, Zia — might be reported hanging about at Kew Bridge station. Such people are inclined to pass the time before arrest in public parks. Routine is to watch the exits. What other clothes have you in your pack?"

"The coat of a suit."

"Splendid! I will show you a patch of lilacs. Go in, put on the coat, drop the pack! I will pick it up. Peculiar — but among us botanists anything goes. Ah, yes, glasses! Take my reading glasses and keep them on while you pass out.

In twenty minutes leave by the gate near the Pagoda over there, cross the road, go straight on and you will see me waiting in a green car. Jump in at once!"

Zia put on her coat in the lilacs and walked away. She watched him pick up her pack, draping it over his arm as if he had been using the sleeping bag for an early siesta or as a protection against damp ground while watching microscopic life among exotic roots. She wondered if he was at all typical of Military Intelligence in this unpredictable country. He preferred to be noticeable rather than inconspicuous and yet whatever he chose to do was unquestioned. The eccentricities of Hungarian noblemen in old days might have had some similarity, effectively disguising active intellect.

Outside the gate she did notice a man hanging about with no obvious occupation. Might be, might not. At any rate he showed no interest in her after one keen glance. The green car was in position and shot off as soon as she shut the door. God alone knew for what disclosure Karel Kren had given his life but now at last it would be welcomed.

"Where are we going?" she asked.

"First of all we shall meet a gentleman called Gerald. He is responsible, Lord help us, for the security of this little nation. It is his pleasure to be known as just Gerald though everyone knows his full name. He has already talked to your friend from Lille. When you have told him about pink Honesty I rather think he will want to make a dash for Alderton Wood. He likes a day in the country."

Whether in Budapest or London conversations which should not be overheard always seemed to gravitate to public parks. This one, she noticed, was called Barnes Common,

188

and it seemed to her that the colonel had twisted unnecessarily through a number of side streets before coming out on a road which ran directly across an expanse of worn but serviceable grass. He pulled in behind a very ordinary, mud-splashed car. A middle-aged man got out and joined the colonel. He looked an office-bound government servant and as if a day in the country would do him good.

"Good afternoon, Zia. Excuse me using your Christian name. I have no official knowledge of any other, you see."

"Thank you, Gerald."

The face was lit up by a gray smile, appreciating the irony of her reply.

"And now what have you to tell me that is so urgent?"

She gave him quickly her adventures of the previous day and night. He turned to the colonel.

"Is it possible? You know the importance of this document, and I do not."

"They believe that Rivac has never had a chance to recover it. Their movements show that. It's quite credible that he would get this Mrs. Taylor to do it for him."

"Shall we be too late to catch them digging, Zia?"

"You might not be. They must have daylight to find the place and the flower and they might have done it this morning. But wouldn't they need time to consult with Appinger? Where is he likely to be?"

"In London. He might be anything — trade delegate, chauffeur to an embassy, courier — but he's sure to be in London where he can get in touch with his bosses. Have you a map with you, Colonel?"

"No, but Zia has."

She gave him a flash of offended eyes.

"Had to take a look in the pack, my dear. It would be

most unseemly to be blown to bits in Kew Gardens. Think of the lilacs!"

Gerald, with the map open on his knees, ignored the exchange.

"Well then, we may not be too late. They will recognize that they are at the right place, which sounds unmistakable from your description, but they'll be puzzled that there is no pink Honesty. So they are bound to spend an hour or two looking for it and probing the ground. Now what I want from you, Zia, is to accompany my team and help them to choose a place where they cannot be seen and will have a clear view of these fellows when they pass. They are bound to go in and out by the route you explained to them because they don't know any other."

"You're going to run them in?"

"Zia, you and your friends have a thing about running people in. We are going to photograph them — including, I hope, your ice-cream man — from two or more angles."

"You know about him?"

"No, but we soon shall. I think from your description that he must be one of the firm's inspectors, not a salesman. That leaves him free to choose what route he will inspect. Now, it will take me half an hour to get the show on the road and it's about an hour and a half's drive. You should be able to hand her over to my men at five-fifteen, Colonel."

"Seventeen-fifteen. Can do."

"In the Home Office, still five-fifteen. You will then be here" — he made a cross on the map — "It looks like a quiet lane and you will find a gray Rover with two men and a driver. Pass over Zia to them."

"And then I must get in touch with Georges Rivac," Zia said.

"Never you mind about young Rivac! He's all right. He doesn't exist."

"But I do worry about young Rivac."

"You leave it to me," Mannering assured her. "Once Gerald has taken his pictures, we can get on with more important business."

At that Gerald asserted himself.

"It is in my interest to cooperate with you, Colonel, but I am bound to ask you for more information. You have, I take it, some connection with Bridge Holdings?"

"Don't know a thing about them!" the colonel replied cheerfully. "I am a simple soldier from MI(S)."

"And what are the duties of that department? MI Secrets?" Gerald asked ironically.

"Nothing so romantic, my dear fellow. MI Supplies. It supplies NATO with whatever is required."

"Hardware?"

"Mostly software."

Gerald let it go at that, returned to his own car and shot off toward the center of London. The colonel remarked that they had plenty of time for a late lunch and that she must be hungry. Zia hesitated.

"My dear girl, the police can't be everywhere," he said, "not the real ones and certainly not the phony fuzz you so cleverly spotted last night. Just enjoy yourself and remember you are — now what? I have it! A charming Hungarian cabaret girl whom I am entertaining with the worst of motives. Hungary used to export beauties to all Europe."

"Well, we don't any longer. That's one good thing," Zia replied proudly.

"There are many good things, my dear. That's why we want you back in Europe more than ever."

Colonel Mannering's confidence was infectious. At the restaurant table Zia had no difficulty in playing up to him, especially since she had not enjoyed a proper meal for the last two days. When, however, she was back again in his car and heading west she was uneasy at returning to the district where police had investigated Mrs. Fanshawe's every move. The only comforting thought was that they knew she had left it. But she had no illusions. Gerald and this genial colonel would sacrifice her discreetly and without hesitation if she became an embarrassment.

Dark Alderton Wood broke up the flat horizon — a miniature of European forest, but lower and more scrubby. A roadside warning showed a picture of deer: another example of the exaggerated care of the English, either for the benefit of the deer or the passing traffic. Probably it was for the deer, she thought, since there was hardly any traffic. Gerald had chosen the rendezvous very well.

The gray Rover was waiting, with a driver and two men in the back surrounded by cameras, some of unfamiliar shape and one marked "infrared." The colonel handed her over and asked them to drop her at the same spot when they had finished. They treated her with marked respect. In their eyes she was, she supposed, the valuable inside agent, the legendary beautiful spy.

The car drove slowly along a side of the wood which was continuous and unfamiliar to her. She picked up her bearings when she saw the brook sliding under the road unromantically confined in a culvert. A little farther on she recognized the overgrown footpath which she had twice followed and had described to the bogus plainclothes detective.

"Would they have left their car near here or in Alderton Abbas?" the driver asked.

"I should think near here. They might not want to be seen walking with spades."

Driving a little way on they came to a timber track disappearing into the hazels on the left of the road. Very evident in the mud was the recent impression of car wheels. Whatever vehicle had gone in had not yet come out. One of her companions silently vanished into the thicket and returned in five minutes to report that a black van was parked out of sight of the road with no driver in it. Zia went back with him to see if she could identify it. It was the same van in which she had traveled to Oxford the previous night.

There was then no reason to hide by the path or the stream or to push through bushes with the risk of being heard. The two cameramen decided that they could conceal themselves and their apparatus within easy range of the van. The driver and Zia were to wait a few miles away until they received a radio signal that the van had left and it was safe to return.

The signal came through within half an hour. Gerald had run it close. The diggers must already have given up and been smoothing the ground by the time the cameras were in position. There had been four of Mr. Appinger's friends; to judge by the description, one was last night's constable, one probably the boatman and two unknown. The triumphant operators had perfect pictures and were justifiably proud of Zia and themselves, for it had been nervous work at short notice without knowing whether the supposed enemy agents were armed or what precautions they might have taken. The three pressed her to have a drink with them in the nearest pub; as it happened to be the White Hart she had regretfully to refuse. She was then handed back to the colonel with two hours of daylight left.

"Where's Gerald?" she asked.

"I think we may find him at the Manor Farm — if a Mr. Longwill has returned from the City."

"But I daren't go there."

"Well, what about this Mrs. Daisy Taylor?"

"If you can get me into her cottage without being seen."

"Will the village recognize you?"

"Not necessarily. I've only been there once in daylight."

"How were you dressed?"

"Lady. Country."

"Then we'll go back to the hitchhiker I met in Kew Gardens, and you can have my reading glasses again if you don't lose them."

"But I was dressed like that last night."

"Never mind! They can't have started another watch on Alderton yet. And they know or think they know that Rivac is not there."

"Shall I get the brochures?"

The colonel hesitated, for once indecisive.

"I think yes. Rivac or you? And as I don't yet know where Rivac is or how far Gerald is willing to protect him, it had better be you."

"But it doesn't matter anymore if either of us is arrested."

"Doesn't it? What about your uncle and his club? What about keeping Appinger in the dark? And how about young Zia's photograph on the front page, real name Miss Terezia Fodor?"

"I'd forgotten. It was all going so well."

"That's just when one trips up, my girl. Will you be safe

if you spend the night with Mrs. Taylor? We may need you, and I've had no time to make sure of your safety in London."

"I think so, provided I stay indoors."

"Then here's our story if we require one. I drove you down from London. I am staying with Longwill. You, for the sake of somewhat old-fashioned propriety, are sleeping at Mrs. Taylor's rather than in a lewd bachelor establishment. I will call for you and the brochures at a natural hour — say, nine o'clock after breakfast. We don't want to arouse curiosity by starting too early. Let something blow over your face and jump straight into the car!"

"And Georges Rivac?"

"Gerald and I will find out from Longwill where he is and the best way of extracting him."

VIII
～

THE SUNDAY AFTERNOON HAD dragged on for Georges through long hours of depression. The brochures were perfectly safe where they were, but nothing could be done with them. He too was perfectly safe where he was and useless to himself, to Zia and her Europe. The more his imagination ranged over village and town, river and mountain and all the trampled and loved earth between the Channel and the Black Sea, the more he felt guilt at hiding in a boyhood hole looked after by an indulgent nanny. The whole position was such a desperate muddle when it came to sensible planning. Mrs. Fanshawe was known to the police, but not to Appinger. M. Rivac was known to Appinger, but not yet to the police.

When dusk came down he was overcome by impatience. Where was the newly aggressive Georges who was going to — going to what? Appinger's scratch organization of outwardly respectable British bourgeois like the ice-cream man could do what they bloody well pleased and go where they liked, whereas M. Rivac dared not show his nose without compromising Paul, Daisy and in the end probably Zia. Not too much French élan, the gray-faced man had warned. The dithering of a frightened mongrel was more like it. And Zia — where was sweet Zia? He had to know.

He told Irata that he was going out for more supplies and would be back after midnight. Irata was not to worry. The days of boredom and the nights when no light could be shown would soon come to an end. The Spaniard, however, seemed to be in good spirits and assured him that sleep was the only remedy and he intended to be content with it.

Georges set off about ten, passing around the head of grandmother's valley and approaching the Manor Farm from the north, avoiding the paddock and the garden. The ground floor was lit up. Paul appeared to be giving a dinner party. The dining room and the front of the house were out of sight, but he could see the kitchen window where Marlene and Muriel, Paul's two trusty women from the village, were washing up. Two guests — a man and his wife, as their voices told him — left fairly early. The beam of their headlights twinkled through black hedges and outlined colorless pyramids of trees as they drove away. Half an hour later more voices at the front door indicated that the rest were leaving. Prolonged silence and lights turned out suggested that Paul was now alone except for his temporary kitchen staff.

He crept close, always out on the open grass across which approach to an objective, provided there was no moon, was safer than by hedge and ditch where one could see less and risked surprise. The back door opened and the two sisters left. In the momentary light the upper leaves of the shrubbery could be seen shivering though there was no wind. Someone else had been watching the house and had just slipped into cover. The first of the dew collecting on the leaves had caught the starlight so that even in pitch-darkness he could distinguish the course of the watcher as he resumed his position.

A detective was unlikely. Police would hardly bother. Paul's guests were sure to be well-known, and Mrs. Fanshawe could hardly be expected to turn up at a dinner party. Appinger then? Well, inquiries would have revealed to him that Paul Longwill had been a close friend in the distant past and was a possible ally in the present. Now that they had time to concert plans which were less hasty, it was sound common sense to detail a man to keep an eye on Longwill. Georges gave up all idea of ever visiting the house and carefully withdrew, belly to grass, until it was safe to stand up and start for home.

On his way it seemed to him odd that the close-knit village should be quite unaware of intrusions in the night. Yet what was odd? The pubs were shut and sleep was sleep. Nocturnal animals were seldom observed at all except by the naturalist on the lookout for them. Few people ever saw any more of a badger than its squashed corpse on the road, or knew the hour when the vixen came and went taking one duck with her and leaving another headless.

When he returned to the icehouse he found it empty. Irata's few possessions had gone as well, proving that this was no temporary absence. Georges, looking back on their recent conversations, realized that he ought to have continued to impress on him the danger of his arrest for murder. Instead, taking pity on this Spaniard as highly strung as himself, he had assured him that the accusation would not stand up. And Irata, torn between his two loyalties, to the Party and to the dear home now at last open to him, had very reasonably decided that any extra loyalty to the unknown prisoner — Spaniard, British secret agent or whatever he was — could be ignored.

Georges went down to the house and was surprised that Irata's motorcycle was in the larder where Paul must have left it. Presumably Irata had come down to recover the bike, but had decided in the end not to risk it. Since the number was known, it could lead to his immediate arrest whereas if he walked or took public transport he could choose time and place to arrange his own voluntary interview with the police. Of Irata himself there was no sign except a broken bottle of dark red wine with half its contents spilled on the floor, which he had intended to take with him for the journey.

Would he give away where he had been hiding? There was no reason why he should and perhaps one could count on that much loyalty to a mysterious friend who might still be useful. All the same, sleep was out of the question. Making the least possible noise and working backward down the slope, Georges repaired the narrow, twisting passage to the icehouse, intertwining bramble and wild rose, gathering up the branches which Paul had cut and sticking their butts into the ground so that they appeared to have withered in place.

Through all of Monday, with short intervals of dozing, he waited for police to arrive at the house below. They did not come. Either Irata had kept his mouth shut or had not been caught. The long June evening was fading the wrack of grandmother's garden into gold and dapple when he saw two men approaching the house, one tall and worn to leanness, one rounded by office life. As they came nearer he recognized the latter as the gray-faced but ultimately cordial crook who had interviewed him on Saturday morning.

They sat down, one on the rusty remains of a garden roller, the other spreading out his length on the grass, and were obviously waiting for him to appear. They must have talked to either Daisy or Paul Longwill. Georges wriggled up the slope along his hidden passage and took a careful look around. Nobody else was in sight. He then came down from the head of the valley, reluctant to give away as yet the exact position of his den, and joined the two.

Gray face introduced his companion:

"Colonel Mannering of MI(S), whatever that may be."

"I can give him better credentials than that, Gerald. Mr. Rivac, I represent the department which Karel Kren was trying to reach."

"You knew him?"

"No, nor Lukash, except as — what shall I call him — our foreign correspondent."

"Thank God we have met at last!"

"That's just what Miss Fodor said."

"She is all right?"

"Like yourself. All right till she isn't."

"Where is she?"

"With Mrs. Taylor."

"But Daisy's cottage may be watched."

"It is not watched by the police, Mr. Rivac. And our other friends, if they saw her at all, will only recognize her as a Swiss friend of Mrs. Taylor."

The inscrutable Gerald asked if Irata could observe them. Georges replied that he had disappeared, leaving his motorcycle in the house, and asked:

"Can you get hold of him before he is arrested?"

"Without the help of the police I doubt if I can get hold of him at all. You remember that I warned you. Once you are connected with Fyster-Holmes the Law must take its course."

"Then our Georges must take his own course back to Lille and quickly," Mannering interrupted.

"What good would that do? There is such a thing as extradition, Colonel. Well, we had better see what can be done with the motorbike. Does nobody ever come here, Mr. Rivac?"

"Only house-hunters sometimes. But Appinger knows it's a likely place for me."

"His men were here last night disguised as police," the colonel said. "They got Miss Fodor but she talked herself out of it. Too long a story for now — all about flowers and Alderton Wood where she was on Saturday night."

"But she couldn't have been here without my knowing. Oh, of course, of course! I was trying to get in touch with Longwill and when I came back Irata had gone. You may like to know that the Manor Farm was watched. If it wasn't police, one of Appinger's team was hoping to grab me coming in or going out."

All three entered the dusk of the house and Georges showed them the bike pushed into the larder where Longwill had hidden it. A few muddy footprints which he had not noticed in darkness were faintly visible on the polished floor.

The colonel showed interest in the black pool of wine, dipped a finger and tasted it.

"Still very drinkable?" Gerald asked ironically.

"Yes, if one must. Try it!"

Gerald too dipped a finger.

"Know the taste?" Mannering asked. "No, I thought you wouldn't. The police and the brutal and licentious soldiery know it quite well, but MI Five can work without it."

"Well, what is it?"

"Blood and wine, Gerald, blood and wine. They had no time or nothing to wash up with. So they spilled what was left of Irata's bottle on it."

The gray-faced man retched and spat, but got his own back.

"It's true," he said, "that police and military are only called in when we have failed. I suppose the body has been removed."

"I don't see how they can have done. According to Zia, somebody disturbed them and they whipped her off. The somebody must have been Irata. She saw only one car, so they must have carried him away on foot or not at all."

"Poor devil! I did like him," Georges exclaimed. "Why, why?"

"Because his evidence would have been invaluable to us and to the police," Gerald answered. "But he was no more use to them."

"Not upstairs, I think," said the colonel, who had been following the traces of mud. "So where, Mr. Rivac?"

"Garden?"

"Garden graves are too obvious. In the house?"

"Try the kitchen."

Irata was on the floor of the cellar. He had been stabbed from behind between the shoulders, once only but deep.

Georges wildly protested that it was madness, sheer madness, that sooner or later the body must have been found.

"And then who did it? Mrs. Fanshawe or her unknown companion who must be on the brink of being identified?"

"It still doesn't make sense. If I'm arrested I tell all I know."

"Perhaps they hoped to get you too last night or didn't care what unprovable spy yarn you told so long as they laid their hands on what Kren gave you. Rippmann, Fyster-Holmes and now Irata — can you talk your way out of all three?"

"Well then, it's up to us," the colonel declared. "We've got to bury the bugger."

"I cannot allow it. I am responsible for the security of the United Kingdom and what I do must always be within the Law."

"And I in my way, Gerald, am responsible for the security of Europe. If no one will protect my agent, I will."

"I will have nothing to do with it. You yourself suggested that the police can discover a fresh grave at a glance."

They were singing in their throats like two angry tom-cats. Georges timidly murmured that he used to hide things under the cellar bricks.

"What sort of things?"

"Oh well — postcards and things."

"A difficult age, dear Rivac. I used to hide them under the mattress until I found it was turned once a month. But we haven't a crowbar."

"The bricks are laid on earth. No concrete. And loose under the wall there."

Gerald objected that the police would spot it at once and he would not permit such folly.

"But since they know nothing at all about Rivac there's no reason why they should search his grandmother's house. I suppose you can't ride a motorbike, Gerald?"

"During the war, Colonel, when I was a mere security corporal in what you rightly describe as the brutal and licentious soldiery, my motorbike was to me what a horse is to a cowboy."

"Didn't walk, eh?"

"Never!"

"Haven't forgotten?"

"Of course I haven't forgotten!"

"It wouldn't be against the laws of the United Kingdom?"

"What wouldn't? About six of them, I should think. What the devil are you talking about?"

"Well, if you were not even here you could not forbid what Rivac and I are thinking of. And if the bike isn't here, the police would never look for Irata."

Gerald's stern face lit up as if he had just heard some witty and scandalous anecdote over the port.

"By God, I've never had a chance for thirty years! Old times! Good old times! But Lord help us if a police car spots the number! Well, the bike looks as if it had some speed. Shoot around a couple of corners before they can catch me up and run for it in the dark, what?"

"Don't go too far and leave yourself a long walk!"

"No, Colonel. I shall do what Irata might have done — leave it in the nearest car park and return to —"

"The security of the United Kingdom. And wipe your prints off everything you touch."

"Do they teach you that in MI(S)? You go ahead and wave to me when the road is clear!"

The dusk had deepened. Mannering went out to watch the lane while Gerald wheeled the bike as far as the gate. Georges closed down the cellar and went out to the dilapidated old toolshed where the best implements he could find were a coal shovel and a discarded billhook which could be used as a pick for loosening the earth. The problem of a lever was more difficult and only solved by a flat iron strip above the door frame, the screws of which had rusted away. Silence at the gate went on and on. There would be bicycles and pedestrians, he guessed, on the way to and from the pub and perhaps a few lucky lovers wandering off into the scented night. At last he heard the bike start at the second kick, and after two smart changes of gear it blasted smoothly off into the distance until rising ground cut off the sound.

To raise the bricks, starting from the wall where they were already loose, was easy, but the earth beneath was nearly as hard as any concrete. Georges picked away with the billhook while the colonel shoveled.

"Hard labor for us till the small hours," he said. "And what do we do with the earth, Georges?"

"Into the septic tank. I hear the sediment is backing up into the well anyway. The plumber will wonder how so much soil got into it, but let him wonder!"

Mannering pointed out that the packing case would do to shift it, tipped the moldy children's books out onto the floor and picked up *The Tale of Samuel Whiskers*.

"I used to enjoy that one," he said. "Tom Kitten lost himself in the flues of a chimney and was nearly put in a pudding just like you."

"Why wasn't I told the right chimney?"

"No one to tell you. Each division has a top-secret flue of its own. There's Gerald's MI Five. Cunning lot of sods! He has now got his claws into a major organization. It may be a year or more before they find out that every movement and every contact of theirs is known. Ruthless — that's what he is. I'll bet he wishes that you and that pretty little hell-cat of yours were down there with poor Irata. Then you could never give the show away in court. And there's his opposite number, MI Six, with their own sooty flue. I believe there are still bits of MI Fourteen about too, but I don't know what they do. And then there are harmless staff officers in MI(S). We just listen to people like Lukash."

"And what is Bridge Holdings?"

"I haven't the least idea, Georges. Probably that question should be put to Her Majesty's Secretary of State for Foreign Affairs. But Herbert Spring likes you and we'll take his advice — for you're in deadly danger from the police and your safety from the KGB can never be guaranteed. I shall now dig a case full and you can do the next."

It was long after midnight when the hole was deep enough for Irata and he was laid in it.

"No salute. No 'Internationale' on a brass band. No priest. What can we do for him, Georges?"

"Nothing. He saved my life and I can give him nothing. I suppose he was an atheist."

"Let's hope that he was wrong, and that something can return to the land he so loved even now."

They filled the grave, stamped back the bricks and swept the floor with Georges's jacket. The surface of course had different irregularities from those that were before, but the general impression, they agreed, would be that age and the seepage of water had loosened what was an amateur job in the first place. Only Daisy might be puzzled by the changed pattern of ups and downs. Dust and cobwebs, however, showed that she never went down there.

"Well, that's that, and I had better be off."

"Where is your car?"

"At the Manor Farm."

"Won't the police ask why, and who you are?"

"Let them! I am an old friend of Paul Longwill from Military Supplies at the War House. You see, Georges, how useful it is to be a simple soldier. We are below suspicion. Now I am taking Zia and the brochures to safety at nine o'clock. Your turn will be at night. Since you are believed to be in Lille, you must not on any account be seen in the village."

Georges consumed the last scraps of food and drink in the icehouse, stretched out his aching limbs and went to sleep. At dawn he heard a car turn into the gate and stop outside the house. Assuming that the colonel had changed his mind and decided to pick him up before Zia, he looked carelessly over the screen of bushes and instantly withdrew his head. A police car had thrown out two officers into the house and sent two more to the far corner to cover the back.

The party inside reappeared in ten minutes, which proved that they had seen nothing wrong with the cellar. The inspector in charge looked disappointed with their report, called in his men at the back and then held a long conversation over the car radio; evidently he had more to discuss than a dawn raid which had drawn a complete blank. Well, that stood to reason. Even a cursory look around would have shown that the badly wanted Irata had wheeled in his motorbike and recently wheeled it out again. The broken bottle was further proof. Georges and the colonel had scrubbed the pool clean and poured pure wine over the stain.

Later in the day, when police returned with their battery of devices, full investigation was likely to reveal the footsteps of Mrs. Fanshawe and the murderer of Fyster-Holmes as well as a regular thieves' kitchen of other visitors. The variety of tracks in an empty house inspected by prospective buyers would muddle the issue, but it was too much to hope that police would leave the overgrown slope unexplored. The icehouse was finished as a refuge.

A plainclothesman was left behind, posted under the

trees above him; so they still suspected that someone might seek safety in the house. All was silent till half past eight when he heard the beat of a horse's hooves cantering past the gate. Paul must be up to something, for nobody else in Alderton or a near village kept horses.

Shortly afterward the car roared up to the house again. The inspector stood up and hailed his sentry on guard under the trees.

"Come down quick! We want every man. She's not far off."

For a moment the constable seemed about to hurl himself at the impenetrable scrub, but he thought better of it and ran directly down to the lane. As soon as he was in the car it shot off northward.

Georges had assumed that he himself or the badly wanted Irata was the object of the raid on the house; but the threat was far worse than that. They had Zia on the run, and since they had reason to suspect she was in Alderton it must mean that they had traced the connection between Mrs. Fanshawe and Rivac and knew very well that he had been her accomplice in the mud of the Thames backwater.

Now that the sentry had gone from the top he crawled up to take a look at the village. He could see Daisy's garden. The colonel was talking to her and in his hand he held something like a book. It could be the two brochures, for he knew where they were hidden and could have picked them out of the drain pipe if Zia had not had time. It sounded as if she hadn't with the police right on her tail. She could not get clear. He himself, who knew every yard of the country, would have little hope in daylight; he'd be picked up before nightfall running across the open or cowering in a ditch.

He guessed where she would go if she could possibly get so far. According to Mannering she had spent Saturday night under hawthorn by a stream, but the colonel did not know where in Alderton Wood it was and would never find her. Georges could imagine her sitting there not once admitting defeat but desolate, well aware that Georges, wherever he was — and it was evident that she did not know — might see no reason to move, never realizing that Mrs. Fanshawe was very near the deadly exposure as Zia Fodor. Paul could not help. If Daisy's cottage and the Manor Farm had also been raided — which seemed pretty certain — Paul would not dare to guide a rescue when his every move might be followed.

No reason to move? To hell with it! He would have a try. The description of Georges Rivac must after all be a little vague. A bad passport photograph was probably the most they could lay their hands on unless one counted a portrait of him at the age of thirteen on Daisy's mantelpiece. It might not be difficult to reach Alderton Wood if he could openly walk the roads instead of inviting capture by rushes from one futile patch of cover to another.

With all his thoughts turned inward to himself and outward to Zia the last thing he had considered was his appearance. He now took stock of himself. His jacket was covered with brick dust, his trousers stained and shapeless. He could take to the road as a tramp, but tramps were no longer common and likely to be questioned by any passing cop when a criminal was loose. No, he had to be something grubby, agricultural and at work. He couldn't think what. The landscape of his bit of England was familiar but its social life had changed. His eyes fell on the billhook. A useful property. He remembered hedgers always carrying with them a personal hook, shaped to and by the hand. There was the shovel too. Who the hell would carry a shovel? Well, a hedger might if he expected to have to clear a few yards of ditch as well. At any rate the solitary walker would not give the impression of a tramp and certainly not that of a French *commerçant* from Lille. Carrying shovel and billhook he wriggled his way up the slope. All was clear. Once on the upper road he settled down to the gait of an old-fashioned farmhand, quickening to a fast stride when hedges hid him.

IX

When Zia was dropped at Daisy's cottage there was no awkward waiting at the front door. It opened, received her and closed. Daisy had observed the car through her lace curtains and recognized her.

"Now you come into the kitchen, Mrs. Fanshawe, and we'll 'ave a nice cup of tea what I expect you could do with."

She picked Zia's pack off the chair where she had laid it down, separated coat from sleeping bag and bag from other possessions and put all away in different cupboards. The action was as immediate and instinctive as that of an experienced criminal.

"I'm going to ask you if I may stay the night, Mrs. Taylor. The man who left me is a colonel in the army and a friend of Georges."

"Of the general too, me dear?"

"Mrs. Taylor, you mustn't tease me. I think you know very well that there isn't any general. When we met before you said Georges might take up with a pair of Siamese twins. Well, I'm the twins and I'm not married and — and I don't know where he is and I must."

"There, there! Don't take on so! I'll take a message for you, Mrs. Fanshawe, when the coast is clear."

"He and Mr. Longwill talked about a cellar in his grandmother's house. He was going to be there with the Spaniard, Irata, but he wasn't."

"You've been looking for 'im?"

"The night before last."

"Well, he is and he ain't in no cellar as you might say."

Cautious old thing. But how right and sweet and trust-worthy!

"What has he told you about me?"

"It were not what 'e said, me dear, but them eyes of his when 'e said it. Now I've known 'im since 'e was three and you can't never make 'im do nothing until 'e ain't jumpy and knows 'e wants to."

"He knows he wants to, all right."

"Well, I only 'opes you treats 'im kind. He 'as a lot to learn about us, 'as Master Georges."

"Mrs. Taylor, I shall treat him very kind. I intend to make him marry me if we are ever safe again."

"That do make a couple of the pair of you! And safe from what, may I ask?"

"So much, Daisy — so much!"

Zia broke down in helpless sobbing. It was as if she had been longing to cry for days, deprived of tears as a prisoner deprived of the sanctuary of the sky and without the warmth and comfort of another woman.

"Now you 'aven't been sleeping, me dear, and in strange places I wouldn't wonder. So upstairs with you and a little supper in bed, like, and then I'm going to turn the light out and sit with you till you're off. Just tell me one thing now, so I can be easy. Will he be out of the trouble?"

"I am sure he will be, Daisy dear, but he can never return to Alderton or Lille."

"Won't I never see 'im again then?"

"Wherever we are, Daisy, there will be a ticket for you and a spare bedroom."

"Now to bed, my darling! And don't you dare to stir till I tell you and we'll be all ready in time for your nice, tall officer."

Zia awoke refreshed and a new woman. She lay in bed listening to the silence and a dawn chorus of birds in which, unlike the full ensemble of Alderton Wood, the village prima donnas could be distinguished. She was at last confident that she was in good hands and her duty done. However many of these mysterious agencies there might be, at least one of them could see her safely and secretly back to Hungary and ensure that Georges Rivac remained unknown to British police.

Long before eight Daisy was in her room, a breathless Daisy.

"Now don't you be alarmed, me dear, but one of the girls what does for Mr. Longwill 'as come over to tell me that the 'ouse is fair swarming with police. They didn't allow no one out, but Master Paul says to 'er: Marlene, 'e says, you get took all over queer and gibber at 'em as 'ow you're that feared of murder and the cops, and keep on screamin' until they turn you out 'ome. And then you nip down to Daisy, 'e says, and tell 'er they got on to a certain person through the 'otel. Telephone and breakfast, she says Master Paul said."

"And what about the colonel?"

"She tells me there was another gentleman 'avin' 'is bath and told 'em to come in, which was 'ardly decent, and said 'e didn't know naught about nothing and would they kindly pick the soap up off the floor where 'e'd dropped it because they give 'im such a turn."

Rivac. It was not a common name. Police knew without a doubt that Mrs. Fanshawe had some connection with Irata and that she had been present at the death of Fyster-Holmes. They also knew, acting on the inquiry from Lille police, that Rivac had stayed in Alderton with Daisy and was a friend of Paul Longwill. And now Mrs. Fanshawe and Rivac had both been in the Regency Hotel when he was supposed to have returned to Lille. He must be as badly wanted as she was herself.

"They'll be here next," Zia said, "unless nobody saw me arrive."

"It was quick enough, but village eyes are quicker. I'll say you're ill and mustn't be disturbed."

Zia got her imagination to work on that one. The colonel must never say that he had driven her down from London; he had picked up a girl on the road, obviously feverish and ill, and had charitably taken her to Mrs. Taylor, having heard from some nameless passer-by that she also was charitable and would give her a bed.

"That lets you out, Daisy, if you stick to it. You never dreamed that the poor thing was Mrs. Fanshawe whom you only saw once. And we must get a message to Colonel Mannering at the Manor Farm so that he knows what to say when they ask him. He is really a colonel and they will have to believe him."

"Then get dressed in case you 'as a chance to run for it, me dear. And if it's any manner of good to drop out of the back window there, you'll land on a nice, soft flower bed and won't 'urt yourself."

Daisy put her, now fully dressed, back in bed and arranged a fairly convincing show. She placed a bottle of medicine and a drink of lemon by the bedside, squirted the room with disinfectant, turned on a wholly unnecessary electric fire, covered up Zia's hair and put a cold compress over forehead and eyes.

"And 'ere they comes!" she said, hearing a car draw up outside.

Zia listened to the rumble of the police apologies and the higher note of Daisy's protests. After searching the ground floor, the tramp of feet started to come upstairs. Somebody entered the room. Zia, groaning and tossing, did not even look up.

"I don't doubt that she's ill, Mrs. Taylor, but this may be the woman we want. I shall not disturb her till the doctor has had a look but I must post an officer outside the door. Meanwhile we will ask Colonel Mannering how and where he picked her up."

The door was locked. Zia crept out of bed and watched the road from the front window of the darkened room. There was a small crowd of a dozen curious villagers outside the house. To her amazement she saw Paul Longwill ride up on the bay mare — the picture of an old-fashioned squire sorting out the troubles of the village. He may have thought he was in character, but the stares proved that nobody else did; she noticed that he was far from a competent horseman.

Waving back the curious, he slipped the reins far too carelessly over the gate post and came in. Well, at least Daisy could make an opportunity to speak to him. The colonel, arriving on foot, joined the onlookers with an air of detached amusement.

But why? What was Paul up to? Was this ridiculous masquerade one of his affectations to impress the police? And then she saw it. Quietly she opened the back window and dropped. She walked steadily around to the front, saying a casual good morning to the bystanders. Before they could recover from their surprise at Daisy's unknown guest, or the police — if they were still inside — could leave the house, she was in the saddle and away. The colonel made a deliberately futile effort to snatch at the bridle. Paul dashed out into the road, shouting that the blasted woman had stolen his horse.

Cantering down the street and breaking into a gallop on the green shoulder of the lane which passed grandmother's house, she headed north. Once over the rise and out of sight of the village she took to the fields and into an inviting fold of the ground just deep enough to cover the mare and herself if she dismounted. She watched two police cars racing up the lane; it was a fair bet that when they came to the crossroads at Alderton Abbas one would turn right and the other left to cut her off. Behind them the lane was fortunately empty. She charged straight down into it, jumping the easy hedge, and was again hidden, provided no traffic passed. There was then no instant way out to the west unless she jumped the opposite hedge. Any of her own horses could have taken a rabbit hop and cleared it, but there was no telling what the mare, seldom exercised and kept largely as a decoration, could or could not do. The jump could only be risked if she had room for half a dozen strides and a firm takeoff from the shoulder.

She rode on desperately, seeking the needed space on the right of the lane and found it in an open gate. Hoping to God that the mare had been trained as a hunter before being used as a rocking horse for Paul's girlfriends, she turned into the gateway and rode at the hedge. The mare, unhappy at the change to tarmac, took off too late, barged her way through the hawthorn, tripped, recovered and was away with a long, easy stride into the cover of willows around a pond.

Zia knew that somebody somewhere must have seen her, but if that somebody had no idea what was going on in Alderton it might be all of half an hour before she was reported. Meanwhile the police were off on the wrong track and she had time to think. Arrest in the end was unavoidable, yet if she could delay it for a few hours Gerald and the colonel might hit on some means of rescue. The right game was to go hard for the edge of Alderton Wood, come out into the long glade and gallop down it where no car, even if it could reach the glade at all, could possibly catch her.

Zia, rejoicing in the speed and excitement of the mare, did just that. Easily clearing a barbed-wire fence — though she could not know it was going to be easy and almost closed her eyes — she arrived in a pasture at the end of the glade where there was a herd of Herefords and three horses among them, two of them bright bays and the third a chestnut. They presented to her the solution of her worst problem: how to get rid of her own dark bay mare. The police, she said to herself contemptuously, would call the whole lot brown and fail to distinguish one from another.

Turning into the trees she slipped off saddle and bridle, hiding them under a pile of rotten hay left over from winter feed, and after a quick rubdown with handfuls of hedge parsley to remove the white salt of sweat turned the mare loose into society. It might well be late afternoon before the owner of the field realized that a stray horse was among his own, and evening before the police contacted him or he the police.

There was now only one place to go and wait for the end. Georges could guess it, but he might know nothing at all of this frantic morning. Keeping in the shelter of the trees she walked on until she came to the stream and could follow up its course to the sanctuary under the canopy of tall hawthorn — the flowers were falling now — with its clumps of Honesty. The sand was ruffled by the ramblings of Appinger's busy gang; patches of bare earth among the trodden stems showed where they had smoothed over their excavations. Their efforts would have been encouraged when they found the clear footmarks of a man and a woman left a week ago by Georges and herself.

She crossed the stream into the jungle of hazels on the other side and worked her way through them into a bird's nest of dead mossy stumps where she would never be spotted unless a line of police combed the wood as mercilessly as beaters on a shoot. But that in fact was their practice. She remembered pictures of police looking for tiny clues to a murderer. Murderer — it was so absurd to think of Georges as a murderer. The word appalled her. Yet anybody in a moment of utter desperation could be one. She was one. She had thought of the drowning of Rippmann as an act of defense like that of a soldier who shoots before he is shot. Had it been really necessary? If only she had known all she knew now, she and Georges could easily have lost Rippmann in London. Yes, indeed they could; but Rippmann on leaving the ferry, standing behind her perhaps when she showed her passport to the Immigration Officer, would have had no difficulty in discovering the name of the woman who had been talking so intensely to Georges Rivac.

And now her name was going to be discovered anyway. Burn her passport — that was the only solution. She should have done it long ago, but exposure had never been so near as now. Police could be a long time finding out who she was and meanwhile the colonel would find some means of warning her mother and her uncle. She built a little fire of dead wood and burned the Hungarian passport then and there.

An hour later she heard someone approaching through the thicket on the opposite bank. Fool! The tiny column of smoke might have attracted one of the searchers. She sank into the hazels, all of her hidden but her eyes. She caught glimpses of a figure uniformly gray, bent low and carrying a spade. It might be police. It might be the ice-cream man returning. It might be Gerald coming to bury her as a nuisance to be got rid of. The recent contemplation of her own guilt reinforced panic. She felt terrified as never before.

The crouching and sinister figure passed out onto the sand and stood up. Zia burst out of the hazels, jumped the stream, throwing up a sunlit sparkle of water as she landed short, and was in his arms.

"How did you know it?"

"Where else could you be? But I was sure I would get here first."

"Paul left a horse for me and I was away like a highwayman."

"Where is it?"

"In a field at the end of the glade with other horses. Do they know I'm in the wood?"

"They must think it likely. But we're safe here for hours perhaps. And it's a very big wood and I know it."

"Have they arrested Paul?"

"Ever tried to land an eel? How did he do it?"

She told him about the formal arrival of the booted squire. Her Georges crowed with laughter. It seemed to her that she had not heard laughter for years. Laughter was safety. Laughter was the eternal present which would become a future.

"Why be uncomfortable?" he suggested. "If they beat the wood we can hear them long before they get here."

He settled down on the sand and spread out his coat for her alongside. She nearly answered that she was glad nobody could telephone this time. Too brazen? Yes! He must be allowed his illusions. Probably he would apologize again.

"I've been so frightened till now," she said, resting her head on his shoulder.

After the kiss he said nothing but Zia . . . Zia . . . Zia, as if her name was worth all the terms of endearment in the world.

"No, Georges, no! We may have to run. How can we in this state?"

"Zia! My lovely Zia!"

Gentle she knew he would be. Too gentle she feared. He might know nothing about women as Daisy had said. But on one point Daisy was wrong . . . very wrong, very wrong.

"Georges! My love! Oh God!"

She lay still at last, twining him with arms and legs and wishing she could grow more of them just to hold him. And such fulfillment was so gloriously unexpected. But at least she had been right about the apology.

"Angel, I cannot forgive myself. You are too beautiful."

"And if you could forgive yourself?"

"I should go mad with love."

"So that was just when you are sane? Poor Zia, how she must suffer! . . . Georges, I beg you, Georges!"

Half-asleep she crooned over him, her child, her lover, her comrade. The white flowers of the hawthorn drifted down on him and she kissed them away, regretting that she had nowhere to secrete a handful of them for memory. A beam of the midday sun piercing the canopy fell on her face and startled her from this scented twilight of love into another reality. Distant bodies were splashing down the stream toward them.

There was no time to cross to the safer hazels. Georges picked her up, hardly giving her time to grab her clothes, and slid with her into cover.

"They are not here," the colonel said. "You're wrong, Longwill."

"Then whose are those trousers?"

"By God, if they've got him . . ."

"There could be other reasons."

Georges crawled silently away from her and spoke.

"I was having a dip in the brook, Paul. You should have given us warning. Kindly pass me my trousers!"

"Mrs. Fanshawe was having a dip too?"

"We were both rather dirty."

"What a revolting expression, Georges!"

Zia, now dressed, decided on the grand manner.

"Would you please get my bra out of the nettles, Paul? It must have blown there when I hung it up to dry."

"With pleasure. Generals' wives must of course preserve their modesty in the water."

She burst out of the bushes, flung a lump of mud at him and followed it by herself.

"You were marvelous, Paul. Thank you, thank you! Did you get away with it?"

"Well, I put on a show for them, slapping my boots and bawling at Daisy and Mannering for being taken in and never seeing that the girl wasn't ill at all."

"And they didn't believe a word of it," the colonel added. "But what could they do?"

He seemed interested only in the clumps of purple flowers which were still standing. Zia assumed that his detachment from the delicate situation was in the best tradition of military politeness.

"So this is Honesty! In fact, Georges, is it ever pink?"

"Never. But there is a white form in gardens. It still comes up among the weeds in grandmother's border."

"Interesting! Now that reminds me — I have the brochures in my truck."

Zia exclaimed with joy. It was a God-given day if ever there was one.

"Hold it, Mrs. Fanshawe! They are meaningless unless you and Georges can throw some light on them. The truck, yes. It's waiting for us. An army fifteen hundredweight with the cover up and one of my staff sergeants driving. But we have first to reach it. Thames Valley Police are taking the Rivac-Fanshawe connection very seriously. A distinguished diplomat has been bumped off in their manor."

He spread Zia's map out on the sand and marked the movements of the searchers. He had watched cars patrolling the road around the northern border of the wood, and a cordon was beginning to work through it from the west. Pickets were on the Alderton–Alderton Abbas road to the east. So they had to break out to the south.

"But I've told him that there's not a hope there," Paul protested. "The right flank of the police line is moving up toward us through the trees along the edge of the glade. We should be in full view of them crossing the open."

Georges murmured as if half his mind was elsewhere —

as indeed it was — that there should not be any need to cross the glade.

"She left Paul's horse there. It depends whether there is any other farmhand in sight."

"What depends?"

"Whether I can get away with it. Do they know I'm here?"

"Hereabouts — unless you and Irata went off on his motorcycle. They have found the hole and have evidence that both of you were in it recently."

"Then it's impossible. No, no, too risky. No way of knowing what I might run into. . . . Yes, so, I'll try it. The horse, you see — I find it and yell to them."

Zia implored him not to show his face outside — not now when they were nearly safe.

"I'd recognize you anywhere," Paul added.

"But the police can't be sure. And when I talk to them . . ."

"That's asking for it!"

"A good thing sometimes. I'm going to talk to them — and agents from Lille don't speak broad Bucks."

"You're too young to speak broad Bucks."

"Oi bain't. Mr. Longwill, 'e says to oi there's a foiver for ee if ee foinds me 'arse. Oi knaws where she'll eat, oi says. Graass 'er wants. Better graass 'n yourn, Mister Longwillie. Longwillie me faather called 'im an' oi could tell ee for why."

"Tell us some other time," the colonel said. "You're in command, Georges. What are your orders for us?"

"Go down the stream to the edge of the glade. Keep as near to the right of their line as you dare, and fall back in

223

front of them if you have to. Paul knows the wood. When you see some of them break away to talk to me, get through the cordon! Then we must leave it to the colonel to bring up his truck."

Carrying his billhook Georges crossed the stream and was instantly lost among the hazels.

"He's got religion again," Paul said, "like the time he insisted on potting a deer. It worked then."

They reached the edge of the wood and crouched down. The cordon was still some distance away, beating the wood slowly and thoroughly. A terrified roebuck dashed through the trees, saw them and changed direction, seeming to pirouette like a ballerina on one tiny hoof. The back of another animal was skittering down the ditch between glade and wood with the undulating movement of a stoat; but it was gray and massive and undoubtedly Georges.

"The mare's too far away," Zia whispered in an agony of fear for him. "He has to go right out over the grass."

Georges had now left the ditch and stopped dead. Knowing where to look they could see his shape clearly, but he had probably satisfied himself that the cops on the right of the line were far enough inside the trees and not bothering with the sunlit expanse of green where an upright human figure would catch the eye without even watching. He was quite still for more than a minute with his head turned toward the wood and then dashed a good ten yards out into the open and dropped. They waited for the triumphant bark of the police, but the only sound was the steady approach of the rustlings and crackings of the undergrowth.

He was wriggling forward now, taking advantage of a hardly perceptible fold of the ground which might once have been an ancient track. From where they were they could see the full length of it, and it seemed unbelievable that the police, though away to the side, could fail to detect his presence. The colonel stretched out a hand and clasped Zia's, both sure that it must be the end.

"He could do it when he was a boy," Paul said, "but, oh God, not now!"

"What time of year?" Mannering asked.

"September."

"Well, it's June, and if his backside is six inches higher, so's the grass."

Georges smoothly rose from the ground and in four strides was at the wire fence which Zia had jumped. At once he started to knock in a staple with the flat of the billhook as if he had been there all along.

"Hi, mister! Lookin' for a 'arse, be ee?"

His hail rang out over the empty glade to them and to the police. They could not distinguish the words of the reply, but again Georges's good Bucks answer carried.

"Oi sees 'un 'ere! Bay mar-re what ain't ourn!"

That did the trick. Two constables ran out from the wood and he pointed out the mare. A third man appeared, whistled and was joined by an inspector. Georges looked as if he were being stupid, slow and persistent, pointing to the horses and describing at length the differences between them. It was now plain why he had said that success depended on no other farmhand being in sight; if there had been, the local man would have joined the party and asked Georges who he was and for whom he was working.

Paul moved cautiously ahead and beckoned them on. By the time two of the police had strolled back to their posts on the right of the line they were through it and lying still as the beat proceeded away from them. In a gap in the trees Zia could see that the remaining two had wriggled under the wire and were standing guard over the mare, finding that without a halter it was impossible to detain her for questioning. Meanwhile Georges was shambling toward the cover on the far side of the glade inspecting posts as he went.

They waited just short of the road until the army truck drove slowly past. The colonel stopped it, raised the hood and pretended to be examining the engine as a patrol car came up. He raised an innocent and interested face, replied to a question and when the car had gone on signaled to Zia and Paul to make a dash for the back. He himself got in alongside his sergeant and they were off to pick up Georges.

Safe in the green twilight of the canvas cover Zia changed into WRAC uniform which was laid out for her — Paul pointedly keeping his eyes on the driver and, she was sure, taking a quick and critical glance while the khaki blouse was over her head. Opposite the other half of the wood they met Georges coolly walking along the road with his billhook, now confident that his farce was acceptable to any spectators. For him too there was a uniform. It was entirely right for him, Zia thought. She had summed him up, with his two opposing nationalities, as less decisive than herself. Was that true? He had so often been decisive, but always at the last moment.

The colonel half-turned toward them.

"Sparks," he said to his driver, "these are friends of Lukash."

"Glad to meet them, sir! We haven't heard from him lately."

"We shan't hear from him anymore. But they have brought a message from him if we can decipher it."

"The computer, sir?"

"I don't think it's the kind of food it's going to eat. Now, we'll drive through Alderton and drop this gentleman in boots and breeches as near as possible to the Manor Farm when the road is clear. Then to our second home!"

Paul slid out when the truck stopped. After half an hour it stopped again. A civilian guard spoke to the colonel, looked into the truck, let it through some unseen barrier and onto an even concrete road.

"You can get out now. You're as safe as in jail, guarded with the utmost efficiency by Gerald and his thugs. *He* doesn't know all of what he is guarding and *I* don't know exactly what he is up against. Everyone to his own galley as Georges would say."

A young officer in uniform passed, and Georges, living up to his new part, supposed he ought to salute him and did.

"Attached to the establishment by Signals," the colonel explained. "My fellows remain civilians unless it's useful not to."

They were outside a low brick building set on a slight plateau of grass with the farming Midlands rolling away in field and copse on all sides. Around them, spaced over a quarter of a square mile, were masts linked by cables to each other and to the central building.

"It doesn't belong to me," Mannering assured them. "I just have a room here in case I need it."

Carrying the brochures he led them into a small office bare as a turret except for a trestle table along one side, hard chairs, a large desk and a formidable safe.

"Sparks, we didn't have time for any breakfast and can't think on empty stomachs. We'll all have a stiff gin first and then you might go around to the canteen and bring us lots

227

of anything edible. By the way, did you have any trouble with the police?"

"Just a few questions. I was an army dendrologist recording the effect of laser guidance passing through thick timber."

"Did they know what a dendrologist was?"

"No, sir. So I was able to blind them with science and cause some delay."

Sparks returned with heaped plates of eggs and bacon, saying that the roast was off and he couldn't see anything else fit for distinguished foreigners.

"How do you know I'm not British, Sparks?" Georges asked.

"You gave the French salute, mate."

When Zia and Georges were restored, the colonel placed the Intertatry brochures on his desk and pulled up chairs for them alongside him.

"Now, first of all, are these two the same?"

"I think so. Kren gave me two in case the Ministry lost one."

"The only oddity I can find is that they are page proofs, not the finished article. There are a few penciled corrections in the diagrams."

"Page proofs would be quite normal if Kren was rushing the new engine onto the market."

The colonel was silent, searching the eastern sky through the window, his thoughts seeming far away from the pages in front of him.

"Now assuming the brochures were intercepted, the first move of the KGB would be to find the printer. There's no name. We must assume that the printer was a friend of

Karel Kren. He need not have known what he was doing — neither do we yet — but he understood that he must destroy the galleys and all other evidence. Well, he couldn't possibly do that if the shop was printing, say, a thousand of the brochures. All his men would suspect something fishy. But he could — couldn't he? — run off a few page proofs and give the lot to Kren. Then the galleys would be burned and the frames emptied. You must have ordered advertisements and leaflets, Georges, in the course of your business. Does that make sense to you?"

"Yes, for a small jobbing printer who could run the presses himself if and when he wanted to and was always short of storage space. As you say, he couldn't possibly do a long run but he could manage half a dozen page proofs and not leave a trace of type and galleys."

"And all this junk at the end — engine spare parts and numbers for ordering — have you ever checked the numbers against former brochures?"

"No. They looked all right."

"Zia, what is the number of your uncle's division?"

"The Third Armored."

"Now this is just a wild shot, Georges. You see, I know what sort of stuff Lukash was sending us and what we hoped his next message or the message after would be. Look through that list of spare parts — it will be familiar to you — and see if there is any 3A anywhere."

Georges ran his finger down five pages, closely printed, of engine spare parts.

"Nothing," he said, "except screw for magneto back plate. Number for ordering is H8923A. And just above it is spring washer for magneto back plate H8922."

"What's the good of the H?"

"It refers to the illustration of engine assembly."

"Have a look for Ps!"

"Drain plug P2642. Filler plug P2643c. Dipstick for filler plug P2645c."

"Karel Kren! By God, I salute him! Ignore the first number, which only draws your attention to P for Poland. Then take the last digits of the next Ps, and read off Polish Third and Fifth Corps. And a very useful addition if they still fight as they did at Monte Cassino! Now R!

"Screw for Inlet Manifold R9082. Gasket for Inlet Manifold R9083. Carburetor R9086. Gasket for carburetor R9091c.

"Romanian Third and Sixth Divisions. First Corps. Corps of course may be quite differently composed if the day comes, but we know the present divisions and their commanders. Now let's see what the Czechs can contribute!"

"Too many Cs around," Georges said.

"Ah, yes! Now what would Kren have done? Try S for Slovakia!"

"Only two Ss in the whole list. Petrol tank S9228. Petrol tank complete S9299."

"No divisions at all? It's impossible. And there is no Ninth Division. Lukaṣh told us it was broken up, so Kren knew that we know it. Complete? God, he means the whole bloody army! Well, that's the optimism of hatred. Impossible to guarantee! But it does mean wholesale surrenders and chaos at GHQ."

"And only one Hungarian division?" Zia asked indignantly. "You told Georges to look for 3A, not H. That's what started you off."

"Let me see. Stud for throttle lever. Nut for throttle lever. Washer for throttle lever. Zia, I am proud to announce that as well as the Third Armored you are offering us Second and Third Corps."

Zia jumped in her chair and called like a silver cavalry trumpet that they were worth all the rest.

"We are talking of a Europe to be, Miss Terezia, not gallant Magyars on bay mares. Patriotism, as another lady said, is not enough. Do you fully realize what you and Georges have delivered? I could crack it only because I was ready for it. These are the units which are ready to come over to us in battle if corps and divisional staffs in what your uncle called the club can carry the regimental officers. And they must be pretty sure they can."

"But Kren could have posted the brochures in Brussels," Georges said.

"Yes, if the club had known the right address. As it was, they could only have ended up in somebody's wastepaper basket."

"And yet you all keep on talking as if my life were in danger."

"It's in less danger than anyone's in Europe, Georges. The KGB must have you alive at all costs."

"Why should they assume that I know all these military details which I can't remember anyway?"

"They cannot assume that you don't. You would be in front of your interrogators right now, my lad, if this Appinger had had enough time and had not been forced to use Fyster-Holmes and a scratch organization. Then there's the little matter of Rippmann. Only an experienced agent could have recognized him."

"You have to protect him," Zia insisted, shrill with guilt. "It's the least you can do."

"Not my department, Zia. And Gerald can't because Georges is as badly wanted by the police as you are. I rather think we should call on your old friends, Bridge Holdings."

"Oh, not Herbert Spring again!"

"He might know the right people to return you to Budapest."

"I've burned my passport."

"Just as well. It would show your visit to this country."

"I never remembered that! Oh, and I took such care with everything else."

"Zia, if secret agents never made simple mistakes they would never be caught at all. Now I was doing a bit of thinking while we were by the stream and I have some questions for Georges."

Georges noticeably blushed and cleared his throat.

"How tall is Appinger?"

"About five foot nine I'd say."

"Long-legged? Short-legged?"

"Short for his height."

"What time does the ice-cream van usually call at Alderton on a weekday?"

"Daisy would know. Get on to Paul and he'll find out for you."

The colonel pressed a button on his desk and Sparks appeared, now looking unmilitary in blazer and checked trousers.

"Sparks, you remember those marvelous Persian melons you gave me for Christmas?"

"Glad you enjoyed 'em, sir."

"You mentioned that your father had friends in the trade."

"Yes. Started off as a porter and ended up a wholesaler in the old Covent Garden."

"Do you think he could sell off a barrow?"

"Christ, yes! The old bugger would knock the rest of them for six."

"Reliable?"

"In all but his scales, sir. But he can keep his mouth shut if that's what you mean."

"Tell him to hire a barrow, fill it up with flowers and fruit and stand by for orders. Expenses no object. Remuneration whatever I can screw out of Gerald if he's still available. Will pa play?"

"Yes, sir. Ex-CSM with military medal and bored at home."

"Just our man. Right! Lay on a truck big enough to carry the barrow and pa! When you have fixed the lot, tell me where to find you and I'll be with you early tomorrow morning. You two will be dropped at my apartment. Here's the key and use it as your own. You may not see me or anyone for a couple of days, but don't go out on any account! Sparks will see that the larder is full and drink is there already."

"You are not married, Colonel?" Zia asked.

An impertinence, but she was intensely curious. So masterful and attractive a man must surely have a woman of equal character.

"Indeed I am, my dear — to MI(S). So be at ease and enjoy yourself, for it may be the last time you will ever see Georges Rivac."

"I will, wherever he is."

"You won't, wherever he is."

"It's a joke?" she asked, turning a little pale after her first flush of anger.

"No. It would be serious and tragic for an ordinary citizen, but for a man whose home is all Europe, a man of courage and enterprise without attachments, it might be a bit of a joke."

Nervously but firmly, as if that were an accusation, Georges retorted:

"I am not . . . not any longer, I mean . . . not without attachments. They come first."

"They do, do they? Then you have both told me what I needed to be sure of. After all, one can't in these days infer a damned thing from Daphnis and Chloe splendidly unembarrassed."

"But you said I should never see him again," Zia reproached him.

"I said you would never see Georges Rivac again."

In the back of that closed and saving truck Sparks drove them away. No questions were asked except by Sparks, who wanted to know what he should buy for dinner and breakfast. Questions among these professionals were so obviously futile and would remain with courteous but unenlightening replies. Even when he told them they had arrived, all they could see was a small square of Georgian houses with a railed and formal garden in the middle of it. The number was 18 and there was a scent of evening lime trees. Name of square unknown. To Georges's eye it could be nowhere else but London.

Mannering's apartment on the second floor was highly civilized compared to what he had called his second home.

When Sparks had left they explored, hand in hand, two bedrooms, a living room and a kitchen–dining room. Zia had expected some bachelor's pad, comfortable as a club and severe in its furnishings. Color and arrangement all showed a woman's hand. The colonel was undoubtedly a man of taste, but not that kind of taste. In each room was a single bed. In one of them marks on the carpet suggested that there had once been a double bed.

"His wife must have left him," Zia said. "That's why he snubbed me by saying he was married to MI(S)."

She was irritated by her own feminine curiosity which there were few clues to satisfy. In the other bedroom, plainly that used by the colonel himself, was a photograph of a glorious fair-haired woman in her early thirties and a glossy print of a press photograph showing Russian tanks rumbling into the main square of a city she recognized as Prague.

"1968," Georges remarked. "You wouldn't think he would need that reminder even in his bedroom."

They left the problem alone as tiredness overwhelmed them. Relaxation there could not be. In foreign uniform, in doubtful safety and with no sure future, all that their temporary refuge allowed was tiredness. They ate a few biscuits, swallowed some wine and collapsed into bed, he in Mannering's, she in the other. If the double bed had still been on its marks they would not have taken it. They were finished, a collection of limbs stripped of humanity and emotion.

The morning was dull and raining, a milder return to the weather when they had sailed from Calais. They were no longer stimulated by one desperate day after another and too conscious of a nameless prison at the mercy of men whose kindness might be only to keep them quiet. They could not manage more than a strained cheerfulness for Sparks, who came in with a shopping basket of food varied and plentiful enough for a small restaurant. Zia maintained at least her curiosity.

"I hope the colonel's wife won't mind our being here," she said.

"I never met her, Miss, but I think she'd like it. She died in 1968."

"Prague?" Georges asked.

"Prague, mate. She got in the way of a Russian tank. Inconvenient for them that was. So they gathered up any awkward corpses and carted 'em off. It's all he ever knew."

"She was . . . well, on business? And a Czech?"

"On holiday, Miss, seeing her parents," Sparks replied uncompromisingly.

When Sparks had gone, Georges remarked:

"That's why he keeps the photograph — her only grave. Sometimes I wonder whether we are helping or making matters worse."

"He doesn't wonder," Zia said. "And Kren didn't."

Georges examined with interest the basket left in the kitchen.

"Forget it, my darling! Look at all this and cheer up! He would never go to such trouble if he meant to let us down."

"And I'm hopeless in the kitchen."

"There are still family cooks in Hungary?"

"Yes, when they are old friends like ours."

"If mademoiselle will wait in the bar, lunch will be ready in half an hour."

"Where did you learn?"

"Trial and error. A woman won't go to much trouble for herself. A man will. And ten times more for Zia, my Zia."

After Georges's lunch, matched to the colonel's admirable claret, there was no difficulty in finding an occupation for the rest of the day. Uniforms hurled away, they returned to their only civilian suits of sleek skin. In the morning his room, being the nearest, was selected; in the afternoon Zia's siesta was interrupted in the other. At dusk the colonel's softest armchair led to a delightful interlude with a long night and a single bed to follow.

Sanity returned with the sun. Day stretched ahead again with nothing to do but look out of the window and wish for more freedom as a setting for the freedom to love. One distraction was fright when a police car stopped two doors away; another when an old gentleman bird-watching in the garden raised his binoculars to observe Zia at the window; a third when Sparks knocked and entered immediately, forcing Georges to rush for a bath towel and Zia — since the colonel had no discoverable dressing gown — for a pair of his pajamas.

Sparks did not turn a hair, saying, with what seemed the constant ability of MI(S) to deal with any situation, that he had always heard that the WRAC uniform was scratchy till the girls got used to it. He added to Georges:

"But what I've come to tell you is that three gentlemen will be calling this evening. So you mustn't be improperly dressed on parade, mate."

They were not. Since time had somehow to be passed, Georges became more ambitious in the kitchen, taking a good two hours to prepare lunch, while Zia listened, first with alarm and then amusement, to the normal flow of excited curses from the craftsman. It was, she decided, too distracting an occupation and would be allowed no oftener than once a month in future. What future and how far away?

Looking aimlessly out of the window which separated them from any future and its folk, she recognized the colonel's familiar green car and let him in. He looked tired. The smile on the face of the tiger was gentle but far from reassuring.

"First to arrive, I see," he said. "I must admit that for a simple soldier a conference with Gerald and Herbert Spring is rather frightening."

"How is Gerald?" Georges asked.

"Alive. That's all I know — and that the police have Irata's bike."

"Poor Irata! He was so fond of it. Where is he?" Zia asked.

"Out of reach of the police, my dear. You can be sure of that. By the way, Georges, I called on your admirable friend Paul Longwill in the City. He's going to buy your grandmother's house."

"He isn't as rich as he makes out, you know."

"I do know. Gerald will help. It's one of the bills I have for him. Damn it, he gets a vote of his own from Parliament! I don't. Have to rattle my begging bowl."

"Is Paul in the clear?"

"He thinks so. He says the police are not even polite to him anymore, and that's a good sign. Ah, here they are!"

He let in Gerald and Herbert Spring.

"Good evening, Spring! Good evening, Corporal! You may sit down."

"I can't sit down, damn you!" Gerald replied.

"Office chair worn out?"

"You're lucky I'm still in it! If you want to know, I was tooling along quite happily looking for a quiet spot to leave the bike when I was picked out by headlights. Blue lamp on top of the car. Hell! So I whacked her up to eighty. They couldn't catch me because I could corner faster, but they stuck to my tail. All right in the lanes, but then there was a long straight. I knew I'd had it. I'm not James Bond."

Zia, kept from knowledge of Irata's fate, was annoyed at the levity of these supposedly responsible English. It was her life and Georges's that mattered, not theirs.

"And then I saw a train. One of those tinpot railways which Beeching kept open for goods traffic. Level crossing with gate still open. It slammed down just behind me and by the time quarter of a mile of train had passed I was in the next county or somewhere near it. A nice, quiet, graveled farm track showed up on the left a bit late. I was so blasted panicky that I turned into it and came off."

"How did you get home with no seat to your trousers?"

"Walked for an hour and took a taxi. Now have you got anywhere with all this nonsense about Kren and Lukash, Colonel?"

"Yes. The brochures were invaluable — so secret, Gerald, that I daren't think of them myself. And have you identified Fyster-Holmes's friends?"

"Some of them. The rest in a week or two. The pity is that we have no way of recognizing Appinger as he calls himself. If the man ever entered this country again, every movement of his could be watched and every contact investigated."

"You'll be able to recognize him. He's only got one eye."

"Then the other is a very good glass one," Georges said.

"I'm sure it will be. But for the moment he will leave

239

with a bandage over it. And meanwhile check all private nursing homes, Gerald! I think the frontal lobe of his brain may not be all it was."

"What on earth are you talking about?"

"Well, you see, he knew the importance of these brochures — not what was in them but the sort of thing that might be. Given a hot clue, I hoped he would decide that his incompetent partners had given up too soon and that he ought to look for the pink Honesty in person. And he did."

Georges mentioned impatiently that it didn't exist. He, like Zia, felt forgotten in the enthusiasm of these competing professionals.

"But you told me the white did, so I found it. And watered red ink is obtainable through MI(S). You remember the ice-cream inspector, Gerald?"

"Suspected Party member since 1962. Contacts under investigation. Suspected . . ."

"In fact a fat file on the way. Well it so happened that a barrow of fruit and flowers pulled up in Alderton near the ice-cream cart. It was a hundred to one that the inspector would be on board, very anxious to get a line on what the police were up to. 'What's this here?' he asks, seeing some pretty pots of pink Honesty among bunches of the purple. ''Arf a quid a pot, Guv'nor,' the hawker answers. 'Where did you find it?' Mr. Vanilla-and-Strawberry wants to know. 'Up yours,' says my old barrow boy. 'Only spot in the Home Counties, but it ain't far away.'

" 'Would a fiver be any use to you?' Ice Cream suggests. So my Covent Garden expert tells him exactly where it is, nearly Zia's description but about twenty yards off and not that easy to see when you get there. And then the inspector nips straight to the village telephone, making the first move a lot faster than I expected. Appinger had to come out from London, but I still had plenty of preparation to do."

"I hope to heaven you have given nothing away, Colonel," Gerald said. "This is surely not the business of your MI(S)?"

"Personal, Gerald, entirely personal. Among other things, let's say I wanted to pay him out for making me lie on my belly in Alderton Wood wondering whether I'd be tried by Court Martial or the Assizes. Well, moving to Act Two, there was I up a tree and Appinger comes out with old Nut Sundae. Of course I cannot be sure that it was Appinger, but he was tearing a strip off his assistant in shocking bad English which was all splutter and the comrade was taking it all as if he was the office boy.

"Operation Appinger so far successful. But one can never be sure what's on the other side of the hill. My guess was that when he found the pink Honesty which his chaps had missed he would lift it with a spade or garden fork, putting his foot on it like everyone else. Height and probable length of leg correctly estimated by Rivac here. Angle of shaft to ground calculable . . . It should have hit him hard in the crotch, but he bent down and used a trowel. So it got him in the eye like King Harold."

"So it's MI(S) which is the real Dirty Tricks Department," Spring exclaimed.

The terrier snapped into the conversation for the first time, somehow emphasizing for Georges the likeness of the other two to a wolfhound and a jealous old sheepdog.

"Will you please explain at length, Colonel Mannering?" Gerald demanded. "The use of explosives could have been disastrous."

"Nasty bangs. I quite agree. It was just a spring-loaded plate. General principle of mousetrap. A light touch and a little metal stake jumps up. End of it just clear of the ground of course, but imperceptible. A slight improvement on the sharpened bamboo booby trap."

"But you could have killed him!"

"With pleasure. But I knew you wanted him kept alive."

"And what happened then?"

"Ice-cream man very sportingly carried him away on his back."

"I suppose you see that you have entirely wrecked my plan of keeping our knowledge secret."

"Not at all, Gerald. They'll stick it onto Rivac, assuming that he must have been an interested observer in Vietnam. I was myself. Poor Georges! What a bloodthirsty, cunning brute! Rippmann, Fyster-Holmes, now this."

"They'll get him, you know, if the police don't," Spring said. "And he'll be lucky if he can take Kren's way out."

"That's just why I wanted you here. Wave your wand and make him vanish!"

Georges impetuously interrupted, saying that it was simple. Both Lille and England were out forever and he was homeless.

"But Zia is not," he added. "You must get her back to Budapest, and she's burned her passport."

"How sensible of her! Then the next time she wants to compete in something international she has only to go to the right commissar in tears and swear she lost it. I can arrange to have her handbag stolen, if necessary, but that's a bit crude and I am sure she can think of something better. She is an important ambassadress of sport as they call it and she should not be stopped from bringing fame to Hungary just because she has been a stupid, careless little girl. Would it work, Miss Fodor?"

"Yes, I think so. But how can I ever go home?"

"You travel on a British passport. An Indian princess, perhaps. Some dark makeup and a pretty sari. That should deceive Gerald's excellent chaps at the airport, watching for Mrs. Fanshawe. What color sari would you like?"

"Pink for Honesty."

"Back to your usual form, I see, Miss Fodor! We shall book you to Vienna. After that leave the rest to Bridge Holdings and for once do what you are told."

"But I must account for my time to the Hungarian Travel Bureau. I'm supposed to be in Switzerland."

"Well, you were. You fell ill and went to a very private nursing home in Zurich. Doctor's certificate can be supplied. But I'm afraid it will have to be an abortion."

"How disgusting!"

"Only in case of official inquiries. Medical details would not be on the certificate. Just think of poor Georges! He has to have an abortion backward and be reborn. Who would want to go through all that again to reach a future without a past? Would you mind being born in Mexico, Mr. Rivac, somewhere out in the wilds — I know just the right little town — where registration is always dubious and hard to check?"

"No. Someday, perhaps, I can come back to Europe."

He was in such a mood of despondency at all this talk of rebirth and nameless future that he could neither suggest nor argue. The colonel revived him by asking sharply: "And what about his Lille agency?"

"I thought of buying it, but the paperwork is too complicated. We'll just let it die. With Rivac on the run, that will appear very natural to police and authorities."

"But he can't live on hand-outs!"

"Bridge Holdings, my dear colonel, is a commercial firm with wide interests and government favor. I shall look after my old Mexican friend. I knew his mother and he has all the requisite qualities to represent our company in Spain."

"By God, he has! Do you ever go show jumping in Spain, Zia?"

"In the autumn. But will I have to defect? I don't want to do that."

"I think if you were simply to get yourself a foreign husband and keep your nose clean afterward," Spring said, "they would let it go at that. Communists or not, your charming people are very reasonable."

"Most unwise!" Gerald exclaimed. "She can't just pick a husband out of the hat."

"That's up to her, Gerald. But Don José Rivero Muñoz y Carvacal, the assistant manager of Bridge Holdings (Iberia) S.A., may be available."

Geoffrey Household
RED ANGER

A young English clerk fakes his own suicide to escape a boring job—then reappears as a Rumanian refugee from a Russian trawler fleet. From the moment Adrian Gurney, alias Ionel Petrescu, is "discovered" on the coast, however, he is caught in a sinister and unexpected intrigue: He is recruited to hunt down Alwyn Rory, fugitive and reputed traitor. Gurney manages to locate Rory's hiding place, and the two soon find themselves on the run together, as the C.I.A., the K.G.B., and M.I.-5 close in. . . .

WATCHER IN THE SHADOWS

Watcher in the Shadows is the story of a manhunt, of a protracted duel fought out in London and the English countryside by two of the most accomplished and deadly intelligence officers to have survived World War II. One of them is a Viennese who served in the British Intelligence; the other is a dangerous fanatic who has already murdered three men. "A thriller of the highest quality"—Anthony Boucher, *The New York Times Book Review.*

Geoffrey Household
ROGUE MALE

His mission was revenge, and revenge means assassination. In return he'll be cruelly tortured, tracked by secret agents, followed by the police, relentlessly pursued by a ruthless killer. They'll hunt him like a wild beast, and to survive he'll have to think and live like a rogue male. "A tale of adventure, suspense, even mystery, for whose sheer thrilling quality one may seek long to find a parallel . . . and in its sparse, tense, desperately alive narrative it will keep, long after the last page is finished, its hold from the first page on the reader's mind"—*The New York Times Book Review*.

HOSTAGE: LONDON

Magma International: ruthless anarchists. *Their aim:* revolution through fear. *Their weapon:* an atom bomb hidden somewhere in the heart of London. Operating under the guise of a publisher's salesman, Julian Despard is a loyal member of Magma—until he discovers the mass-murder plot threatening London. Breaking with his former comrades, he sets out to prevent the catastrophe even as the terrorist blackmail of Downing Street begins. But will he be able to locate and defuse the bomb before Scotland Yard arrests him . . . before Magma itself finds and kills him?

Geoffrey Household

DANCE OF THE DWARFS

"Have you ever seen one? . . . What did it look like?"
"They don't come out in the day?"
"All such things dread the sun."

Dr. Owen Dawnay had set up an agricultural station in a ranch house at the edge of the Amazonian jungle. It is a remote place inhabited only by primitive half-Indian cattlemen. At first he is puzzled by the cattlemen's fear of the dark. Then he learns that they are afraid of elusive dwarfs who are supposed to dance among the trees by moonlight. A rationalist and a scientist, Dawnay resolves to confront the unknown; but he will finally realize that he has entered a region beyond reason—the twilit terrain of nightmare. . . . "Brilliantly imagined, intellectually provocative, strangulatingly paced"—*The New Yorker*.

Graham Greene

THE END OF THE AFFAIR

This frank, intense account of a love affair and its mystical aftermath takes place in a suburb of wartime London.

THE POWER AND THE GLORY

In one of the southern states of Mexico, during an anti-clerical purge, the last priest, like a hunted hare, is on the run. Too human for heroism, too humble for martyrdom, the little worldly "whiskey priest" is nevertheless impelled toward his squalid Calvary as much by his own efforts as by the efforts of his pursuers.

THE QUIET AMERICAN

The Quiet American is a terrifying portrait of innocence at large, a wry comment on European interference in Asia in its story of the Franco-Vietminh war in Vietnam. While the French Army is grappling with the Vietminh, back at Saigon a young, high-minded American begins to channel economic aid to a "Third Force." The narrator, a seasoned foreign correspondent, is forced to observe: "I never knew a man who had better motives for all the trouble he caused."

Also:

BRIGHTON ROCK
A BURNT-OUT CASE
THE COMEDIANS
THE HEART OF THE MATTER
IT'S A BATTLEFIELD
JOURNEY WITHOUT MAPS
LOSER TAKES ALL
MAY WE BORROW YOUR HUSBAND?
THE MINISTRY OF FEAR
OUR MAN IN HAVANA
THE PORTABLE GRAHAM GREENE
SHADES OF GREENE
TRAVELS WITH MY AUNT

Erskine Childers

THE RIDDLE OF THE SANDS

The Riddle of the Sands is regarded by many critics as one of the best spy novels ever written; it is certainly the first modern espionage story and remains a classic of the genre. Its unique flavor comes from its richly detailed technical background of inshore sailing in the Baltic and North seas, from its remarkable air of authenticity, and from its evocation of the world of the late 1890s, with its atmosphere of intrigue and mutual suspicion that was soon to lead to war. Erskine Childers died before a firing squad in Dublin, denounced as a traitor, yet his book was an expression of his loyalty to England and his concern for the nation's defense. With its suspense-packed plot and breathtaking climax, it is a novel that will appeal to scores of readers brought up on the realism of Eric Ambler, Graham Greene, and John le Carré.

Stuart Kaminsky

MURDER ON THE YELLOW BRICK ROAD

The yellow brick road ran through the famous *Wizard of Oz* sound stage at M.G.M. studios. On November 1, 1940, a dead man lay upon it, blood from the knife wound in his chest flowing along the cracks of the bricks. Summoned by the young and frightened starlet Judy Garland, private detective Toby Peters tries to hold off the police and the reporters, protect M.G.M. from unpleasant notoriety, and make sense of the few slim clues. Before long, he realizes that he is confronting nothing less than a plot against the life of Miss Garland herself. Enlisting her help (as well as that of Clark Gable and Raymond Chandler), Peters uncovers further clues. He knows he is near to the shocking truth when shots are fired at him from a passing car, he is attacked in a motel, is almost demolished by a muscle-man, and falls victim to an outrageous frame-up, with the police closing in. "Toby Peters is a tough guy, faced with some tough opponents. . . . It's a cute idea, if any murder can be described as cute, and Mr. Kaminsky has a high old time with his Hollywood characters"—*The New York Times Book Review*.

Gwen Robyns

THE MYSTERY OF AGATHA CHRISTIE

Agatha Christie—Queen of Crime, Duchess of Death, First Lady of Mystery—was the most successful English writer of all time. Translated into 103 languages (14 more than Shakespeare), her books have sold four hundred million copies, earning her a fortune in every currency on earth. Mrs. Christie herself was more mysterious than her fictions, however. On December 3, 1926, she vanished—only to be found ten days later, living under an assumed name in a resort hotel. *The Mystery of Agatha Christie* fully explores this still unsolved case, as well as every other aspect of Mrs. Christie's closely guarded life. We learn that she wrote her first novel because her sister bet her that she couldn't; that her first marriage was stormy, and her second, to archaeologist Max Mallowan, blissful; that she loved buying and redecorating houses and at one time owned eight; and that her loathing of publicity was so extreme that she refused even to attend parties in honor of her books. Her autobiography, published in 1977, is reticent; the current novel about her disappearance is highly speculative. Only Gwen Robyns's book tells us the inside story of this demure woman who, more than anyone else, made murder familiar.

Frank MacShane

THE LIFE OF RAYMOND CHANDLER

Raymond Chandler murdered more people than Dashiell Hammett did—and he murdered them brilliantly. Dismissed from his job with an oil company for heavy drinking, Chandler did not begin to write detective fiction until he was forty-four; yet within a few years he published *The Big Sleep* and created in Philip Marlowe one of the century's most popular and durable heroes. Marlowe's exploits were filmed, and Chandler himself went to Hollywood as a scriptwriter. Drawing on Chandler's voluminous and lively correspondence and on conversations with members of his circle, Frank MacShane has given us the definitive account of the life and times of this unique literary figure.

John Boyd
THE LAST STARSHIP FROM EARTH

Mathematicians must not write poetry—above all, they must not marry poets, decrees the state. But Haldane IV, mathematician, and Helix, poet, are in love. They are also puzzled, for they have been studying the long-hidden poetry of Fairweather I, acknowledged as the greatest mathematician since Einstein. As they explore further, the danger for them grows; the state has eyes and ears everywhere. Will they find, before it is too late, the real meaning of the following words by Fairweather I? "That he who loses wins the race,/That parallel lines all meet in space." "Terrific . . . it belongs on the same shelf with *1984* and *Brave New World*"—Robert A. Heinlein.

THE POLLINATORS OF EDEN

The coldly beautiful Dr. Freda Caron has waited too long for her fiancé, Paul Theaston, to return from Flora, the flower planet. Determined to learn what has happened, she begins a study of plants from Flora, and slowly she is warmed by her communion with them. Eventually she makes the trip from Earth to Flora for further research and to see Paul. What she finds is the secret of the flower planet, but in her initiation she too becomes a pollinator of Eden.

THE RAKEHELLS OF HEAVEN

In the future there will be colonial imperialism—in space! Two space scouts, John Adams and Kevin O'Hara, are sent to explore a distant world called Harlech. The Interplanetary Colonial Authority prohibits human colonization and control of those planets whose inhabitants closely resemble *Homo sapiens,* as the Harlechians do. Thus, relations with their women are strictly forbidden. But such rules were not made for Red O'Hara. From the Adams-O'Hara Probe, only John Adams returns. . . .